領隊英文

隨書收錄每章「綜合練習」及「領隊英文」歷屆試題

English for Tour Leaders

黃榮鵬 著

五南圖書出版公司 印行

自 序

緣　起

　　1990年自陸軍「預備軍官」退伍後，從事「自由領隊」的工作，一邊就讀於中國文化大學觀光事業研究所碩士班，於1993年順利以第一名畢業後，專職於旅行社擔任「線控」工作，工作之餘也在學校教授「觀光學」、「觀光行銷學」、「旅行業經營與管理」與「領隊與導遊實務」等相關課程。當時在教學過程深感國內有關教科書之不足，使得自己有提筆的動機。雖然明知在主、客觀條件下，要完成一本令自己滿意的書，實屬不易。更何況要令旅遊從業前輩滿意、觀光旅遊學術先進認同，更非是一件容易的事。隨即考取公費赴美夏威夷進修，課餘之時也從事「導遊」服務的工作。一年後返台，任教於國立高雄餐旅專科學校。離開「旅行業界」轉任「學術界」，使自己更積極從事撰寫工作，於1998年出版第一本《領隊實務》一書。受到師長與業者的肯定，同時也獲得先進的指正，一併感謝。

　　時光飛逝十多年來，有些學生已成為旅行業中、基階主管，大學及研究所同學也有的任職旅行業高階主管或企業主、觀光主管機關之官員，甚至曾任領隊協會理事長。不論在產、官、學三方面，對於旅遊消費市場上許多看法分歧，但有一共同理念「人才」是攸關旅行業經營成功的關鍵因素。更因為當時任教於國立高雄餐旅學院旅運管理系，同時也破紀錄二年八個月畢業於國立中山大學企業管理研究所博士班，順利取得「博士學位」與「副教授」資格，隨即以罕見的速度三年後順利升等「教授」資格。在恩師蔡憲唐教授諄諄教誨下，更加體會「教育訓練」的重要，也愈加催促自己及早完書及提供最新研究成果與讀者分享。儘管深感惶恐與不安，「學得愈多、帶團出國；帶得愈多團，愈加深感覺自己學問之不足」。但是，與其一直等待前人、前輩出書以供盛享，不如自己繼續踏出另一步。

期　望

　　身為「觀光旅遊管理」教育之「工作者」，不敢自稱是「學者」。希望藉著本書能幫助讀者經由透明化的過程，習得有系統、有組織之領隊應具備的「關鍵字彙」，與相關旅遊業者溝通時所應掌握「關鍵會話」的能力。此外自2004年「導遊」與「領隊」考試已修正為國家級考試，同時將「領隊英文」列入考試內容的一部分，國內相關書籍均屬於「觀光英文」或「旅遊英文」，都是從消費者的角度撰寫；相對的針對領隊帶團所需要的領隊專業英文相關書籍卻闕如。過去忙於準備「考博士」、「修博士」、「取得博士學位」；從追求世俗的「講師」、「副教授」；進而未滿40歲的前夕，升等至學術終點「教授」資格；無不戮力完成，就好像領隊一天一天實踐旅遊契約書內容與完成所有行程表工作任務一樣，實在無瑕編撰《領隊英文》一書。至此，上述階段性目標均以罕見速度達成，才著手實現多年的願望之一：完成本書。本書希望對於準備「領隊」考試有所助益；尤其考上之後許多非本行之新進旅遊同儕，不僅在「帶團」或從事旅遊工作時皆能有所精進。

特　色

　　為達到以上的預期目標，本書在撰寫與排版上分成以下四方面：

一、首先以領隊的角度正確掌握「關鍵字彙」，俾使有志從事領隊工作人員在此行業中，有基本專業字彙的能力。

二、有基本字彙能力後，要勇敢表達出來，特別是帶團工作時時需要與國外相關旅遊業者溝通，因此第二部分加入「關鍵會話」，奠定基本領隊溝通會話能力。

三、除此之外，為因應國家考試於第三部分增列「語詞測驗」與「文法測驗」，並提供相關測驗題與「帶團技巧」分享，以利讀者應付領隊考試與實務帶團工作。

四、最後，本書內容是從領隊帶團標準作業流程切入，第一章「機場服務」
　　至「返國」等作業流程共計十二章，使讀者不僅「考得上」更能「用得
　　上」，而非僅「考得上」卻不知「如何帶團」的窘境。

為使讀者有更實際的體驗與深刻印象，在每章均加入相關「照片」與「圖表」，期望「理論」與「實務」相結合。最後本書──《領隊英文》特別加入綜合測驗題，以利準備「國家考試」。預祝讀者取得帶團資格，早日實踐「不花自己一毛錢，遊遍世界七大奇景的願景」。

感　謝

本書的完成有賴諸多師友協助，在未寫書之前對於他人之大作偶爾可抒發己見，但自己在撰寫的過程中才知其艱辛。更重要是從付梓那一刻起，不僅喪失評論之機會，更淪為旅遊業前輩與旅遊學術界先進無情嚴厲之考驗。若以純經濟利益的考量，撰寫的工作與出國帶團收入的相對比較利益之下，更是令我提不起勁，本書之完成是遙遙無期。在此要衷心感謝引我入此行的雄獅旅行社董事長王文傑、旅遊先進陳嘉隆理事長；帶我沐浴在學術殿堂的恩師李瑞金、唐學斌、廖又生及李銘輝教授；完成此書最大無形推動力量的國立高雄餐旅大學容校長繼業、國立中山大學蔡憲唐、盧淵源教授；國立高雄應用科技大學戴貞德教授；旅遊管理研究碩士生陳佳妏、李玉蓮、楊雅涵、楊縈潔與吳蕙蓁同學的協助校稿、打字；特別是時時給予我成長機會與鼓勵的凌董事長瓏。

國立高雄餐旅大學旅遊管理研究所教授兼觀光院院長／所長

黃榮鵬 於高雄小港

2012.3.28

CONTENTS

在機場時——辦理登機與出境手續

一、工作程序（Working Procedures）

　　領隊交班工作完成後，確認護照會由送機人員攜帶至機場或親自攜帶。於出發當天應至少比團體集合時間早半小時以上，至機場辦理登機手續，若遇到特殊狀況，例如：農曆過年、美國線加強安檢等因素時，應至少比團體集合時間早1小時以上。

　　辦理登機手續過程時，如有特殊狀況，例如：夫妻度蜜月、父母親帶小孩、親屬帶祖父母或年紀稍長者。由於團體機位是依照英文姓氏A至Z的順序排序，所以有時一家人並未能坐在一起，若碰到上述情形時應委婉協調航空公司地勤人員，給予座位上的彈性調整。

　　關於行李部分，應提醒團員個人貴重東西要隨身攜帶，但管制物品一定要放置在託運大行李箱，且務必請團員親自看著托運行李經X光機掃描檢查通過後，再行離開前往出境關口。

二、關鍵字彙

　　身為領隊應熟悉專有字彙，掌握「關鍵字彙」，於溝通時自然能順暢無虞。因此，在此階段共分為下列十一大類關鍵字彙：

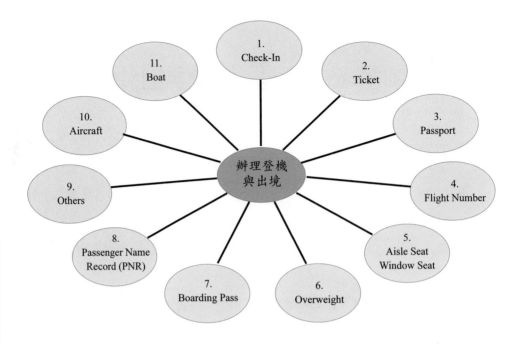

1.Check-In　辦理登機手續

‧ Passport	護照	‧ Status	訂位狀態
‧ Ticket	機票	‧ Ticket Counter	辦理出境手續櫃檯
‧ Departure Lobby	出境休息室	‧ Group Visa	團體簽證
‧ Arrival Lobby	到達休息室	‧ Visa Free	免簽證
‧ Time Zone	時區	‧ Visa On Arrival	落地簽證
‧ Flying Time	飛行時間	‧ Visa Fees	簽證費
‧ Transit Without Visa (TWOV)	過境免簽證		
‧ Greenwich Mean Time (GMT)	格林威治標準時間		
‧ Daylight Saving Time (DST)	日光節約能源時間		
‧ Minimum Connecting Time	最少轉機時間		
‧ Travel Information Manual (TIM)	旅行資料手冊		
‧ Charter Inclusive Tour (CIT)	包機全備式行程		
‧ General sales Agent (GSA)	總代理		
‧ Flight Information Board	航班資訊顯示板		

2.Ticket　機票

‧ Manual Ticket	手寫機票	‧ Audit Coupon	審計聯

· Electronic Ticket	電子機票	· Agent Coupon	開票單位存根聯
· One Way (OW)	單程票	· Flight Coupon	搭乘聯
· Round Trip (RT)	來回票	· Passenger Coupon	乘客存根聯
· GIT Fare (GV)	團體票	· Economy Class	經濟艙
· Excursion Fare	旅遊票	· Business Class	商務艙
· Full Fare	全票（12歲以上）	· First Class	頭等艙
· Half Fare	半票（2-12歲）	· Endorsable Ticket	可轉讓機票
· Infant Fare	嬰兒票（2歲以下）	· Not Valid Before	此效期之前為無效票
· AD Fare	旅行社折扣票	· Not Valid After	此效期之後為無效票
· Quarter Fare	四分之一票價	· Void	作廢
· Free of Charge (FOC)	免費	· Ticket Center	票務中心
· Currency Code	幣制代號	· Sticker	改票貼紙
· Automated Ticket and Boarding Pass	自動化機票含登機證		
· PTA-Prepaid Ticket Advice	預付票款通知，以便取得機票		
· Neutral Unit of Construction (NUC)	機票計價單位		

3.Passport　護照

· Name	姓名	· Date of Birth	出生日期
· Surname	姓	· Date of Issue	發照日期
· Given Name	名	· Date of Expiry	效期截止日期
· Nationality	國籍	· Place of Birth	出生地
· Personal Id. No.	身分證統一編號	· Republic of China	中華民國
· Sex	性別	· Signature of Bearer	持照人簽名
· Authority	授權機關	· Visa Type	簽證種類

4.Flight Number　航班號碼

· Flight Number	航班號碼	· Online	航班有服務點
· City Codes	城市代號	· Offline	必須轉接航班服務
· Aircraft Codes	機型代號	· Tax-Free Shop	免稅店
· Airport Codes	機場代號	· Stewardess	空中小姐
· Code Sharing	共用班號	· Pilot	飛機駕駛員

・Extra Fly	加班機	・International Date Line	國際換日線
・Charter	包機	・Incentive Traffic Right	航權
・International Air Transport Association (IATA)	國際航空運輸協會		

5.Aisle Seat / Window Seat　選位——走道座位 / 靠窗座位

・Aisle Seat	走道座位	・A Seat Close to the Front	前面座位
・Smoking Seat	吸菸座位	・Non-Smoking Seat	非吸菸座位
・Window Seat	靠窗座位	・A Seat over the Wing	靠機翼座位
・Middle Seat	中間座位	・A Seat by the Emergency Exit	靠緊急出口座位
・A Seat away from the Lavatory	遠離洗手間座位		

6.Overweight　行李超重

・Luggage=Baggage	行李	・Suitcase	行李箱
・Checked Luggage	托運行李	・Baggage Tag	行李牌
・Carry-On Luggage	手提行李	・Fragile	易碎品
・Free Luggage Allowance	免費托運行李重量	・Overnight Bag	過夜簡易小包
・Baggage Claim Tag	托運行李收據	・Compensation	賠償
・Porter	行李員	・Excess Baggage	超重行李
・Charge for Overweight Luggage	行李超重費		

7.Boarding Pass　登機證

・Boarding Gate	登機門	・Boarding Time	登機時間
・Briefing Before Departure	行前說明會	・Seat Number	座位號碼

8.Passenger Name Record (PNR)　訂位紀錄

・Computer Reservation System (CRS)	電腦訂位系統		
・Billing and Settlement Plan (BSP)	銀行清帳計畫		
・Official Airlines Guide (OAG)	航空公司資料查詢簿		
・World Airways Guide (ABC)	航空公司資料查詢簿		
・High Season	旺季	・Space Confirmed (OK)	確認機位
・Shoulder Season	平季	・On Request (RQ)	候補機位

· Overbooking	超賣	· Subject to Load (SA)	空位搭乘
· Elapsed Journey Time	實際飛行時間	· Infant Not Occupying a Seat (NS)	嬰兒不占位
· Meal Coupon	餐券	· Open	回程未預訂

9.Others　其他

· Affinity Tour	同性質團體	· Badge	胸章
· Local Contact	當地聯絡人	· Travel Mart	旅遊交易會
· Sender-Off	送客者	· Travel Fair	旅展
· Limousine Article	接送旅客車	· Booth	攤位

10.Aircraft　飛行器

· Single Engine Airplane	單引擎飛機		
· First Class Section	頭等艙區		
· Adjustable Air Outlet	空氣調節器		
· Overhead Reading Light	正上方閱讀燈		
· Attendant Call Button	呼喚鈕		
· Claim Tag	行李寄存提單		
· Helicopter	直升機	· Cockpit	駕駛艙
· Flight Deck	駕駛室	· Radar Cone	雷達罩
· In-Flight Meal	機內食物	· Galley Modules	空中廚房
· Channel Selector	調頻開關	· Volume Control	音量調整器
· Earphone Jack	耳機插座	· Foldaway Table	折疊桌
· Cabin Lavatory	機艙化妝室	· Oxygen Mask	氧氣罩
· Airsickness Bag	污物處理袋	· Space Shuttle	太空梭
· Launch Pad	發射台	· Lunar Lander	登月小艇

11.Boat　船

· Passenger Boat	客輪	· Fishing Boat	漁船
· Freighter	貨輪	· Pleasure Boat	遊艇
· Ferry Boat	渡船	· Motor Boat	快艇
· Waterline	吃水線	· Row Boat	划艇
· Inflatable	充氣式橡皮艇	· Sail Boat	帆船
· Compass	羅盤	· Outboard Engine	船外引擎
· Power Boat	機動船	· Tanker	油輪
· Life Boat	救生艇	· Fire Boat	消防艇
· Hover Craft	氣墊船	· Hydrofoil	水翼船

三、關鍵會話

(一)航空團體櫃檯辦理登機手續

【Scene：Check-in counter】

Airline employee: Good morning, ma'am! May I have your passports and tickets of your group, please?

Tour Leader : Yes, here you are. There are 30 people in my party. Can I have an aisle seat? I don't want to disturb other passengers if I need to leave my seat. Besides, I need to take care of my group during the flight.

Airline employee: Let me check.... Ok, no problem. How many pieces of luggage in your group need to check in?

Tour Leader : Yes. We have 25 pieces of baggage.

Airline employee: Would you tell your clients to check in their baggage by themselves?

Tour Leader : Of course. They are not overweight, are they?

Airline employee: Alright. You are all set. Here are your 30 boarding passes and your tickets with your 25 baggage claim tags. Your seat is 36C and your boarding time is 8:45 p.m. at Gate 20.

Tour Leader : Thank you.

Airline employee: Have a nice flight.

圖1-1　航空公司辦理團體Check-In 櫃檯

(二)詢問航空公司櫃檯

【Scene：Check-in counter】

Airline employee: Good morning, sir. What can I do for you?

Tour Leader 　　　: Is this the counter for BR087 to Paris?

Airline employee: Yes, sir. Are you the tour leader of Leo Tour?

Tour Leader 　　　: Yes, I am.

Airline employee: Please go to the next counter for group check-in.

圖1-2　機場航空公司櫃檯

Tour Leader	: Hello, we are a group of 30 people going to Paris by BR087.
Airline employee	: May I have your tickets and passports, please?
Tour Leader	: Sure, here you are.
Airline employee	: How many pieces of luggage would you like to check in?
Tour Leader	: 25 pieces altogether.
Airline employee	: Here are your tickets, passports and boarding passes.
Tour Leader	: Thank you.
Airline employee	: You're welcome.

圖 1-3　領隊於團體櫃檯辦理登機手續

(三)團體行李超重

【Scene：Check-in counter】

Airline employee: Excuse me, sir. Do you have any pieces of luggage to check in?

Tour Leader　　: Yes. We have 25 suitcases.

Airline employee: Would you please put them on the scale?

Tour Leader　　: Of course. They are not overweight, are they?

Airline employee: I am sorry. They are 6 kilograms over.

Tour Leader　　: That's too bad. Could you explain the free baggage allowance to me?

Airline employee: Of course. The flight to Paris, your free baggage
allowance is not more than 20 kilograms each.

Tour Leader　　: Oh, ok.

Airline employee: Maybe you could pick something out of your luggage
and take them with you.

Tour Leader　　: Good idea.

圖1-4　航空公司行李輸送帶與重量過磅

Airline employee: Alright. Here are your baggage claim tags, flight tickets, boarding passes and passports.

Tour Leader　　　: When is the boarding time?

Airline employee: The boarding time is 8:45 p.m. and you will board from Gate 20.

Tour Leader　　　: Thank you very much.

圖 1-5　海關人員使用X光機檢查托運行李

四、語詞測驗

1. **at**（某個時點）「幾天幾分」

I eat breakfast at seven in the morning.

我早上7點吃早餐。

2. **in**（較長的一段時間）「年、月、週、季節等」

We will have a nice Italy tour in a few days.

幾天後我們將會有一個非常愉快的義大利之旅。

3. **on**（特定日）「星期幾、幾月幾日那天」

My next tour will be departed on the 19th.

我下一團是19號出發。

4. 表原因、理由介系詞：**at、from、of、through**

I was surprised at the ICE accident news.

我對德國高速火車ICE意外事件那消息感到驚訝。

5. 表目的的介系詞：**after、for、on**

Those tourists of my group thirst for knowledge.

這一團團員求知慾很強。

6. 表材料的介系詞：**of**

The Sorrento music box made of wood is the most famous souvenir in Italy.

蘇連多木製的音樂盒是義大利最有名的紀念品。

7. 表原料的介系詞：**from**

Wine is made from grapes.

葡萄酒由葡萄製成。

8. 表工具的介系詞：**with**

French enjoy snails with snail fork.

法國人用田螺叉享用法式田螺。

9. 表方法、手段的介系詞：**by**、**on**、**with**

Do not eat lobsters by hand.

不要用手吃龍蝦。

10. 表關係的介系詞：**about**、**for**、**on**、**over**、**with**

This is a local agent fax for the tour leader from Taiwan Leo Tour.

這封當地代理旅行社的傳真是給台灣Leo旅遊的領隊。

11. 表樣態的介系詞：**after**、**by**、**in**、**with**

Do not talk to the members of your group in this impolite way.

不要對你的團員以這種不禮貌的方法講話。

12. 表行為者的介系詞：**by**

This message was written by local guide.

這留言是當地導遊寫的。

13. 表起源的介系詞：**from、out of**

Where do your people of your group come from?

你們這一團團員是從哪裡來？

14. 表計量、範圍的介系詞：**at、by、for、in、to**

amount to~　總共~

at full speed　以全速

by the pound　以磅算的話

for one's age　論年齡

I bought this Swatch for 100 US dollars.

我花了100元美金買一隻Swatch手錶。

15. 表條件的介系詞：**for、with**

With your help, this group's shopping power is amazing.

靠你的幫助這一團的購買力驚人。

16. 表比較、對照的介系詞：**to、with**

compare A with B　將A與B比較

Comparing the performance of last group's tour leader with yours, you are better.

拿上一團領隊的績效與你比較，你較優秀。

17. **Compare A to B**～　把A比喻成B

Tour leader is often compared to a friend of tourist.

領隊經常被比喻成團員的朋友。

18. 表反對 / 贊成的介系詞：**against**（反對）、**for**（贊成）

Are you for or against the local guide's suggestions?

你贊成或是反對當地導遊的意見？

19. 表示穿著的介系詞：**in**

The girl dressed in white skirt is our local guide.

穿著白色裙子的女生是我們當地的導遊。

20. 表附帶狀況的介系詞：**with**

Don't speak to your tourists with your mouth full.

對團員講話時嘴巴裡不要有東西。

21. **be absorbed in** ～ 全神貫注於某事

I was so absorbed in leading tour that I forgot to order lunch (in advance).

我全神貫注於帶團而忘了訂午餐。

22. **be amazed [astonished] at [about, by]** ～ 使吃驚

I was amazed at the sight of the Grand Canyon.

我看見大峽谷時感到很驚訝。

23. **be annoyed at [by, with]** ～ 使困擾

I am annoyed at the noise from the next room.

隔壁房間的噪音令我感到困擾。

24. be clued-up ～　熟知的

Are you clued up on playing poker?

你熟悉打撲克牌嗎？

25. be contented [content] with ～　滿足的

Most tour leaders are not contented with their escort per diems.

大部分領隊不滿意領隊出差費。

五、文法測驗

本章重點：五大基本句型分析

句型一　S+V

S+V	Fire burns. 火燃燒。
S+V+M（修飾語）	A lot of relatives came to see me off at the airport. 許多親戚來機場為我送行。
It+V+S	It matters little whether my colleague comes or not. 我的同事是否會來都無關緊要。
There+V+S	There are many tourists sitting on the Seine River bank. 有許多觀光客坐在塞納河邊。

句型二　S+V+C（complement 主詞補語）

S+V+C	They are happy tourists. 他們是快樂的觀光客。
S+V+O+假補語（可以是現在、過去分詞、名詞或形容詞）	Tour leader left the hotel unobserved. 領隊離開飯店沒被發現。
形容詞+to-原形動詞	Tour guide is eager to push shopping. 導遊急著推銷購物。 Tour leader is anxious to see local guide. 領隊急著要找當地導遊。
be+形容詞+介系詞	The Italian driver is very fond of Chinese food. 那位義大利司機非常喜歡中國菜。

不定詞的受詞→句子的主詞	It is difficult to please drivers. 司機很難取悅。
不定詞補語和動名詞補語	My ambition is to become a tour leader. 我的抱負是成為一位導遊。 My hobby is collecting foreign coins. 我的嗜好是蒐集國外錢幣。
主詞+被動語態+主詞補語	He is said to be a great musician. 據說他是個偉大的音樂家。
seem之後可接不定詞當補語	He doesn't seem to like oyster. 他似乎不喜歡生蠔。
介系詞片語作補語	Local guide's advice will be of some help to you. 當地導遊的忠告會對你有些幫助。

句型三 S+V+O

及物動詞和受詞、副詞的位置	Tour leader reads the working itinerary carefully every morning. 領隊每天早上都仔細地看工作日誌表。
動詞片語和副詞	Tourists listen carefully to their local guide. 團員仔細聽當地導遊的解說。
以不定詞為受詞的動詞	Drivers want to rest. 司機想要休息。
以動名詞為受詞的動詞	Do you mind smoking here? 你介意我在這裡抽菸嗎?
動名詞意義上的主詞	I don't like driver knowing my secrets. 我不希望司機知道我的祕密。
以動名詞或不定詞為受詞,但意義不同的動詞: (1)（動名詞表示動作已發生）	I remember seeing him while I was on tour in Paris. 我記得帶團在巴黎期間曾見過他。
(2)（不定詞表示動作尚未發生）	You must remember to see local guide this morning. 你必須記得今早要去見當地導遊。
以that子句為受詞的動詞	Tour leader insisted that tour guide (should) be on time. 領隊堅持導遊要準時。
以疑問句,whether,if所引導的子句為受詞	Do you know whether tour guide said so? 你是否知道導遊這麼說的嗎?

同系動詞+同系受詞	They lived a happy life. 他們過著快樂的生活。
反身動詞+反身受詞	Don't praise yourself too much. 別過分自誇。

句型四　S+V+IO+DO

動詞+間接受詞+直接受詞	I gave the driver the tips. 我給司機小費。
動詞+間接受詞+介系詞+直接受詞	Tour leader informed company of the accident. 領隊通知公司那件意外事故。
間接受詞+that子句	Tour guide told us (that) it was a lie. 導遊告訴我們，那是個謊言。
間接受詞+wh子句	Driver asked me where I came from. 司機問我來自何處。

句型五　S+V+O+C（受詞補語）

S+V+O+C	They elected him group leader. 他們選他為團體領袖。
受詞+to be	We know this story to be true. 我們知道這個故事是真的。
受詞+to-V	Tour leader advised me to stop complaining. 領隊勸我別再抱怨。
感官動詞+受詞+原形動詞	We heard the actor sing on the stage. 我們聽到演員在舞台上唱歌。
使役動詞+受詞+原形動詞	The sad story made us move to tears. 那個悲傷的故事讓我們感動落淚。
感官動詞+受詞+現在分詞	We could hear her singing in the bathroom. 我們可以聽到她在浴室裡唱歌。
使役、感官動詞+受詞+過去分詞	I could make myself understood in Italian. 我可以用義大利語表達意思。
get, etc. +受詞+V-ing	He got the slot machine going. 他使吃角子老虎運作。
形式受詞	I found it impossible to keep up with him. 我發現不可能趕上他。

附件 1　電腦訂位紀錄（PNR）

FD 1.1CHEN/YUCHINMS

QGPBRSRS

23OCT AE6I44

   1 BR　902　G　SA　25JAN　KHHTPE　HK1　X　0750　0830

   2 BR　　67　G　SA　25JAN　TPELHR　HK1　　　1000 1955

   3 BR　68　　G　TU4FEB　LHRTPE　　HK1　X　2210 2200*1

   4 BR　911　G　WE　5FEB　TPEKHH　HK1　　　2245 2325

TKT-E REFD / RERTE REF TO ISSG OFC 2.E NONENDORSABLE

3.E GTT/KHHLON 4.E REBKG CHRGE TWD5000 5.F BSR 1GBP/45.95TWD

6.C23JANTPE BRTD 6954451237583

FD 1.1CHEN/HUIYAMS

QGPBRSRS

23OCT AABPNL

   1 BR　　902　G　SA　25JAN　KHHTPE　HK1　X　0750　0830

   2 BR　　67　G　SA　25JAN　TPELHR　HK1　　　1000 1955

   3 BR　　68　G　TH　30JAN　LHRTPE　HK1　X　2210 2200*1

TKT-E REFD / RERTE REF TO ISSG OFC 2.E NONENDORSABLE

3.E GTT/KHHLON 4.E REBKG CHRGE TWD5000 5.F BSR 1GBP/45.95TWD

6.C23JANTPE BRTD 6954451237584

FD 1.1HUANG/JUNGPENGMR 2.1CHANG/YUNGHSIANG MR

3.1CHEN/GRACEHSIUHUIMS

QGPBRSRS

23OCT AE6NC2

1 BR   67 G SA 25JAN TPELHR HK3   1000 1955

2 BR   68 G TH 30JAN LHRTPE HK3 X2210 2200*1

TKT-X1 E REFD / RERTE REF TO ISSG OFC 2.X1 E NONENDORSABLE

3.X1 E GTT/TPELON 4.X1 E REBKG CHRGE TWD5000 5.F BSR 1GBP/45.95TWD

6.1 E VALID ONLY ON DATE/FLT SHOWN

7.X1 C23JANTPE BRTD 6954451237585-586

8.1 C23JANTPE BRTD 6954451237607

F 1.1HSU/WENYIMS 2.1TSAO/CHINGHUIMR 3.1CHUANG/SHUHUAMRS

4.1LIU/HSUSENMR 5.1SHIH/CHENSUMS 6.1CHOU/YALINMS

7.1TSAI/CHIAMINGMR 8.1LEE/HUISHENGMS 9.1TSAI/PIFENMS

10.1HSIEH/YAOHSIENMR 11.1YANG/MALIMS 12.1HSIEH/YIJUMSTR

13.1CHOU/HSUEHCHIMS 14.1CHOU/KUEIHSIENMS 15.1CHENG/HUEICHUMS

16.1CHEN/YUNMINGMR 17.1CHEN/MINGHUIMS 18.1TSENG/JENHSIANGMR

19.1WANGHUANG/CHINCHIHMRS 20.1WANG/YENCHINGMS

21.1WANG/HONGWENMR

QGPBRSRS

23OCT AEI6TC

1 BR   67 G SA 25JAN TPELHR HK21 1000 1955

2 BR   68 G TH 30JAN LHRTPE HK21 2210 2200*1

TKT- E REFD / RERTE REF TO ISSG OFC 2.X1 E NONENDORSABLE

3.E GTT/TPELON 4.E REBKG CHRGE TWD5000 5.F BSR 1GBP/45.95TWD

6.12 N HSIEH/YIJUMSTR 27JAN1993

7.X12 C23JANTPE BRTD 6954451237587-606

8.12 C23JANTPE BRTD 6954451237608

(　) 1. It seems very difficult _____ on the plane.

    (A) to stop the child to cry   (B) restraining the child to cry

    (C) to stop the child from crying   (D) holding the child's crying

(　) 2. It is necessary _____ the earphone immediately.

    (A) for tourists to return   (B) that he returns

    (C) his returning   (D) to him return

(　) 3. It is no _____ arguing about it because the long distance coach driver will never change his mind.

    (A) use   (B) help   (C) time   (D) while

(　) 4. _____ only five hours to finish the city tour.

    (A) I took myself   (B) It needed me

    (C) It required me   (D) It took me

(　) 5. Aswan power stations employ _____ water to produce electricity.

    (A) falling   (B) fallen   (C) filling   (D) filled

(　) 6. "I'd like to buy an expensive Rolex watch in Bucherer."

    "Well, they have several models _____."

    (A) to choose from   (B) of choice

    (C) to be chosen   (D) for choosing

(　) 7. Some tour members haven't got chairs _____ in the Chinese restaurant.

    (A) to sit   (B) for sit on   (C) to sit on   (D) for sitting

(　) 8. The tour leader tried to silence the _____ tour members in vain.

    (A) exciting   (B) excited   (C) to excite   (D) excite

(　) 9. One of the slot machines stopped _____ and caused a lots people complaining in the casino lobby.

    (A) to work   (B) work   (C) worked   (D) working

( ) 10. Tour leader bitterly regretted _____ him other tour member's private secret yesterday.

(A) to tell   (B) to be telling   (C) to have told   (D) telling

( ) 11. We went _____ to take a vacation.

(A) aboard   (B) absurd   (C) abandon   (D) abroad

( ) 12. Leo filled out the _____ to receive a new passport.

(A) apply   (B) landmark   (C) application   (D) appreciation

( ) 13. Leo got a _____ to travel overseas.

(A) visa   (B) vote   (C) receipt   (D) invoice

( ) 14. We are _____ for Japan next fly.

(A) leaving   (B) going   (C) coming   (D) taking

( ) 15. "We've been looking for you everywhere. Where did you go?"

"I went to the airport to _____ my friend off."

(A) see   (B) look   (C) watch   (D) talk

( ) 16. I'd like to make a _____ on a flight to Japan.

(A) decision   (B) reservation   (C) ticket   (D) description

( ) 17. How many _____ do you have?

(A) pieces of luggage   (B) piece of luggage

(C) pieces of baggages   (D) luggages

( ) 18. The Paris Rapid Transit System _____ public transportation.

(A) facilitates   (B) migrates   (C) restrain   (D) operates

( ) 19. London is the _____ city of the United Kingdom.

(A) capital   (B) big   (C) solid   (D) similar

( ) 20. The President vowed to _____ down on illegal drug trade.

(A) strike   (B) purge   (C) crash   (D) crush

解答

1.C 　2.A 　3.A 　4.D 　5.A 　6.A 　7.C 　8.B 　9.D 　10.D 　11.D 　12.C

13.A 　14.A 　15.A 　16.B 　17.A 　18.A 　19.A 　20.D

綜合解析

1. difficult 常見接不定詞to。

   領隊帶團最好不要坐在經濟艙第一排，通常第一排是安排嬰兒吊床或小孩與父母同行的座位區，若坐於此較易碰到上述困擾。

2. 基本句型 It -----for ----to ---- 。

   耳機一般不可隨意取走，國際線通常不需額外付費，但是歐洲與美國國內線，有時使用耳機需另外付費，領隊應事先確認清楚後，告知團員。

3. 慣用語法 It is no use 加 Ving。

   長程線司機特別是歐洲線司機，往往台灣團體所用的多數為義大利司機，因此領隊除了英文為基本溝通語言外，義大利文也是重要的學習目標，將有助促進彼此尊重與提升領隊的專業，因為也常發生司機路況不熟，如果與司機語言無法溝通又路況不熟，那領隊這一路將是危機重重。

4. 慣用語法It take人 to V（原形）。

   市區觀光如有當地導遊，則事先應與導遊、司機協調，導遊有工作時間、司機有Bus Hours限制，必須在一定時間內完成，因此領隊一定要全力完成中文行程表的內容，以免客訴。

5. 動名詞當形容詞用。

   亞斯文水壩位於尼羅河上游，供應埃及與鄰國蘇丹重要的水力與電力，目前一般埃及團都有中文導遊隨行，領隊重點工作在於照料團員。

6. 習慣用語，主動非被動，(C)不選。

   Bucherer為勞力士的專門代理店，領隊應事先向團員說明清楚退稅規定，與離開瑞士邊境通過海關時應注意事項。

7. 補語，sit on 是慣用語，(A)(D) 不選，(B) for 加原形錯。

團體用中式餐廳，原則上是十人一桌，有些餐廳桌次安排因為空間限制，有些大桌有些小桌，但無論如何一定是要讓每一位團員都有位置坐，而且食物量一定要補充足夠，以免團員感覺不公平而產生不悅。

8. 過去分詞當形容詞。

領隊帶團應注意國際禮儀，公共場所或秀場應事先委婉告知團員應注意事項，以免有失國際禮儀，說明時應注意措辭遣字，以免得罪團員。

9. Stop Ving 停止動作；Stop to V（原形）停止去做某事。

在賭場時，領隊一般禁止與團員一起賭博，但對於賭場相關設備或遊戲規則，領隊應向團員解說介紹，最忌諱的是與團員有私人借貸行為。

10. regret 後加Ving 為慣用語，意思為後悔已告知的事。

身為領隊因職務上關係擁有團員個人資料，此資料大多為私人事務，領隊不宜向第三人談論此事，如有團員彼此需要對方個人資料，例如：婚姻狀況、工作詳情等，領隊皆不宜透露，應由團員自行處理。

11. 慣用語 go abroad 出國。

團員出國動機不同，對於團體旅遊的需求也有所不同，有人是為購物觀光、醫療觀光、賭博觀光、知性觀光等，因此身為領隊應分析每一位團員之需求，以盡力符合團員的期待為目標。

12. 應熟記字彙 application 申請表。

團員護照遺失是較麻煩的事，事前準備影印本與照片，帶團中隨時提醒團員注意；遺失時應冷靜以對，根據相關程序申請補發。

13. 應熟記字彙Visa 簽證。

簽證分為團體簽證與個別簽證，如為團簽領隊應妥善保存，個簽領隊應事先將影本留存，以防團員遺失簽證。

14. 慣用語leave for 前往。

搭機前領隊應隨時確認登機門、航班是否正確，以免搭錯飛機，或早已更

改登機閘口卻在錯誤的登機閘口空等。

15. 慣用語 see off 送行。

領隊出發當天最好勿自行開車前往，選擇搭乘大眾交通工具較好，如有友人送行最佳，實務中曾發生領隊前往機場途中不幸發生車禍，卻身懷整團護照、簽證、機票，而又無人得知領隊為何遲到，導致整團延遲出發。

16. 慣用語 make a reservation 訂位。

不論是航空公司、飯店、火車、餐廳、秀場、當地導遊等所有旅遊相關行業，都需事先訂位，而訂位不一定代表一切沒問題，領隊應做好再確認工作，特別是旺季時。

17. 慣用語 many pieces of 單數名詞。

不論是出國或返國托運行李，領隊一定要確認所有行李件數、保管好收據，團員也嚴禁幫陌生人托運行李。

18. 應熟記字彙 facilitate 加速。

團體旅行除非有自由活動時間，一般很少有機會搭乘地鐵等大眾運輸交通系統，一方面不易掌握團體，另一方面在治安狀況不佳的某些城市或區域，領隊無法照顧團員，易發生意外；除非在不得已或治安無虞狀況之下，領隊才可帶領團員搭乘大眾運輸交通系統，但也要盡量避開尖峰時段與隨時注意扒手。

19. 應熟記字彙 capital 首都。

各國首都是觀光的重點，因此，領隊對於城市觀光的地理、人文、歷史等，應要下功夫自行研讀相關旅遊資訊。

20. 慣用語 vow to 誓言。

毒品是違法物品，但少數國家列為三級毒品的大麻，在荷蘭卻是合法的。因此，領隊應嚴禁團員從事非法行為，對於團員要道德勸說，切勿違法，儘管入境隨俗，但不應違反台灣的道德規範、風俗習慣、宗教禮法與法律標準，當然領隊也要以身作則。

( ) 1. The plane leaving for Tokyo from Hong Kong will _____ at seven p.m..

    (A)depart   (B)departing

    (C)departure   (D)departed   【98外語領隊】

( ) 2. You will have to pay extra _____ for overweight baggage.

    (A)tags   (B)badges

    (C)fees   (D)credits   【98外語領隊】

( ) 3. You will get a boarding _____ after completing the check-in.

    (A)pass   (B)post

    (C)plan   (D)past   【98外語領隊】

( ) 4. People traveling to a foreign country may need to apply _____ a visa.

    (A)for   (B)of

    (C)on   (D)to   【98外語領隊】

( ) 5. Mike forgot to save the file and the computer _____ suddenly. It was a real disaster.

    (A)broke up   (B)was broke

    (C)was plugged in   (D)crashed   【99外語領隊】

( ) 6. John has to _____ the annual report to the manager before this Friday; otherwise, he will be in trouble.

    (A)identify   (B)incline

    (C)submit   (D)commemorate   【99外語領隊】

( ) 7. Millions of people are expected to _____ in the 2010 Taipei International Flora Expo.

    (A)participate   (B)adjust

    (C)emerge   (D)exist   【99外語領隊】

( ) 8. We arrived at the airport _____, so we had plenty of time for checking in and boarding.

    (A)at the best of times   (B)in our own time

    (C)dead on time   (D)in good time   【99外語領隊】

( ) 9. The prosperity of _____ tourism is related to the policy of our government.

    (A)domestic   (B)duplicated

    (C)dumb   (D)detour   【100外語領隊】

( ) 10. The travel agent _____ the delay.

    (A)astonished at   (B)astonished

    (C)apologized   (D)apologized for   【100外語領隊】

( ) 11. You must check the _____ date of your passport. You may need to apply for a new one.

    (A)explanatory   (B)exploratory

    (C)expiry   (D)expository   【100外語領隊】

( ) 12. If you're travelling to the United States, you may need a _____.

    (A)vicar   (B)villa

    (C)vista   (D)visa   【100外語領隊】

( ) 13. Now you can purchase a seat and pick up your boarding pass at the airport on the day of departure _____ simply showing appropriate identification.

    (A)together   (B)for

    (C)by   (D)with   【101外語領隊】

( ) 14. If you carry keys, knives, aerosol cans, etc., in your pocket when you pass through the security at the airport, you may _____ the alarm, and then the airport personnel will come to search you.

    (A)let on   (B)let off

    (C)set on   (D)set off   【101外語領隊】

( ) 15. Tourist: What is the baggage allowance?

Airline clerk: _____

(A)Please fill out this form.

(B)Sorry, cash is not suggested to be left in the baggage.

(C)It is very cheap.

(D)It is 20 kilograms per person. 【101外語領隊】

( ) 16. I would like to express our gratitude to you _____ behalf of my company.

(A)at (B)on

(C)by (D)with 【101外語領隊】

解答

1.A	2.C	3.A	4.A	5.D	6.C	7.A	8.D	9.A	10.D	11.C	12.D
13.C	14.D	15.D	16.B								

於登機閘口前

一、工作程序（Working Procedures）

　　於航空公司團體櫃檯辦理完成登機手續，並向團員簡短說明出入關程序後，如時間許可再做一簡單說明會，向團員再次說明此次旅遊行程的重點注意事項。此時若仍有少數團員未到，則可請已有出境經驗的團員先行離開，最後再到登機閘口集合，領隊則留下來等尚未到的少數團員。等待至起飛前1小時仍有未到集合地點的團員，則應將該團員的護照、機票、簽證與其他證件留給送機人員，請送機人員繼續等待並積極再一次聯繫未到團員的現況。

　　領隊此時應盡速通關至登機閘口，確認團員是否全數到齊進行最後清點，並逐一認識團員以加深印象，領隊應最後登機，以確認所有團員均已上機；如有少數團員仍未到登機閘口，或許在免稅店、在航空公司貴賓室或餐廳，領隊應協調航空公司地勤人員給予廣播，如有團員手機號碼應盡速聯繫。待全團上機後，領隊再協助座位安排與必要設施服務說明。

二、關鍵字彙

　　領隊應熟悉重要關鍵字彙包含下列七大項：

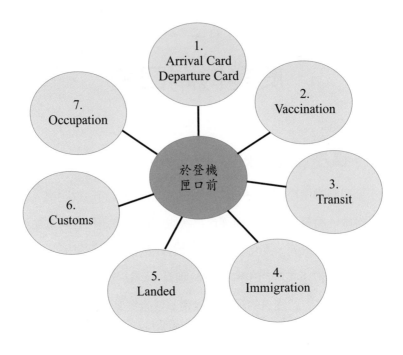

1.Arrival Card / Departure Card　入境卡 / 出境卡			
・Full Name	姓名	・Purpose of Visit	拜訪目的
・Nationality / Citizenship	國籍	・Holiday / Pleasure	渡假 / 玩樂
・Sex	性別	・Visit Friends / Relatives	拜訪朋友 / 親友
・Male / Female	男 / 女	・Convention	會議
・Place of Birth	出生地	・Business	商務
・Date of Birth	出生日期	・Accommodation	住宿
・Passport Number	護照號碼	・Intended Length of Stay	停留時間
・Country of Residence	居留國家	・Signature	簽名
・Occupation	職業	・Use Block Letters	使用大寫字體
・Accompanying Number	同行人數	・Permanently	長期
・Last Place / Port of Embarkation	最後離開地點 / 港口		
2. Vaccination　預防接種			
・Health Certification	健康證明	・Certificate	證明

3.Transit　轉機

・Transit Visa	過境簽證	・Flight Schedule Monitor	班次顯示銀幕
・International Flights	國際航線	・VIP lounge	貴賓室
・Domestic Flights	國內航線	・Visitor Information	旅客服務處
・Airport Terminal	機場航廈	・Ground Transit	地面轉乘地點
・Flight Information Board	飛機資訊顯示板	・Airport Shuttle	機場接駁車

4.Immigration　移民局

・Official Use Only	官方填寫處	・Section	部分

5.Landed　降落

・Exit/Way Out	出口	・Delayed	延誤

6.Customs　海關

・Customs Inspector	海關檢查員	・Dangerous Article	危險物品
・Goods to Declare	申報物品	・Luggage Claim	行李領取處

7.Occupation　職業

・Teacher	老師	・Architect	建築師
・Engineer	工程師	・Fireman	消防員
・Carpenter	木匠	・Dentist	牙醫師
・Pharmacist	藥劑師	・Farmer	農夫
・Nurse	護士	・Fisherman	漁夫
・Artist	藝術家	・Priest	和尚、教士
・Actor	演員	・Housewife	家管
・Dancer	舞者	・Painter	畫家
・Designer	設計師	・Barber	理髮師
・Hairdresser	美容師	・Salesman	推銷員
・Housemaid	女僕	・Businessman	企業家
・Patrol	小販	・Salesclerk	店員
・Public Official	公務員	・Statesman	政治家
・Lawyer	律師	・Pilot	飛機駕駛員
・Manual Worker	勞工、勞力者	・Unemployed people	無工作者

三、關鍵會話

(一)登機閘口——航空公司登機廣播詞

Ladies and gentlemen, Leo Airlines flight 888 will now be boarding at gate 66.

We invite those passengers with small children or those requiring special assistance to the boarding gate.

We now invite first class passengers to board.

We now invite those in business class to board.

We will begin boarding passengers seated in the main cabin now and will be boarding by row numbers from the back of the aircraft towards the front.

We now invite passengers from rows 50 to 62 to board.

We now invite passengers from rows 36 to 49 to board.

We now invite all remaining passengers to the boarding gate.

圖2-1　機場出境大廳航班狀況顯示板

(二)航空公司班機延誤廣播詞

　　Air Leo regrets to announce the Flight 777 to Geneva, scheduled to depart at 3:00 p.m. has been delayed on account of a big fog. This flight will depart at 3:45. Passengers with connecting flights will be met by an Air Leo ticket agent on arrival in Geneva.

圖2-2　機場出境檢查

(三)航空公司最後登機廣播

　　This is the final call for CX flight 260 to Bangkok, now boarding at Gate 21. Please have your boarding pass ready.

圖2-3　機場登機閘口

四、語詞測驗

1. **be delighted with [at, by]**～　對……感到高興

   The Italian driver was very delighted with his tips from Taiwan tour groups.

   那一位義大利司機對於台灣旅行團給他的小費感到高興。

2. **be disappointed in [at, by, of, with]**～　對……感到失望

   I was disappointed at the results of the local agent's arrangement.

   我對於當地代理旅行社的安排感到失望。

3. **be disposed to** ～　願意

I was disposed to help waiters to serve my group members.

我願意協助服務生去服務我的團員。

4. **be frightened at [by, of]** ～　使驚恐

I was frightened at the dreadful sight from the Ghost Tour in Edinburgh.

愛丁堡鬼之旅沿途景象令我驚恐不已。

5. **be offended at** ～　觸怒（**to take offence at**）

The driver was offended at tour leader's instructions of city tour in Paris.

那位司機對於領隊操作巴黎市區觀光的行程指示而感到生氣。

6. **be prepared to** ～　準備

We are prepared to take off.

我們準備好要起飛。

7. **be satisfied with [at]** ～　使滿意

I am not satisfied with flight attendant's service.

我不是很滿意空服員的服務。

8. **be surprised at [about, by]** ～　使驚訝

I was surprised at the shopping commissions from this group.

我對於這一團的購物佣金收入感到驚訝。

9. **be trouble with [by]** ～　使煩惱

I am trouble with the overbooking problems in hotel reservations tonight.

我對於今晚飯店超賣感到煩惱。

10. **be acquainted with** ～ 認識

I am acquainted with the Italian driver of this ten-day tour.

我認識這一次十天之旅的義大利司機。

11. **be convinced of** ～ 使（某人）明白

I am convinced of the difficulty of being through guide in East Europe.

我明白要擔任東歐團的全程領隊兼導遊是一件困難的工作。

12. **be determined to** ～ 使決心

I was determined to be a good tour leader.

我決心成為一位好領隊。

13. **be inclined to** ～ 使傾向

I was inclined not to push the night tour in Rome when my group members were tired.

當我的團員都累了，我傾向不推薦羅馬夜遊。

14. **be opposed to** ～ 反對

I am opposed to local guide's arrangement in London.

我反對倫敦當地導遊的安排。

15. **be jammed with** ～ 塞滿

The duty-free shop was jammed with the Chinese tourists.

免稅店擠滿中國觀光客。

16. **be accustomed [used] to ～** 習慣於

I am accustomed to leading the driver where to go in Europe because some drivers are newcomers.

因為一些司機是新手，在歐洲我已習慣於指示司機該往哪走。

17. **be concerned with ～** 關心到某事

Tour leader must be concerned with the crime in red-light district.

領隊應關心紅燈區的犯罪問題。

18. **be confronted with ～** 遭遇

I was confronted with many difficulties when I lead tour in Paris first time.

當我第一次帶法國團時，我遭遇到很多困難。

19. **be engaged in [on] ～** 著手某事

He has been engaged in escorting tour for thirty years.

他當了三十年的領隊。

20. **be tired after [from] ～** 疲倦的（**to be weary after [from , with]**）

Tourists are always tired from walking for a long distance.

觀光客通常走太久而感到疲倦。

21. **be abundant in ～** 擁有豐富的（某物）

The Loch Ness is not abundant in fish.

尼斯湖漁產並不豐富。

22. **be accessible to ～** 易接近的

Tour leader is accessible to tourists.

領隊應易於接近團員。

23. **be alive [sensitive] to ～** 對……敏感

Glowworms are alive to sound and light in New Zealand.

紐西蘭螢火蟲對於聲音與光敏感。

24. **be ambitious for ～** 熱切期望的

Tour leader should not only be ambitious for money.

領隊不應只有熱切期望於賺錢。

25. **be angry at [about, over, with] ～** 憤怒的

I was angry at tour leader's behavior.

我對於領隊行為感到生氣。

五、文法測驗

本章重點：疑問句分析

疑問句what, which	What happened? 發生了什麼事？
疑問句who	Who came first, the tour guide or driver in airport? 誰先到機場，是導遊或司機？
疑問句how	How do you like Budapest? 你覺得布達佩斯怎麼樣？
疑問句how, what	How's your company? 你的公司好嗎？
How many, how much	How many people are there in your group? 你這一團多少人？
how often	How often do you visit Paris? 你多久來巴黎一次？
how far, how long	How far is it from here to the TGV station? 從這裡到子彈列車車站有多遠？
介系詞+疑問句	To whom are you speaking? 你正在和誰講話？

why, what for	Why did you visit London? 你為什麼去倫敦觀光？
where +介系詞	Where do you come from? 你是從哪裡來的？
when	When does show begin? 秀什麼時候開始演？
附加問句	It is very fine, isn't it? 天氣非常好，不是嗎？

本章綜合練習

( ) 1. "Did you write to tour guide last month?"

"No, but I'll _____ her over Christmas vacation."

(A) be seen (B) be seeing

(C) have seen (D) have been seeing

( ) 2. Who's that girl tour guide's talking with? I _____ her before.

(A) never had seen (B) had never seen

(C) was never seeing (D) never saw

( ) 3. Tour leader keeps talking about the optional tour, she had a very good time,

_____ she?

(A) hadn't (B) had (C) didn't (D) weren't

( ) 4. "They don't seem to answer their phone when tour leader call."

"There isn't anyone at room, _____?"

(A) isn't there (B) is there (C) is it (D) isn't it

( ) 5. He's taken his medicine, _____?

(A) hasn't he (B) didn't he (C) doesn't he (D) isn't he

( ) 6. Tour leader said she _____ her lunch when the driver came.

(A) finishes (B) had finished

(C) has finished (D) had been finished

( ) 7. We had to wait a long time to get our visas, _____?

(A) don't we　(B) didn't we　(C) couldn't we　(D) shouldn't we

( ) 8. Tour leader had done that before, _____?

(A) wouldn't he　(B) shouldn't he　(C) hadn't he　(D) didn't he

( ) 9. We ought to go Grand Canyon National Park by plane, _____?

(A) shouldn't we　(B) wouldn't we　(C) should we　(D) would we

( ) 10. Tour leader never dared to go gambling, _____?

(A) daren't he　(B) dare he　(C) didn't he　(D) did he

( ) 11. We should _____ the Rhine River cruise at least ten minutes before departure.

(A) arrive　(B) book　(C) board　(D) go

( ) 12. They had to _____ their fly because of heavy raining.

(A) go to　(B) delay　(C) forward　(D) board

( ) 13. Won't you have a seat? _____

(A) Yes, please do.　　　　　　(B) I am sorry.

(C) No, I will.　　　　　　　　(D) Thanks, I will.

( ) 14. Have you _____ the cost of the hotel?

(A) figured out　(B) figured at　(C) figured in　(D) figured

( ) 15. Whenever I _____ these days in Oslo, I always carry my raincoat.

(A) shall go out　(B) am going out　(C) would go out　(D) go out

( ) 16. "Was the driving pleasant when you vacationed in Australia last summer?"

"No, it _____ for four days when we arrived, so the roads were very muddy."

(A) was raining　　　　　　　(B) would be raining

(C) had been raining　　　　　(D) have rained

（　）17. "What were you doing when local guide phoned you?"

　　　　"I had just finished my work and _____ to take a bath."

　　　　(A) starting　(B) to start　(C) have started　(D) was starting

（　）18. How many people _____ the travel conference of London Travel Fair?

　　　　(A) attended　　　　　　　　(B) is attending

　　　　(C) do they attend　　　　　(D) was attending

（　）19. When I arrived in Sorrento the sun _____ .

　　　　(A) has been shining　　　　(B) shone

　　　　(C) has shone　　　　　　　(D) was shining

（　）20. "Leo is taking a month's vacation in June."

　　　　"That's nice. Did he say where _____?"

　　　　(A) is he going　(B) he goes　(C) he's going　(D) will he go

解答

1.B	2.D	3.C	4.B	5.A	6.B	7.B	8.C	9.A	10.D	11.C	12.B
13.D	14.C	15.D	16.C	17.D	18.A	19.D.	20.C				

綜合解析

1. 文法測驗，未來進行式。

　隨時與旅遊相關行業的從業人員保持良好互動，而身為領隊應在平時做好個人人際關係的建立，出外靠朋友是領隊體會最深的一句名言。

2. 文法測驗，過去式。

　領隊應注意基本帶團禮節，稱呼團員應加稱謂，不可直接叫出團員名字，指示方向或點名時，應將手的五指併攏，而不宜用單一手指方式，指點團員。

3. 附加問句，根據動詞而來，had為過去式。

　適度的自費活動與具特色的自費活動，對於整體旅遊滿意度是有提升的作

用，但是如果是為降低成本，把應該原來包在團體旅遊活動的項目切割成許多自費活動，再迫使由領隊推銷自費活動，當然身為領隊壓力也隨之增加。

4. 附加問句，根據動詞而來，isn't 為動詞。

領隊分房後應盡速查房，確認所有團員房間設施是否正常，團員是否了解所有房間設備如何操作，電話查房也是可行之道，特別是異性房間或團員住宿單人房時，領隊不宜獨自前往查房較宜。

5. 附加問句，根據動詞而來，has 為動詞。

身為領隊不論任何狀況下，都不應拿口服藥品給予團員，除非有醫師在場或經過醫師的同意，有狀況時則應盡速送醫。

6. 時態：過去完成式。

領隊應招呼團員用餐後，始可自行用餐，一般會與司機同桌；如有導遊同行用餐，可以一齊討論行程內容。如遇停車不易或治安不佳旅遊地區，應請司機待在車上照料，以免車上東西失竊或車子遭破壞。而領隊應事先詢問司機是否要帶便當與飲料給他，再煩請司機利用空檔再進餐。團員用餐完畢，領隊也應結束用餐，也就是說比團員晚用餐，早結束。

7. 附加問句，根據動詞而來，had 為動詞。

少數國家為落地簽證或外站取簽證，領隊出國前要確認清楚，並將落地簽證之必要證件準備妥當，減少作業時間，避免團員不耐煩。

8. 附加問句，根據動詞而來。

帶團旅遊非靠記憶與背誦，唯有不斷的實務操作累積經驗才是上策，你做過嗎？你去過嗎？你吃過嗎？你玩過嗎？你聽過嗎？

9. 附加問句，根據動詞而來或習慣用語。

旅遊市場激烈競爭的結果，許多行程拉車時間過久，此時領隊車上帶團技巧就格外重要，一方面要掌握時間不能超過司機工作時間(Bus Hour)，有時甚至要中途換車或司機，以避免超時違法。因此，領隊遇到行程拉車過久

時，事先準備功夫就要強化。旅行業者也應避免一味殺價取量，而忘了人性化的考量。美西大峽谷國家公園一天拉車來回拉斯維加斯，就是非人性化的行程安排。

10. 附加問句，根據動詞而來或習慣用語。

領隊要以身作則不要介入賭博，但要說明賭場相關注意規則，讓團員清楚賭場遊戲規則與禮節。

11. 慣用語board 登機、登船。

飛機、火車、輪船的出發時間都不等人，因此領隊要提前抵達，避免延誤行程，又要善後處理，往往所費不貲。根據相關法令規定，延誤行程超過5小時，要算一天團費賠償給團員，因此領隊帶團時間掌握不可不慎。

12. 關鍵字彙 delay 延誤。

遇到緊急事件，領隊首先要冷靜以對，之後要站在團員的角度設想，將損害減至最低。如果去程飛機延誤，後續則要聯繫國外代理旅行社、導遊、司機、餐廳與飯店等等一系列的行程變動，不管是由於人為疏失或非人力所能控制的因素，最高原則是讓行程走完。相對的，如果是返國時遇到延誤，所衍生事端較少；但如果轉機接不上，那領隊臨場應變能力就愈顯重要。

13. 附加問句，根據動詞而來或習慣用語。

領隊帶團要以服務至上，服務好與壞較難以量化，但切記不要有明顯瑕疵，成為客訴的主要原因。

14. 習慣用語 figure in計算、figure out 了解。

領隊帶團不僅是把團帶好，關於所有相關旅遊成本也要了解，有時團員會比較別團，甚至同一團的團員，為何價格有所差異的問題，領隊應有正確回答的能力，偶爾團員有加開房間或延回時，飯店房價也是團員所關切的問題之一。

15. 原形動詞。

領隊出國前必備的旅行用品應備妥，若因缺少的旅行用品而造成領隊身體不佳，必定影響帶團效果。除此之外，說明會時應向團員說明清楚，避免旅行不便，領隊也困擾。

16. 過去完成進行式。

不論是雨天或風雪天，領隊要注意行車安全，每日出車前確認車子狀況。行車中要注意司機精神狀況，並囑咐團員盡量不要坐在第一排較安全。

17. 過去進行式。

領隊應至少前一天與當地導遊聯繫，以利隔天行程順利進行。

18. 習慣用語 attend conference 參加會議。

世界知名旅展，身為旅行業從業人員有機會也應積極參與，掌握市場趨勢與潮流，有機會可以開發新的旅遊行程與景點。

19. 過去進行式。

義大利蘇連多是著名海邊渡假遊樂區，也是名謠「歸來吧！蘇連多」描述地點，搭乘水翼船前往卡布里島更是義大利南部重要的行程，但是「藍洞」是否能親自目睹則要靠運氣，天氣不佳，導致風浪太大，則往往要敗興而歸。

20. 未來進行式。

自由領隊（Freelance）一年超過一半都在帶團，自我調適與休息也是非常重要的事，否則團帶多、帶久，往往會彈性疲乏，影響帶團服務品質。適度休假陪伴家人與親友是必要的，同時也可以學習新東西，甚至不同國家語言，以利再度出發帶團環遊世界。

( ) 1. We are sorry. All lines are currently busy. Please _____ on for the next available agent.

(A)keep (B)hold

(C)call (D)take 【98外語領隊】

( ) 2. All passengers shall go through _____ check before boarding.

(A)security (B)activity

(C)insurance (D)deficiency 【98外語領隊】

( ) 3. He got his visa at the eleventh hour.

(A)at the last moment (B)at eleven o'clock

(C)before noon (D)by midnight 【98外語領隊】

( ) 4. I was supposed to meet John at the concert hall, but he stood me up.

(A)kept his promise (B)knew it well

(C)canceled the reservation (D)didn't show up 【98外語領隊】

( ) 5. Tom was _____ from his school for stealing and cheating on the exams.

(A)exempted (B)expelled

(C)exported (D)evacuated 【99外語領隊】

( ) 6. Mary is _____ divorce because her husband is having an affair with his secretary.

(A)controling to (B)filing for

(C)calling for (D)accustomed to 【99外語領隊】

( ) 7. This express train _____ at 9:30 am every day. You can plan a short walk before that in the itinerary.

(A)is about to leave (B)will leave

(C)will be leaving (D)leaves 【99外語領隊】

( ) 8. The number of independent travelers _____ steadily since the new policy was announced.

(A)rose
(B)has risen
(C)arose
(D)has arisen 【99外語領隊】

( ) 9. Our parents were high on love and patience, and therefore we followed their instructions willingly.

(A)rejoiced
(B)transcended
(C)valued
(D)taught 【100外語領隊】

( ) 10. She is not so stupid _____ not to understand that.

(A)so
(B)with
(C)as
(D)for 【100外語領隊】

( ) 11. What shall we do _____?

(A)after a dinner
(B)after dinner
(C)after we dinner
(D)after the dinner 【100外語領隊】

( ) 12. I am so happy that Nick is coming to visit us. Please tell him to make himself _____ home.

(A)inside
(B)in
(C)on
(D)at 【100外語領隊】

( ) 13. There was a slight departure delay at the airport due to _____ weather outside.

(A)forbidden
(B)inclement
(C)declined
(D)mistaken 【101外語領隊】

( ) 14. In the interests of safety, passengers should carry _____ dangerous items nor matches while on board.

(A)either
(B)or
(C)neither
(D)not 【101外語領隊】

（　）15. All of the students cried out excitedly ＿＿＿＿ knowing that the midterm ex-

amination had been canceled.

(A)for example　　　　　　　　(B)because

(C)as long as　　　　　　　　(D)upon　　　　　　【101外語領隊】

（　）16. All the employees have to use an electronic card to ＿＿＿＿ in when they ar-

rive for work.

(A)clock　　　　　　　　(B)access

(C)enter　　　　　　　　(D)apply　　　　　　【101外語領隊】

解答

1.B	2.A	3.A	4.D	5.B	6.B	7.D	8.B	9.C	10.C	11.B	12.D
13.B	14.C	15.D	16.A								

第三章

搭機時

一、工作程序（Working Procedures）

團員清點確認無誤後，如有需要小幅度座位調整，領隊應即時完成，以利航空公司機上服務人員，起飛前作業。對於必要之設施應事先向團員說明清楚，領隊切勿認為登機後，所有服務工作都是空服人員的工作，而自己卻倒頭就睡。

本階段重點工作是對於「座位的調整」、「特殊餐食的安排」與「飛行途中的照料」。即時貼心的關心與服務、第一時間的與團員接觸，從「沒見過」、「不認識」、「認得」、「感覺還不錯」、「有事就找領隊」、「找領隊準沒錯」、「熟得像多年老友」是領隊帶團應努力的目標。

二、關鍵字彙

搭機時領隊所應熟悉的關鍵字彙包含下列八項：

1.In-Flight　飛行用語

• Jet Aircraft	噴射客機	• Assigned Seat	指定座位
• Upper Deck	上層客艙	• Buckle	帶釦
• Upright Position	椅背豎直	• Ozone	臭氧
• Straps	帶子	• Control Tower	塔台
• Playing Cards	玩撲克牌	• Diversion	降落備用機場
• In-Flight Service	機上服務	• Apron	停機坪
• Pre-Boarding	優先登機	• Runways	跑道
• Recline	斜倚	• Crash	墜機
• Open Seat	先上先坐	• Maintenance Area	維修區
• Center Seat	中央位置	• Sky Kitchen	空中廚房
• Off Load	被拉下座位無法搭機	• Lavatory Paper	衛生紙
• Denied Boarding Compensation		被拒絕登機而要求之賠償	

2.Aircrew　機組員

• Captain	機長	• Cabin Crew	機艙空服員
• First Officer	副機師	• Stewardess	空姐
• Chief Purser	空服長	• Steward	空少
• Purser	座艙長	• Ground Staff	地勤人員
• Flight Attendant	空服員	• Pilot	飛行員

3.Cabin Interior　機內設備

• Overhead Compartment	頭頂置物箱	• Lavatory	洗手間
• Seat	座椅	• Smoke Detector	煙霧偵測器
• Armrest	扶手	• Emergency Door	緊急出口
• Tray Table	折疊餐桌	• Reading Light Switch	閱讀燈開關
• Seatbelt	安全帶	• Attendant Call Button	服務鈴
• Movie Screen	電影銀幕	• Headphone Jack	耳機插座
• Headset=Headphone	耳機	• Volume Control	音量控制鈕
• Window Shade	遮光窗簾	• Channel Selector	頻道選擇鈕
• Escape Slide	逃生滑梯	• In-Flight Magazine	機上雜誌
• Oxygen Mask	氧氣罩	• Toilet Flush	沖水按鈕
• Bassinet	嬰兒搖籃	• Blanket	毯子
• First-Aid Kit	急救箱	• Pillow	枕頭

4.Signs on the Flight　機艙內標誌

· No Smoking	禁菸	· Occupied	洗手間使用中
· Fasten Seat Belt	繫安全帶	· Vacant	洗手間可使用

5.Flight Information　飛行資訊

· Distance to Destination	離目的地距離	· Outside Air Temperature	機外溫度
· Local Time at Origin	出發地目前時間	· Altitude	高度
· Local Time at Destination	目的地現在時間	· Longitude	經度
· Estimated Arrival Time	預估到達時間	· Latitude	緯度
· Speed	速度	· Refuel	加油

6.Situation on the Plane　機上狀況

· Airsickness	暈機	· Life Vest= Life Jacket	救生衣
· Sickness Bag	嘔吐袋	· Turbulence	亂流
· Disposal Bag	廢物袋	· Life Raft	救生艇
· Hijack	劫機	· Jet Lag	時差失調
· Hostage	人質	· Descent	下降

7.Weather　天氣

· Weather Forecast	氣象預測	· Cloudy	陰天的
· Hurricane	颶風	· Foggy	起霧

8.Meal　餐食

· Light Meal	簡餐	· Child Meal	兒童餐
· Hindu Meal　（HNML）	印度餐（無牛肉）		
· Moslem Meal　（MOML）	回教餐（無豬肉）		
· Kosher Meal　（KSML）	猶太教餐食		
· Orient Meal　（ORML）	東方式餐（葷食）		
· Vegetarian Meal　（VGML）	西方素食（無奶、無蔥、薑、蒜）		
· Asian Vegetarian Meal　（AVML）	東方素食（無奶、無蛋、無蔥、薑、蒜）		
· Low Salt Meal　（LSML）	低鈉無鹽餐		
· Baby Meal　（BBML）	嬰兒餐		
· Snack	點心	· Drink	飲料
· Instant Noodles	泡麵	· Orange Juice	柳橙汁
· Sugar	糖	· Tomato Juice	蕃茄汁
· Fish	魚肉	· Coffee	咖啡

• Veal	小牛肉	• Tea	茶
• Chicken	雞肉	• Ginger Ale	薑汁汽水
• Beef	牛肉	• Seven-Up	七喜汽水
• Rice	米飯	• Coke	可樂
• Cream	奶油	• Pepsi Cola	百事可樂
• Hot Towel	熱毛巾	• Mineral Water	礦泉水

三、關鍵會話

(一)飛行中服務

【Scene：In flight】

Stewardess：Do you need anything to drink, sir?

Tour Leader: What kind of drink do you have?

Stewardess：We have coffee, tea, juice, Coke, Spirit, and water.

Tour Leader: Coke for the two children by the window and tea for me, please.

Stewardess：Anything else?

Tour Leader: May I have two pieces of lemon slices?

Stewardess：Here you are.

Tour Leader: Thank you. By the way, give me one more pillow, please.

Stewardess：OK.

Tour Leader: One more question. How long does it take to get to Rome?

Stewardess：We will be on schedule, in about 3 hours.

Tour Leader: Thanks.

圖3-1　確認登機門與所搭乘的航班

㈡點飲料服務

【Scene：In flight】

Tour Leader　：Miss, may I have something to drink?

Stewardess　：Of course, what kind of drink do you want to drink?

Tour Leader　：I want a glass of wine.

Stewardess　：Red wine or white wine?

Tour Leader　：Red wine, please.

Stewardess　：Here you are.

Tour member：What did you drink, tour leader?

Tour Leader　：Red wine. Do you want to drink?

Tour member: Please order another one for me.

Tour Leader ：No problem. Excuse me, Miss. Could you give this gentleman for a glass of red wine?

Stewardess ：Here you are.

圖3-2　事先確認座位配置，登機時協助安排調整座位

㈢用餐服務

【Scene：In flight】

Stewardess ：Excuse me. It is time for dinner. Would you mind putting down the tray?

Tour Leader ：Of course not, what kind of food can I have?

Stewardess ：We offer chicken with rice and stewed beef with noodles.

Which one do you prefer?

Tour Leader : stewed beef with noodles, please.

Stewardess : OK. Would you like something to drink?

Tour Leader : I want to have a glass of red wine.

Stewardess : No problem. Is there anything else I can do for you?

Tour Leader : May I also have a cup of Chinese tea, please?

Stewardess : Tea will be served by the other attendant. Please wait for a while.

Tour Leader : No problems. Excuse me, Miss. Could you give this lady for a glass of white wine?

Tour member: Tour leader, it's very considerate of you.

圖 3-3　協助團員行李置放機上置物箱

機上廣播詞

狀況一

各位女士、各位先生，（早、午、晚）安：

這是機長（副機長、座艙長謹代表機長） ___ 廣播，歡迎搭乘 ___ 航空公司第 ___ 次班機，由 ___ 到 ___ 。我們現在的飛行高度是 ___ 呎，（相當於 ___ 公尺），平均的飛行速度，每小時 ___ 哩（相當於每小時 ___ 公里）。根據今天預定的飛行計畫，飛行時間需要 ___ 小時 ___ 分鐘。預計在 ___ 月 ___ 日星期 ___ 的（清晨、下午、晚上） ___ 點 ___ 分到達 ___ 機場。 ___ 與 ___ 兩地的時差是 ___ 小時，現在當地的時間是（清晨、下午、晚上） ___ 點 ___ 分。根據天氣預測，當我們抵達 ___ 的時候是（晴、陰、雨、下雪）天，地面的溫度是攝氏 ___ 度，相當於華氏 ___ 度。沿途天氣預測（相當好、可能有輕微亂流），請各位在座時，確實將安全帶繫好，祝您旅途愉快，謝謝！

Good (morning, afternoon, evening), ladies and gentlemen:

This is captain ___ speaking (on behalf of captain ___, this is your first officer, purser speaking). Welcome aboard ___ airlines, flight No. ___ from ___ to ___ . We are now flying at an altitude of ___ feet (equal to ___ meters) and with an average ground speed of ___ miles per hour (equal to ___ kilometers per hour). According to our computerized flight plan, the flight time is ___ hour(s) and ___ minutes. The estimated time of at ___ airport is ___ : ___ in the (morning, afternoon, evening) on ___ (Day) ___ (Month) ___ (Date). The time difference between ___ and ___ is ___ hour(s). The local time is ___ : ___ in the (morning, afternoon, evening). The weather forecast at ___ airport upon our arrival is (fair skies, cloudy, raining, snowing) and the ground temperature is ___ degrees Centigrade, or ___ degrees Fahrenheit. According to the enrollee weather report, we might experience some (mile, light) turbulence. I would strongly recommend that while you are seated keep your seat belt fastened. I hope you will enjoy this flight. Thank you.

狀況二

　　各位女士、各位先生，（早、午、晚）　安：這是機長（座艙長）　　　 報告。

　　由於通關手續（機械故障／天氣因素／航管限制／餐點裝載／貨物或行李裝載／旅客人數不符／艙單作業／班機銜接）之原因，我們將再等待 ___ 分鐘才能啟程，謝謝您的耐心與合作。

Good (morning, afternoon, evening), ladies and gentlemen:

This is your captain ___ speaking (this is your purser ___ speaking).

Due to Immigration Formalities (Mechanical Difficulties/ Weather Below Minimum/ Air Traffic Control Restriction/ Meal loading/ Cargo/ Luggage Loading/ Passenger Count/ Ship Paper Handling/ Passenger's Connecting), we shall be waiting on the ground for ___ minutes. Thank you for your patience and cooperation.

狀況三

　　女士們、先生們：早上好／下午好／晚上好：

　　歡迎您乘坐 ___ 航空公司 ___ 號班機前往 ___ 。預計空中飛行的時間是 ___ 小時 ___ 分鐘。我們的機長是 ___ 先生。座艙長／資深空服員是 ___ 小姐／先生。

　　在起飛前，請您繫好安全帶，豎直椅背，扣好小桌板。由於這是一架禁菸班機，在整個飛行途中都不准吸菸，在洗手間裡吸菸不單會觸動煙霧警報器，而且是違法的。

我們很榮幸與您一起飛行，祝您旅途愉快，謝謝！

Good Morning/Afternoon/Evening, ladies and gentlemen:

Welcome aboard our ___ airlines flight No. ___ to ___ . Travel time to ___ will be ___ hour(s) and ___ minutes, Captain ___ is in command and your Chief/Leading Flight Attendant is ___ .

Before we take-off, please make sure your seat back is upright, tray table stowed and seatbelt fastened. As this is a "NO SMOKING" flight, please do not smoke in the cabin or toilets throughout the flight. Smoking in the toilets will activate the smoke alarm and is prohibited by law.

We are glad to have you on board and we wish you a pleasant flight. Thank you.

狀況四

各位女士、各位先生：

航機很快就會在 ___ 降落了，請回到您的座位上，把椅背調直、餐桌鎖妥、繫好您的安全帶。我們希望您對機上的娛樂節目感到滿意，請您將耳機準備好，以便空服員前往收取。

在此，請您關掉所有的手提電子設備。再次提醒您，在抵達機場的候機大廳之前，請不要使用手提電話，謝謝！

Ladies and Gentlemen:

In a short while, we will be landing at ___ . Please return to your seat, put your seat back upright, tray table stowed and fasten your seatbelt. We hope you have enjoyed our in-flight entertainment. Please have your headsets ready for collection by the cabin crew.

At this time, all electronic devices must be switched off. Please be reminded that all mobile phones must not be switched on until you are in the terminal building.

Thank you.

狀況五

各位女士、各位先生：

我們現在已經降落在 ＿＿ 機場，在飛機還沒有完全停妥及機長未將「請扣安全帶」的指示燈熄滅以前，請您不要解開安全帶。

再次提醒您，在客艙內請勿使用行動電話及所有電子儀器用品。同時，當您打開行李箱時，請小心箱內物品，以免滑落下來。下機時，請不要忘了您的手提行李。

＿＿ 航空公司感謝您的惠顧，希望您能再度搭乘。謝謝！

Ladies and Gentlemen:

We have just landed at ___ airport. Please keep your seatbelt fasten until the aircraft has come to a complete stop and the seatbelt sign is turned off.

May we remind you again that using the mobile phones or any electronic devices in the cabin is strictly prohibited? Meanwhile, please be careful while opening the overhead compartment as any items stowed inside might fall out, and take all your personal belongings with you.

Thank you for flying ___ and we hope to have you join us again soon.

四、語詞測驗

1. **be anxious for** ～ 渴望的

Tourists are anxious for good service from tour guide.
觀光客渴望來自導遊的好服務。

2. **be apt to** ～　易於

Tour leaders are apt to make money but forgot to offer good service.

領隊易於只想賺錢，卻忘了提供好的服務。

3. **be available for** ～　有用的、能出席的

The Chinese-speaking guide wasn't available for the Taiwanese tour groups in high season.

旺季時，說中文的導遊往往不足服務台灣旅遊團體。

4. **be aware of** ～　曉得的、意識到的

Are you aware of the difficulty of promoting the optional tours?

你意識到推自費活動的困難性嗎？

5. **be bound for** ～　前往的

This plane is bound for Seoul.

這班飛機飛往首爾。

6. **be bound to** ～　一定、必須（有義務的）

Tour leaders are bound to obey their travel agencies' rules when leading tours.

領隊一定要遵守旅行社的規定帶團。

7. **be careful of** ～　留意某事

Be careful of your valuables in flea market.

在逛跳蚤市場時，小心你的貴重東西。

8. **be caught in** ～ （被雨）淋濕

We were caught in a shower on our way to hotel.

我們返回飯店途中被雨淋濕。

9. **be cautious of** ～ 謹慎的

You must be cautious of not giving offence to tourists.

你必須小心謹慎勿冒犯團員。

10. **be sure of** ～ 確信

I am sure of local guide will be on time.

我深信當地導遊將會準時。

11. **be clever [good] at** ～ 擅長的

This tour guide is clever at Franch history.

這位導遊擅長法國歷史。

12. **be useful to** ～ 有助益的

Red wine is useful to good health.

紅酒有益於健康。

13. **be conscious of** ～ 知道的

Are you conscious of the result of the drama？

你知道這齣戲劇的結局嗎？

14. **be consistent with** ～ 一致的

This tour leader's conduct is not consistent with what he says.

這位領隊言行不一致。

15. be cross with ～　不高興的

Tour leader was cross with the driver for being late for picking up group.

領隊因為司機接團遲到感到不悅。

16. be curious to ～　好奇的

I am curious to know what poker dealer will do.

我很好奇撲克牌發牌者接下來會做什麼。

17. be due to ～　預定

I am due to go shopping tonight.

我預計今晚去購物。

18. be eager to ～　渴望的

I'm eager to work with you.

我渴望與你一起合作。

19. be empty [vacant] of ～　缺乏

The room was completely empty of air conditioner.

這房間沒有冷氣。

20. be essential to ～　必要的

Tips are essential to good servers.

小費對提供好服務者是必要的。

21. be familiar with ～　熟識

I am familiar with this local guide.

我對這位當地導遊很熟悉。

22. **be famous for ～** 聞名的

This Fontainebleau Palace is famous for its scenic beauty.

楓丹白露宮是以它的風景之美而聞名。

23. **be fit for ～** 適合於

You are fit for the job as a tour leader.

你適合當領隊。

24. **be fresh from ～** 剛出來的

He is fresh from tour leader training program.

他剛受完領隊訓練計畫。

25. **be good for ～** 有效的

This ticket is good for one month.

這張票有效期間是一個月。

五、文法測驗

本章重點：祈使句、感嘆句、祈願句分析

祈使句	Come over here.
	來這裡。
	Shut the door.
	關上門。
	Let tourists come in.
	讓觀光客進來。
祈使句+and/or	Hurry up, and you'll catch the last train.
	趕快，那麼你就能趕上最後一班火車。
	Hurry up, or you'll miss the last ferry.
	趕快，否則你會錯過最後一班渡輪。

感嘆句、祈願句	How beautiful tour guide is! 導遊多麼漂亮啊! May you have a good time in Rome! 願你在羅馬玩得愉快!

本章綜合練習

( ) 1. Come here a moment, _____?

    (A) will you   (B) shall you   (C) do you   (D) don't you

( ) 2. Don't put off _____ the work on account of my being unable to solve the problem.

    (A) to do   (B) having done   (C) to have done   (D) doing

( ) 3. "Would you like something more to eat?"

    "No, let's just have our flight attendant _____ some more tea."

    (A) bring   (B) brought   (C) to bring   (D) bringing

( ) 4. Hoteliers asked us _____ any noise.

    (A) don't make   (B) not to make   (C) to not make   (D) make not

( ) 5. Look at tour guide! What _____?

    (A) does he   (B) he is doing   (C) is he doing   (D) does he do

( ) 6. Look at these clouds. _____.

    (A) It'll rain.   (B) It's going to rain.

    (C) It'll be raining.   (D) It is to rain.

( ) 7. Hand in your reports when you _____ the tour.

    (A) are finishing   (B) will finish

    (C) will have finished   (D) have finished

( ) 8. Do not disturb me. I _____ e-mail all morning and have written ten so far.

(A) write (B) have written

(C) was writing (D) have been writing

( ) 9. Let's start city tour as soon as he _____.

(A) would come (B) will come (C) came (D) comes

( ) 10. _____yourself at home.

(A) Making (B) Make (C) Get (D) Do

( ) 11. Would you please _____ your seatbelt?

(A) tie (B) fasten (C) pack (D) hold

( ) 12. The high speed train is _____.

(A) on schedule (B) in schedule

(C) on the schedule (D) up to schedule

( ) 13. They had to _____ their fly because of tornado.

(A) delete (B) sign (C) postpone (D) recommend

( ) 14. Put out your cigarette _____.

(A) in no time (B) no time (C) not in time (D) on time

( ) 15. The plane will_____soon.

(A) take care (B) take apart (C) take away (D) take off

( ) 16. Let's go swimming, _____?

(A) will we (B) don't we (C) are we (D) shall we

( ) 17. Calm down! You can't think carefully if you are too _____.

(A) emotional (B) pleasant (C) respectful (D) speechless

( ) 18. Hurry up or you will _____ the bus.

(A) lost (B) miss (C) loose (D) lose

( ) 19. Let him alone, _____?

(A) shall he (B) will you (C) must he (D) let he

（ 　）20. You had _____ your seats today if you want to be on the train.

(A) better to reserve (B) better reserve

(C) to better reserve (D) the best reserve

解答

1.A	2.D	3.A	4.B	5.C	6.B	7.D	8.D	9.D	10.B	11.B	12.A
13.C	14.A	15.D	16.D	17.A	18.B	19.B	20.B				

綜合解析

1. 附加問句，客氣用語。

   領隊與司機、導遊或團員互動，應使用最尊敬的語氣與詞彙。

2. 習慣用語 put off 加Ving。

   領隊遇到事情應盡速處理，不應抱著鴕鳥心態，得過且過，拖到不可收拾的地步。

3. 習慣用語 have someone do（原形） something。

   隨時注意團員的需求，飛機上服務工作不單是空服員的事，領隊更要協助空服員服務團員，特別是有訂特別餐的少數團員更換座位時，領隊應即時告知該區服務空姐或空少；如團員有特殊需求，領隊要協助處理。

4. 習慣用語 ask someone to do something。

   團員至飯店應保持安靜，勿干擾其他團員，領隊安排房間應將同行家人或夫妻帶小孩或祖父母帶兒子、孫子的團員，安排緊鄰房間；如遇特殊狀況也應排在同一樓層，以減少噪音產生的機會，也利於團員彼此間的互動。Connecting Room 與 Adjoining Room 是領隊應善用的房間。

5. 慣用語。

   領隊是團員之友、團員之師，所作所為應以身作則。

6. 未來式。

天氣會影響旅遊團體的操作，特別是操作自費活動時。一旦下雨，夜遊不適宜、搭機看不清楚景色、出海風浪大、遊船也不方便等，因此領隊要懂得取捨，若天氣不佳強硬進行，自費活動效果當然好不到哪去，反而一切應先以旅遊安全為考量、團員滿意為優先之原則。

7. 慣用語 hand in 繳交／finish tour 結束。

領隊要養成每天記帳的習慣，否則返國後記憶再佳，也會忘記，特別是天數長、牽涉零用金、外幣匯率等。此外，除了應有帳目要清楚外，行程意見與報告也是領隊提供公司修改行程與產品的寶貴意見來源。

8. 現在完成進行式。

領隊帶領長程線團體往往少則十天多到十七天，有時應善用資訊科技，隨時與公司或家人保持聯繫，手機、輕型筆記型電腦、GPS也都是領隊必備之工具。

9. let 祈使句後加原形。

市區觀光應先完成中文行程表的所有內容，如有額外時間，也可以協調導遊或司機在不增加成本的前提下，帶領團員至行程外的景點，增加團員滿意度。

10. 祈使句句首使用原形。

領隊或導遊帶團都應讓團員有賓至如歸的感覺，特別是人在國外，領隊是團員最佳的朋友；行程中如遇到屬於團員的特別日子，也應該為團員慶祝，例如：生日、結婚週年紀念日等。

11. 慣用語 fasten seatbelt 繫緊安全帶。

搭機不論氣流平穩與否都應繫緊安全帶，特別是長途飛行要就寢時。

12. 慣用語 on schedule 按時刻表。

搭乘高速火車，例如：新幹線、德國ICE、法國TGV、西班牙AVE或歐洲之星等，務必提早到達，團體行李太多應規劃置放不同車廂，一般列車停靠

時間很短，要提醒團員盡速上車。否則應建議公司包含行李托運服務，以免行李來不及上火車。上了火車後應再次提醒團員注意貴重行李與隨身物品，小心扒手。

13. 慣用語 postpone 延期。

盡速確定交通工具延誤的原因並安撫團員情緒，爭取應有權益，包括：必要餐食與休息場所，如果時間超過6小時，應有飯店休息或住宿地點，領隊應站在團員立場，盡力以合法、合理、合情、有禮貌的方式爭取團員權益。

14. 片語 in no time 立刻。

法定規範場所當然嚴禁抽菸，特別危害公共安全之地方，例如：飛機、船上、餐廳與飯店房間等，但有時秀場、部分火車車廂或咖啡廳仍可以抽菸，但要注意禮節。也不可諱言，菸有時是領隊與導遊，甚至是司機之間，重要「溝通工具」，有時可以帶一條菸以備不時之需。

15. 慣用語 take off 起飛。

領隊於飛機起飛前要再三提醒團員，扣緊安全帶、豎直椅背、收好餐桌等三部曲，這也是搭機的基本禮節。

16. 慣用語。

海邊、游泳池、湖邊、河邊等戲水場所，領隊都需事先多宣導注意事項，就算有安全救生員時仍需要注意團員安全；若有禁止下水的警告標誌或無救生員值班時，應告誡團員勿輕易下水。

17. 必備單字emotional 感性的。

身為專業領隊要冷靜沈著，不要過於感性處理緊急或意外事件，以Trouble Dealer自許，時時為團員著想、處處為團員解決困難。

18. 慣用語 miss the bus。

寧願早到，也不要遲到，是領隊最高守則，否則後續處理工作有可能傷財、傷身、傷信譽且傷自我專業形象。

19. 附加問句也是慣用語。

領隊自我情緒控制與心理建設也是必要的，遇到不順利的人、事、時、地、物，仍要樂觀以對，尋求解決與最佳的結果，不僅要有效率也要有效果，因為領隊是團員在國外最值得信賴的領導者與朋友。

20. 慣用語 had better 最好。

餐廳、交通工具等事先要訂位且要再確認（reconfirm），特別是旺季時，儘管部分當地代理旅行社（Local Agent）或導遊服務親切，會幫你做再確認動作，但相信自己往往勝過別人，忙忙忙是旅遊業者的困境，忘忘忘也是旅遊業者有時必犯下的錯誤。

歷居試題

（　）1. Please keep your seat belt ＿＿＿＿ during the flight for safety.

    (A)fasten   (B)fastened

    (C)fastening   (D)fastener   【98外語領隊】

（　）2. Jumbo jet had made ＿＿＿＿ for people ＿＿＿＿ for a long distance comfortably.

    (A)possible...to travel   (B)possible it...travel

    (C)it possible...to travel   (D)it is possible...travel

                                                 【98外語領隊】

（　）3. All drinks served on the airplane are complimentary.

    (A)for extra cost   (B)of self service

    (C)free of charge   (D)first come, first served

                                                 【98外語領隊】

（　）4. As the flight to the Bahamas was delayed for eight hours, all passengers were going bananas.

(A)buying fruits   (B)going to the market

(C)getting very angry   (D)disappointed   【98外語領隊】

(   ) 5. Please remain _____ while the plane takes off.

   (A)seated   (B)sitting

   (C)sat   (D)seating   【99外語領隊】

(   ) 6. If you take a _____ holiday, all your transport, accommodation, and even

   meals and excursions will be taken care of.

   (A)leisure   (B)business

   (C)package   (D)luxury   【99外語領隊】

(   ) 7. People _____ fireworks to celebrate New Year.

   (A)get off   (B)take off

   (C)let off   (D)put off   【99外語領隊】

(   ) 8. This trip starts _____ Easter Sunday and lasts for five days.

   (A)at   (B)on

   (C)in   (D)for   【99外語領隊】

(   ) 9. I found myself _____ an airplane.

   (A)in broad   (B)on board

   (C)abroad   (D)with boarding   【100外語領隊】

(   ) 10. After the plane touches down, we have to remain in our seats until we ____

   __ to the gate.

   (A)pass by   (B)stop over

   (C)take off   (D)taxi in   【100外語領隊】

(   ) 11. Before the plane leaves the ground, we must _____ a video related to flight

   safety.

   (A)glance   (B)look

   (C)notice   (D)watch   【100外語領隊】

(　) 12. The newlyweds are on their ＿＿＿＿ tour.

(A)blossom (B)bosom

(C)begotten (D)bridal 【100外語領隊】

(　) 13. For safety reasons, radios, CD players, and mobile phones are banned on board, and they must remain ＿＿＿＿ until the aircraft has landed.

(A)switched on (B) switch on

(C)switch off (D)switched off 【101外語領隊】

(　) 14. During take-off and landing, carry-on baggage must be placed in the over-head compartments or ＿＿＿＿ the seat in front of you.

(A)parallel (B)down

(C)underneath (D)lower 【101外語領隊】

(　) 15. "We are approaching some turbulence. For your safety, please keep your belts ＿＿＿＿ until the 'seat belt's sign goes off."

(A)fasten (B)fastened

(C)fastening (D)be fastened 【101外語領隊】

(　) 16. I was overjoyed to learn that I had accumulated enough ＿＿＿＿ to upgrade myself from coach to business class.

(A)loyalty points (B)credit cards

(C)grades (D)degrees 【101外語領隊】

解答

1.B	2.C	3.C	4.C	5.A	6.C	7.C	8.B	9.B	10.D	11.D	12.D
13.D	14.C	15.B	16.A								

第四章

轉機時

一、工作程序（Working Procedures）

領隊帶團並非每一次都是搭乘本國籍直飛（Non-Stop Fly）航班，有時必須至國外機場轉機，常見的轉機地點為新加坡、香港、澳門、曼谷、吉隆坡、東京，甚至濟州島，領隊於台灣桃園機場或小港機場時就應事先向團員說明清楚，為了「安全檢查」的理由，不論是否更換航空器，都必須將所有手提行李拿下飛機。

領隊應確實清點人數，如遇原班機繼續搭乘至下一目的地，則必須確認所有團員是否都已領取「轉機卡」（Transit Pass），而後引領團員至「候機航站」與正確離境「登機門」樓層，並應說明廁所、免稅店、貴賓室等團員會經常前往之處的所在位置，以及說明當地與台灣時差轉換的差異性，請團員調整手錶時間，與告知正確當地登機時間後，才可以讓團員解散。

如需更換航班，或轉機時間過長，則應帶領團員至可以稍作休息之處，請團員於一定時間後再回來集合，領隊再攜帶所有辦理轉機手續之「機票」、「護照」、「簽證」與「行李收據」等；盡速辦理取得下一段之登機證，如轉機時間超過4小時，宜根據公司規定帶領團員至餐廳用餐，或發放餐費請團員自行用餐。上述工作程序，領隊都應將自己行蹤及個人手機號碼一併宣布，以免發生令團員找不到領隊的窘境。

二、關鍵字彙

轉機時領隊應熟悉的重要關鍵字彙包括下列七項：

• International Airport	國際機場	• Hand Luggage	手提行李
• Domestic Airport	國內機場	• Bonded Baggage	存關行李
• Airport Terminal	航站大廈	• Personal Belonging	隨身物品
• Baggage Claim Area	領行李區	• Customs Inspector	海關檢查員
• Boarding Gate	登機門	• Firearms	槍砲、武器
• Duty-free Shop	免稅店	• Smuggled Goods	走私品
• VIP Room	貴賓室	• Seat Chart	機艙座位表
• Airport Bank	機場銀行	• No Show	該報到未到
• Connecting Fly	連接航班	• Stand By	後補
• Non-Stop Fly	直飛（不落地）	• Block the Seats	鎖位置
• Direct Fly	直飛（有中停）	• Expire Date	截止日期
• Daily Flight	每天飛的班機	• Validity	有效期
• Departures	離境	• Assigned Seating	對號入座
• Upgrade	升等	• Free Seating	不必對號入座
• Transit Pass	轉機證	• Trolley	手推車
• On Time	準時	• Quarantine	檢疫
• Remind	提醒	• Meal Coupon	餐券
• Local Time	當地時間	• Courtesy	招待

· Transfer in, Transfer out	· 接送服務
· Estimated Time of Arrival (ETA)	· 預定抵達時間
· Estimated Time of Departure (ETD)	· 預定起飛時間
· Stop-over Paid by Carrier (STPC)	· 轉機食宿招待
· Customs Declaration Form	· 海關申報單

三、關鍵會話

(一)辦理轉機手續

【Scene：Check-in counter】

Airline employee: Good morning. May I help you?

Tour Leader　　　: Yes, we want to transfer to flight TG 888 to Cairo. May we check in now?

Airline employee: May I have your tickets and passports, please?

Tour Leader　　　: Certainly, here are 30 tickets. May we have our seats close to each other.

Airline employee: Let me check for you. This flight is quite full now. I can hardly give 25 seats together. But I will do my best to make it for you.

Tour Leader　　　: Thanks.

Airline employee: Here are your 30 tickets, passports and boarding passes. I have arranged your seats as close to each other as possible. The departure time for the flight is 12:30 p.m. Please board at gate 30.

Tour Leader　　　: Would you please show me the way to the boarding gate?

Airline employee: Of course, sir. Just take the escalator up to the next door, and you will easily find the gate 30. You still

pass through the security check again and wait in the
departure floor for boarding since there is a lots time for
duty free shopping.

Tour Leader　　: I got it. Thank you very much for your considerate
information.

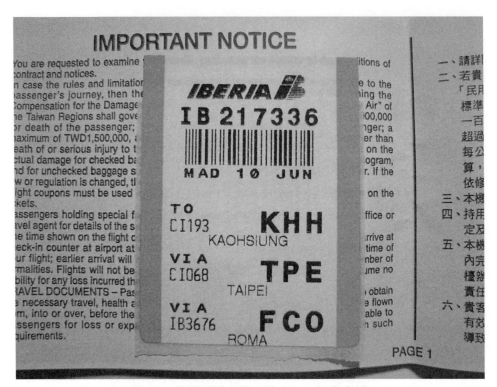

IMPORTANT NOTICE

圖4-1　轉機手續必備文件之一，行李收據

(二)回答團員轉機手續的疑問

【Scene：Airport terminal】

Tour member: Sir, I thought what we took was a "non-stop flight". Why do we have to transit in BKK?

Tour Leader : I am sorry, ma'am. Our flight will fly directly to Vienna. We do not have to change flights, but we have to stop over BKK for about two hours.

Tour member: I am a little confused. Do you mean "non-stop flight" and "direct flight" are not the same?

Tour Leader : No, they are not. Non-stop flight will not make any stops during the flight.

Tour member: What about direct flight?

Tour Leader : Direct flights just mean you do not have to make any connection on the way to the destination.

Tour member: Oh. Now I see. Well if I have to transfer in BKK and continue my journey to JNB, what should I do?

Tour Leader : Then, you would have to go to the Transfer Counter and recheck in.

Tour member: Will I get other boarding pass?

Tour Leader : Yes, you will.

Tour member: Thanks for your information. Now, how long should we wait here?

Tour Leader : About 1 hour.

Tour member: Since there is still one hour to wait, could you show me the way to have Thai massage?

Tour Leader : It is an amazing experience. Do you see the sign over there?

Tour member: Yes. The green one?

Tour Leader : Yes. Just go straight and then turn right. You will see a snack bar right on your left-hand side.

Tour member: I see. What time do we board again?

Tour Leader : Our flight will depart at 11:30 p.m. However, you might need to come back for boarding 30 minutes before the departure.

Tour member: OK. I will be back at that time.

Tour Leader : Enjoy it.

圖4-2　無需辦理轉機手續時航空公司所發過境旅客登機證

圖 4-3　國外轉機指示牌

圖 4-4　桃園機場轉機作業

四、語詞測驗

1. be impatient of [at]～　無耐性的

Tour leader is impatient at tour guide's behavior.

領隊對於導遊的態度感到沒有耐性。

2. be impatient to～　急躁的

I am impatient to board the TGV at Nice station.

在尼斯車站我急著登上子彈列車。

3. be independent of～　不依賴他人的

The driver is independent of his GPS on the long distance coach.

這位司機不依賴他長程遊覽車上的衛星定位系統。

4. be indifferent to～　冷淡的

Tour leaders should not be indifferent to the members of group.

領隊不應該對團員冷漠不理。

5. be indispensable for [to]～　不可缺少的

Local agent's help is indispensable to our tour group.

當地代理旅行社對於我們旅遊團的協助是不可或缺的。

6. be innocent of～　無辜的

Tour leader is innocent of the overbooking for hotel rooms.

領隊對於飯店房間超賣問題是無辜的。

7. **be particular about** ～   對……很講究

I am very particular about Italian food.

我對於義大利食物很講究。

8. **be popular in [among, with]** ～   受人歡迎的

The Paris local guide is popular with tourists of my group.

巴黎當地導遊受我們團員所歡迎。

9. **be relevant to** ～   有關聯的

This fly cancellation was relevant to bad weather.

這班飛機的取消和惡劣氣候有關。

10. **be responsible for** ～   應負責任的

I am responsible for selling tickets.

我是負責售票的。

11. **be short for** ～   ……的縮寫

FOC is short for Free of Charge.

FOC 是免費的縮寫。

12. **be sick for** ～   渴望的

I am sick for leading European tours.

我渴望帶歐洲團。

13. **be sick of** ～   厭倦的

I am sick of the cold weather.

我討厭寒冷的天氣。

14. **be subject to 〜** 使易患、易受

I am subject to colds.

我容易感冒。

15. **be true to 〜** 忠實的

Tour leader is true to his (her) words.

領隊要信守承諾。

16. **be willing to 〜** 樂意的

I am willing to be part-time tour guide.

我願意擔任兼任導遊。

17. **be yet to 〜** 迄今尚（未）

The time is yet to come.

時間尚未到。

18. **be to blame for 〜** 應受譴責

The driver is to blame for the accident.

司機應為此次車禍受到譴責。

19. **abide by 〜** 遵守某事（**to submit to**）

The tour leader will abide by his promise.

領隊會信守諾言。

20. abstain from ～　戒絕（to refrain from）

Tour leader always tells the driver to abstain from smoking on the coach.

領隊常常提醒司機不要在遊覽車上抽菸。

21. account for ～　說明（to explain）

There is no accounting for Tax Refund regulations.

沒有人說明退稅規定。

22. be adapt to ～　使適應

I was able to adapt to the climate in Egypt quickly.

我可以很快地適應埃及的氣候。

23. add to ～　增加（to increase）

It adds to my pleasure to see you in Paris.

在巴黎見到你讓我更高興。

24. add up to ～　總計達……（to reach a total of）

This group shopping amount added up to more than $5,000 Euros.

這一團購物金額總計超過5,000歐元。

25. adjust A to B ～　調整A 使適合B

I adjusted my room to the same floor with my group members.

我調整我的房間與團員在同一個樓層。

五、文法測驗

本章重點：動詞分析

現在式	Our fly takes off at 9:20 this morning. 我們搭的那班飛機將在今晨9點20分起飛。
現在進行式	Tour leaders are always complaining their working conditions. 領隊老是在抱怨他們的工作環境。
現在進行式表未來	I am going abroad next Saturday. 下星期六我要出國。
未來式 be going to	My father is going to apply a new passport. 我的父親將申請新護照。
過去式	Columbus discovered America in 1492. 哥倫布於1492年發現美洲。
過去進行式	I was taking a bath when local guide phoned me. 當地導遊打電話給我時，我正在洗澡。
現在完成式	I have never been to Australia in my life. 我一生從未去過澳洲。
現在完成進行式	How long have you been waiting? 你已經等多久了？
過去完成式	When we got to the Nice station, the train had already left. 當我們到達尼斯車站時，火車已經開走了。
未來式	Will tour leader be thirty five years old on his next birthday? 領隊下一個生日就35歲了嗎？
未來進行式	In ten minutes we will be flying over the Pacific. 再過10分鐘，我們將飛越太平洋。
未來完成式	Tour guide will have left this hotel by the time tour leader gets here. 領隊到這裡的時候，導遊將已經離開這家旅館了。
現在式表未來	If it rains tomorrow, the optional tour will be put off. 若明天下雨，自費活動將延期。
現在完成式表未來 完成	When he has finished the work, he'll be free for some time. 他完成工作之後，將有段空暇時間。

本章綜合練習

( ) 1. Tour members are looking forward to _____ from tour leader again.

(A) hear   (B) hearing   (C) listen   (D) listening

( ) 2. "Do you have any clothes _____ today?" the housekeeper asked.

(A) to wash   (B) be washed   (C) wash   (D) to be washed

( ) 3. My local agent has not confirmed my reservation yet, but she promised

_____ by tomorrow.

(A) for me to have it ready   (B) it was ready for me

(C) me it was ready   (D) to have it ready for me

( ) 4. Do you know _____ the repairs?

(A) to do   (B) how to do   (C) to make   (D) how to make

( ) 5. I remember my father _____ me to the Manly Beach in Sydney when I

was a very small child. We forgot _____ a towel and I felt very cold.

(A) taking/ to take   (B) to take/ taking

(C) take/ taking   (D) take/ taken

( ) 6. "Is everyone here?"

"Yes, everyone _____ Mary."

(A) not   (B) but   (C) without   (D) with

( ) 7. Tour guide likes hearing his own voice. He never stops _____.

(A) telling   (B) talking   (C) to tell   (D) to talk

( ) 8. Are you _____ to the weather in Oslo?

(A) pleased   (B) joined   (C) accustomed   (D) devoted

( ) 9. The tour leader _____ photographs.

(A) enjoys taking   (B) enjoys to take

(C) amuses taking   (D) amuses to take

( ) 10. "When does local guide want to see you?"

　　　"She expects _____ me the day after tomorrow."

　　　(A) on seeing　(B) seeing　(C) for seeing　(D) to see

( ) 11. Do you know _____ a cheese cake?

　　　(A) to do　(B) how to do　(C) to make　(D) how to make

( ) 12. I would appreciate _____ it a secret.

　　　(A) you to keep　　　　　　　(B) that you would keep

　　　(C) your keeping　　　　　　(D) that you are keeping

( ) 13. I am considering _____ your offer.

　　　(A) to accept　(B) accepted　(C) accept　(D) accepting

( ) 14. Although he doesn't like most sightseeing places, he _____ in the resort hotel.

　　　(A) enjoys swimming and golfing　(B) is a swimmer and a golfs

　　　(C) likes swimming and he golfs　(D) likes to swim and a golfer

( ) 15. We think the GPS _____ one of the most useful tools for drivers and tour leaders in use today.

　　　(A) being　(B) to be　(C) be　(D) have been

( ) 16. I found Las Vegas completely _____.

　　　(A) changed　(B) changing　(C) to be changed　(D) to change

( ) 17. They want the cable car station _____ as soon as possible.

　　　(A) to set up　　　　　　　　(B) to be set up

　　　(C) being set up　　　　　　　(D) to have been set up

( ) 18. A rock rolling down a hillside strikes other rocks and makes them _____.

　　　(A) roll　(B) rolled　(C) to roll　(D) to be rolled

（　）19. Did you notice the little Gypsy boy _____ away?

(A) took the candy and run

(B) taking the candy and run

(C) take the candy and run

(D) when taking the candy and running

（　）20. I want to have tourist _____ this fact.

(A) know　　(B) knew　　(C) known　　(D) being known

解答

1.B	2.D	3.D	4.B	5.A	6.B	7.B	8.C	9.A	10.D	11.D	12.C
13.D	14.A	15.B	16.A	17.B	18.A	19.C	20.A				

綜合解析

1. 慣用語 look forward to 加Ving。

   根據旅行業管理規則規範，領隊應從頭至尾服務團員，帶團過程中不宜脫隊處理私人事務或不隨團返國。

2. 被動語態，housekeeper 服務員。

   一般出國旅遊領隊都應攜帶足夠盥洗衣物或免洗式個人內褲，隨個人偏好，整套標準西裝或襯衫如有正式場合才穿著，此類衣物交飯店清洗需求較大。會將衣物繳交飯店房務部清洗，通常是住宿同一飯店兩晚以上，否則儘管是「快洗」都會來不及就要離開該飯店。

3. 慣用語 promise to V（原形）。

   確認訂位工作常委託當地代理旅行社代為執行，但領隊要時時關心進度，如果時間許可自己作確認較適宜。

4. 慣用語 how to do the repairs。

   搭機如遇到座位設施有故障，應先協調機組員確認是否正常，如果無法排

除故障，則應協調換位置。經濟艙已客滿時，可協調升等的可行性或甚至將自己位置與團員互換，總之，以團員利益為優先。

5. remember 加 Ving，代表記住曾做過的；forget加 to V 不定詞，代表忘記去做應該做的。

領隊帶團的過程中有些特殊的景點、餐廳、飯店等，應記錄、拍攝或蒐集相關資料，以利後續帶團所需或公司修正行程的參考依據。

6. 轉折語氣連接詞後省略動詞。

轉機時領隊要確認所有團員是否到齊，登機時也要正確清點人數，一般是提早於登機閘口前一一清點上機人數後，領隊最後才上機。

7. Stop加Ving，代表停止做某事；Stop to V原形，代表停止後做某事。

領隊應善用解說的技巧，解說需因團員性質不同而有所不同，解說過程要有彈性、規劃性，通常午餐後可以令團員稍事休息，放點當地音樂或與景點相關之背景音樂。忌諱自己如滔滔江水說個不停，卻忽視聽者的感受。相對的，團員有不聽的權利，但當導遊或領隊卻沒有不說的權利。

8. 慣用語 be accustomed to 習慣於。

領隊隨身應攜帶多功能性的外套，長程線領隊往往南征北討，台灣出發是夏天，轉機地點是沙漠氣候，抵達地點是天寒地凍。因此，除本身適應力要強外，必備工具也不可或缺。

9. 慣用語 enjoy 加Ving ； take photograph 照相。

攝影服務工作也是領隊必備工作之一，因此基本的攝影技巧與操作能力也是必須的。於行程中找一個合適的地點、時間，拍一張團體照是領隊一生重要且值得回憶的紀念照片。

10.慣用語 expect to V （原形）。

事先與當地導遊聯繫，商談預定的市區觀光行程，特別是有容納量限制（Carrier Capacity Limitation）的博物館、觀光景點，更要確認團體預約時

間，準時提前到達；事前取得導遊個人聯絡方式，甚至手機號碼都是必要的。

11. 慣用語 how to V（原形）；make a cake 做蛋糕。

主題之旅或一般深度旅遊，風味餐的安排是不可少的。因此領隊對於各國風味餐的背景故事、內容、做法與享用方式，也必須加以了解。

12. 慣用語appreciate 加 Ving。

領隊的工作常會接觸團員個人的私人資料甚至於私密，基於職業道德應予保密，非業務需要不必觸及個人私事。

13. 慣用語considering 加Ving。

長程線領隊有時需要親自訂餐付費，因此需按公司預算與協議價格，支付必要的餐費、門票、停車費或其他行程中必須支付的費用，並取得正式收據或憑證，返國後盡速於三天內報帳。如果遇特殊狀況，原契約餐廳停業或適逢公休日，也應在不影響團員利益下，尋找安排同等級餐食，並爭取業者提供（Offer）相同付費條件。

14. 慣用語 enjoy 加Ving。

飯店不僅是睡覺休息的地方，行程中部分飯店具有一定特殊歷史、建築風格或設施，領隊應帶領團員瀏覽或說明相關重點設施，使團員有機會享受此設備，更能提高整體旅遊的滿意程度。

15. to be 成為。

歐洲地理區域涵蓋範圍極廣，且橫跨不同語區，司機工作年資參差不齊，經驗也不一，領隊經驗也有所不同。因此，如有全球導航系統（GPS），可以輔助司機或領隊的經驗不足，減少找路的時間，但有GPS不一定全然是正確的，完全仰賴它，有一定的風險，資料更新與再次確認實際路況是必要的。

16. 被動且省略，changed 正確。

美西內華達州Las Vegas城市發展日益蓬勃，市區範圍不斷向外擴展，飯店

與娛樂設施不斷增建與更新，領隊一兩年沒帶美西團，往往因改變進步太快而驚訝不已，所以領隊應掌握最新旅遊資訊。

17. 被動 to be set up 建立。

興建纜車對於觀光景點的運輸效率可以改善，但往往在旺季時因團員排隊時間過長而耽誤行程；如果團員有部分堅持搭乘纜車，有部分堅持自行登山，此時，領隊對於團員人數掌握就要格外注意。

18. make someone/something V（原形）。

旅遊安全是最重要的，旅遊地區因季節變化，有些並不適合一年四季安排旅遊，但相對的在旅遊淡季，則是因價格較低吸引更多旅客參加，因此，領隊此時更需要注意旅遊安全。例如：亞洲地區的雨季；北美、加拿大、歐洲的嚴冬時期，都是風險係數較高的時期。

19. 疑問句後加原形；對等連接詞 and，前後動詞要一致，(A)(B)錯， (D)when 錯。

吉普賽人散居在歐洲各地，特別是集中在旅遊重點城市如巴黎、羅馬、佛羅倫斯等地，領隊在上述地點應加強團員的安全，並特別注意扒手。

20. 慣用語have someone V（原形）。

領隊除了必要景點解說外，適度深入剖析每一國家的優劣勢，並與台灣做比較，令國人了解台灣所處的國際地位與優劣勢的事實。學習他國的優點，借鏡他國的缺點作為本國人改善的依據，如此，可以將「淺層的觀光」提升至「深層觀光」。

歷屆試題

（　）1. The flight to Chicago has been _____ due to heavy snow.

(A)concealed　　　　　　　　(B)cancelled

(C)compared　　　　　　　　(D)consoled　　　【98外語領隊】

( ) 2. You will need to take a ＿＿＿ flight from Taoyuan to Kaohsiung.

(A)contacting   (B)connecting

(C)competing   (D)computing   【98外語領隊】

( ) 3. Government officials have <u>overlooked</u> the impact of inflation on the economy.

(A)highly expected   (B)failed to notice

(C)found ways of   (D)forgave   【98外語領隊】

( ) 4. After three years, the most wanted criminal <u>is still at large</u>.

(A)is finally kept in prison   (B)is living miserably

(C)is released   (D)has not yet been caught

【98外語領隊】

( ) 5. Expo 2010 ＿＿＿ in Shanghai, China from May 1 to October 31, 2010.

(A)will hold   (B)will be holding

(C)will be held   (D)is holding   【99外語領隊】

( ) 6. Although the unemployment rate reached an all-time high in mid-2009, it has fallen for four ＿＿＿ months by December.

(A)consecutive   (B)connecting

(C)continual   (D)temporary   【99外語領隊】

( ) 7. Our guided ＿＿＿ around the farm lasted for two and a half hours.

(A)voyage   (B)journey

(C)tour   (D)crossing   【99外語領隊】

( ) 8. Tourism has helped ＿＿＿ the economy for many countries, and brought in considerable revenues.

(A)boast   (B)boost

(C)receive   (D)recall   【99外語領隊】

( ) 9. Mr. Jones has got the hang of being a tour guide.

(A)Mr. Jones quit his job.

(B)Mr. Jones needs our help now.

(C)Mr. Jones met some strangers on his way home.

(D)Mr. Jones has learned the skills of being a tour guide. 【100外語領隊】

( ) 10. Mr. Brown was the president, and now Mr. Bean steps into his shoes.

(A)Mr. Bean stamps on Mr. Brown's feet.

(B)Mr. Brown orders Mr. Bean to try his own shoes.

(C)Mr. Bean has replaced Mr. Brown.

(D)Mr. Bean offends Mr. Brown. 【100外語領隊】

( ) 11. The interpreter talked as if he _____ how to fly like a bird.

(A)knew   (B)would know

(C)had known   (D)has known   【100外語領隊】

( ) 12. _____, I will try to correct it.

(A)If I've done a mistake   (B)If I've done wrongly

(C)If I've done something wrong   (D)If I've done something mistake

【100外語領隊】

( ) 13. Passengers _____ to other airlines should report to the information desk on

the second floor.

(A)have transferred   (B)transfer

(C)are transferred   (D)transferring   【101外語領隊】

( ) 14. I am sure that if he _____ the flight to Paris, he would have arrived there by

now.

(A)makes   (B)made

(C)is making   (D)had made   【101外語領隊】

( ) 15. The flight will make a _____ in Paris for two hours.

(A)stopover   (B)stepover

(C)flyover (D)crossover 【101外語領隊】

( ) 16. Our flight _____ to Los Angeles due to the stormy weather in Long Beach.

(A)was landed (B)had averted

(C)had been transformed (D)was diverted 【101外語領隊】

解答

1.B	2.B	3.B	4.D	5.C	6.A	7.C	8.B	9.D	10.C	11.C	12.C
13.D	14.D	15.A	16.D								

第五章

辦理入境手續

一、工作程序（Working Procedures）

　　辦完登機手續，出境前領隊應先將出入境的程序向團員報告，如果有出入境卡或海關申報單，則一併向團員說明清楚且協助填表，但切勿幫團員簽名。此外，如是「直飛班機（Non-Stop flight）」，則行李收據建議由團員自行保管，如果過程中必須轉機或更換航空公司，則由領隊做登記後統一保管，以利轉機時辦理登機手續。

二、關鍵字彙

　　領隊應熟悉關鍵字彙包括下列七項：

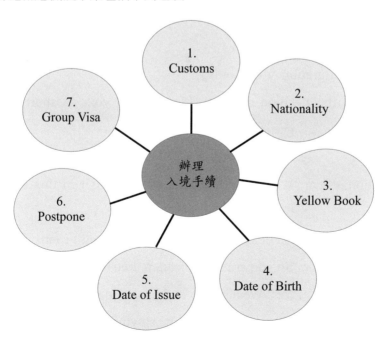

· Customs of Declaration	· 海關申報
· Accompanying Number	· 同行人數
· Nationality (Country of Citizenship)	· 國籍
· City Where You Boarded	· 登機城市
· City Where a Visa was Issued	· 簽證簽發處
· Quarantine Formalities	· 檢疫手續

· Security Check	安全檢查	· Departure to	前往……
· Customs	海關	· Damage	損壞
· Goods to Declare	申報物品	· Group Visa	團體簽證
· Obverse	表格正面	· Postpone	延期
· Reverse	表格背面	· Passport Control	護照檢查
· Customs Duty	海關稅	· Expiry Date	失效日期
· Prohibited Items	違禁品	· Endorsement	轉讓背書
· Banned	禁止	· Immunization	免疫
· Baggage Cart	行李推車	· Yellow Book	黃皮書
· Baggage Service	行李服務	· Complete	完成

三、關鍵會話

(一)領隊於移民關入境時

【Scene：Immigration & Customs】

Immigration officer: Good morning. Please show your passport and immigration card.

Tour Leader ： Here you are.

Immigration officer: What's the purpose of your visit in this country, on business or for pleasure?

Tour Leader ： On business. I am here with a tour group.

Immigration officer: So you are a tour leader, aren't you?

Tour Leader ： Yes. We have several places to visit.

Immigration officer: How long will you be staying in South Africa?

Tour Leader　　　　: 10 days.　We'll be leaving on November 23th.

Immigration officer: Where do you intend to stay while you stay in the country?

Tour Leader　　　　: At the local hotels.

Immigration officer: How much currencies have you got?

Tour Leader　　　　: I have 3,000 US dollars in cash.

Immigration officer: Do you have a return ticket?

Tour Leader　　　　: Yes, here you are.　Can I leave now?

Immigration officer: Just a second, do you remember when you got your last vaccination?

Tour Leader　　　　: Four days ago, just before I came here.　You may check my health certification.

Immigration officer: Ok. I think you are cleared.　Thank you for your cooperation and welcome.

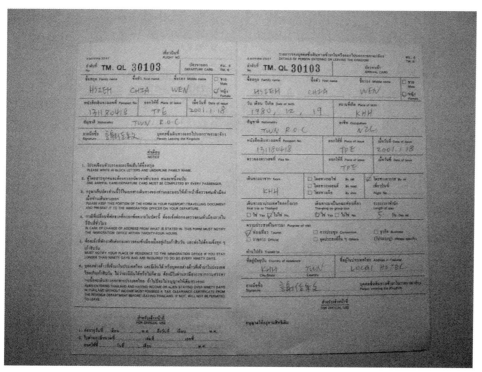

圖5-1　入境必備文件之一，入境卡

(二)領隊於國外辦理入境手續

【Scene：Immigration & Customs】

Immigration officer: Good afternoon, sir. May I have your passport and arrival card, please?

Tour Leader　　　　: I am the leader of a tour group. We have a group visa.

Immigration officer: Please show it and all the members' passports to me.

Tour Leader　　　　: Certainly, sir. Here you are.

Immigration officer: Leader, why is this passenger's date of birth is different from that in his passport?

Tour Leader　　　　: Let me have a look. Oh, I had made a mistake when I filled in the visa form. Sorry would you please correct it for me?

Immigration officer: Sure. Please let me have the address, telephone number and the contact's name of the local travel agency.

Tour Leader　　　　: Yes, can I be the last one to pass, sir?

Immigration officer: Sure, you can.

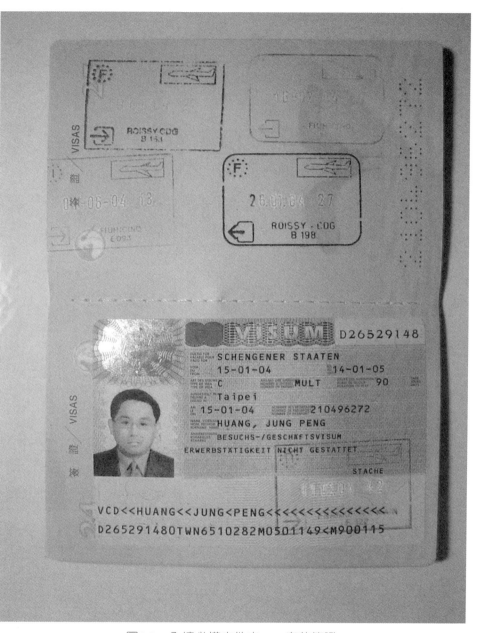

圖5-2 入境必備文件之一，有效簽證

【Scene：Immigration & Customs】

Immigration officer: Passport, please.

Tour Leader　　　： Here you are.

Immigration officer: What's the purpose of your visit?

Tour Leader　　　： I'm here on vacation.

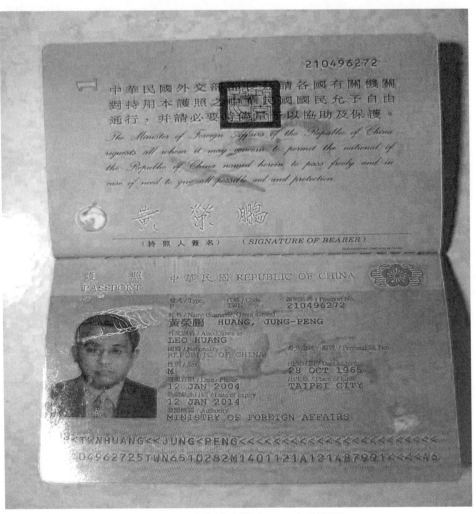

圖5-3　入境必備文件之一，有效護照

Immigration officer: How long do you plan to stay?

Tour Leader　　　: 5 days.

Immigration officer: Ok. You may go now.

Tour Leader　　　: Thank you.

㈣詢問提領行李處

【Scene：Baggage claim】

Clerk of the airport: Good afternoon. What can I do for you?

Tour Leader　　　: Yes. I came from Kaohsiung, Taiwan by CI087. Where can I get my luggage?

Clerk of the airport: The luggage claim area is downstairs.

圖5-4　行李提領區──行李推車

Tour Leader　　　　: Which carousel is for the luggage from Kaohsiung, Taiwan?

Clerk of the airport: You may go straight, and on the left, No. 3.

Tour Leader　　　　: Thank you.

㈤詢問提領行李處

【Scene：Baggage claim】

Tour Leader　　　　: I can't find my baggage. It is missing.

Clerk of the airport: Do you have a ticket and claim tag?

Tour Leader　　　　: Here is my claim tag and ticket.

Clerk of the airport: Would you please fill out this form?

Tour Leader　　　　: Sure. Do I have to come back here for my baggage?

Clerk of the airport: No, we'll send it to you.

Tour Leader　　　　: Really! That's great.

Clerk of the airport: Where would you like your baggage to be delivered?

Tour Leader　　　　: Ritz Hotel in downtown. How soon could you deliver my baggage?

Clerk of the airport: Hopefully by tomorrow afternoon.

Tour Leader　　　　: Ok. Please send my baggage to me as soon as possible.

圖5-5　行李提領區轉台

㈥海關查驗

【Scene：Baggage claim】

Customs inspector: Anything to declare?

Tour Leader 　　　: I suppose no, except a carton of cigarettes.　That's duty-free, isn't it?

Customs inspector: Yes, one can bring in one carton duty-free.　Open your suitcase, please.

Tour Leader 　　　: Yes, ma'am.

Customs inspector: What are those?

Tour Leader 　　　: Those are gifts for tour guides.

Customs inspector: Ok, you can go through now.

Tour Leader　　　: Thank you, ma'am.

圖5-6　海關檢查免稅或應稅檢查通道

四、語詞測驗

1. **agree to** 物 【**with** 人】～　同意

   I agree to your idea.

   我同意你的意見。

2. **answer to** 〜 符合

The tour guide answers to my colleague's description.

那位導遊符合我同事對他的描述。

3. **ask for** 〜 請求（**to request**）

Why don't you ask for tour guide's help?

你為何不請求導遊的協助？

4. **average out** 〜 平均分配（**to arrive at an average**）

Those tips will be averaged out.

這些小費會平均分配。

5. **back up** 〜 支持（**to support**）

My boss will back me up one hundred percent.

我老闆對我百分之百的支持。

6. **bargain for** 〜 議價（**to try to get cheap**）

Tour guide bargained for the diamond.

導遊為了這鑽石跟商家議價。

7. **beg** 人 **for** 物〜 懇求

I beg you for help.

我祈求你的幫忙。

8. **believe in** 〜 相信

Do you believe in what the tour guide said?

你相信導遊所說的嗎？

9. **belong to 〜** 是……的一員（**to be part of**）

This gentleman belongs to my tour group.

這位紳士是我的團員之一。

10. **beware of〜** 當心

Beware of the steps.

小心階梯。

11. **blame 人 for 事〜** 因某事而責備某人

The tourists blamed tour leader for his neglect of the work.

團員就領隊工作上的疏失責怪領隊。

12. **boast of 〜** 自誇

Don't boast of your shopping power.

可別自誇自己的購買力。

13. **call down 〜** 斥責（**to scold; rebuke**）

The tour guide called down the driver for drinking too much.

導遊斥責司機喝太多了。

14. **bottle up 〜** 隱藏（**to hold in**）、蓋住（**to shut in**）

Don't bottle it up; speak out what the tour guide's service performance is！

不要隱藏，將導遊服務績效說出來。

15. **get away 〜** 離去（**to leave**）

Tour leader can not get away from his group all the time.

領隊隨時都應與團員在一起。

16. **break down** 〜　故障、破壞（**to go out of working order**）

Our long-distance coach broke down and had to be towed to the gas station.

我們的長程遊覽車故障，必須拉到加油站修理。

17. **break up** 〜　結束

The city tour broke up at noon.

市區觀光在中午結束。

18. **bring forward** 〜　展示、介紹、提出（**to show**）

May I bring forward a new optional tour for your group?

我可以提出新的自費活動給你的團員嗎？

19. **bring in** 〜　提出（**to give**）、引進（**to import**）、產生、掙得（利益等）

The European long-distance coach brings in new GPS system.

歐洲長程遊覽車引進新的GPS系統。

20. **bring on** 〜　引起（**to cause to happen**）

Tour leader's overwork will bring on an illness.

領隊工作過量引起疾病。

21. **bump into** 〜　偶遇（**to meet unexpectedly**）

I'm glad that I bumped into an old tour guide in London.

我很高興在倫敦巧遇一位老導遊。

22. **burn down** ～　燒掉（**to burn to the ground**）

The famous castle burned down last night.

那著名的城堡在昨晚燒掉了。

23. **burst [break] into** ～　突然開始

The audience burst into frantic applause.

所有觀眾突然開始瘋狂地拍手。

24. **call at** [on 人] ～　拜訪（**to visit**）

I will call on the local agent tomorrow.

我明天將拜訪當地代理旅行社。

25. **book up** ～　預訂

You had better book up if you want to visit Moet & Chandon factory during Christmas vacation.

你如果在聖誕節假期想去參觀最著名的法國香檳酒廠最好先預約。

五、文法測驗

助動詞

can	He can speak French, can't he? 他會講法語，不是嗎?
could	This tour leader could speak Italian at the age of twenty. 這位領隊在20歲時就會說義大利文。
may	May I come in? 我可以進來嗎?
might	She said it might rain tomorrow. 她說明天可能會下雨。

will/won't	We will not accept your gifts. 我們絕對不接受你的禮物。
will	He will often sit up all night. 他今晚將通宵熬夜。
would	Tour leader thought that her members of group would soon get well. 領隊認為團員很快就會康復。
should	You should be more careful in night market. 在夜市你應該更小心。
ought to	Tour leader ought to follow the rules at all times. 領隊應當一直遵守規則。
had better	You had better stay at hotel tonight. 你今晚最好留在飯店。
must	Tour leader must keep his promise. 領隊必須遵守諾言。
have to	Tour leader always has to get up early. 領隊常常必須早起。
had to	Tour leader had to put up with driver's rudeness, sometimes. 領隊有時必須忍受司機的無禮。
be to	You are to do as tour leader tells you. 你必須照領隊所說的去做。
used to	He used to drink a lot; now he hardly ever drinks. 他從前常酗酒，現在幾乎滴酒不沾。
need	Tour guide needn't do the work. 導遊不必做那件工作。
助動詞+have過去分詞	It must have rained during the night. 晚上一定下過雨。

本章綜合練習

( ) 1. Tour leader can't help _____ anxious about the situation.

    (A) feel   (B) to feel   (C) felt   (D) feeling

( ) 2. When tour guide fell off the slide, the other children _____.

    (A) couldn't help laughing   (B) weren't able to stop laughter

    (C) could not avoid to laugh   (D) could not stop but laughing

( ) 3. "I can't see the fly monitor board very well."

"Perhaps you need _____."

(A) to examine your eyes   (B) to have your eyes examined

(C) to have examined your eyes   (D) to be examined your eyes

( ) 4. There was so much noise that the tour guide couldn't make himself

_____.

(A) hearing   (B) to hear   (C) heard   (D) being heard

( ) 5. I knew I could not finish my schedule _____.

(A) by tour guide had come   (B) until tour guide has come

(C) when tour guide comes   (D) before tour guide came

( ) 6. The construction of the theme park _____ before the end of next month.

(A) must have completed   (B) must have been completed

(C) must be completed   (D) must complete

( ) 7. Since they aren't answering their telephone in the hotel rooms, they

_____ .

(A) must have left   (B) should have left

(C) need have left   (D) can have left

( ) 8. Tour leader said that we _____ .

(A) arrived in the station by noon

(B) should arrive in the station till noon

(C) was to arrive at the station till noon

(D) would arrive at the station by noon

( ) 9. My wallet is nowhere to be found. I_____ when I was in the coach.

(A) must drop it   (B) should have dropped it

(C) must have dropped it   (D) had dropped it

( ) 10. I wondered _____ to come to the party.

(A) whether tour guide should have been asked

(B) whether tour guide should asked

(C) whether tour guide is asked

(D) should tour guide been asked

( ) 11. A: Does it snow a lot in New York?

B: _____

(A) Yes, it was.　　　　　　　(B) Yes, It will be.

(C) It did.　　　　　　　　　(D) No, it doesn't.

( ) 12. A: Do you have anything special to declare?

B: _____

(A) No, I don't think so.　　　(B) Sure, I will open it now.

(C) No, I have one.　　　　　(D) What's this?

( ) 13. Don't _____ large amount of cash with you to United States.

(A) carry　(B) carries　(C) cashed　(D) take

( ) 14. In most countries the sale of cigarette to children is _____

(A)ban　(B) allowed　(C)allow　(D) banned

( ) 15. The long distance coach was found _____ near the Seine river bank.

(A) urban　(B) abandoned　(C) addicted　(D) alone

( ) 16. Tour leader should _____earlier in order to catch the TGV.

(A) set off　(B) take place　(C) make sure　(D) get lost

( ) 17. This driver and tour leader's dialogue happened most likely in the_____

(A) airport VIP room　　　　(B) front desk of a hotel

(C) office of immigration　　　(D) cabin of airplane

( ) 18. To help boost the travel and tourism industry, the government is willing

to_____ restrictions on visits from Mainland Chinese tourism.

(A) prohibit　(B) ease　(C) dodge　(D) rid

（　）19. "When should we come back?" "Let's meet_____ in 30 minutes"

(A) at here　(B) in here　(C) over here　(D) here

（　）20. A: Which line should we take?

B:_____

(A) Let's check the Metro map.　(B) The Metro is over there.

(C) Let's not take the Metro.　(D) Where is the Metro?

解答

1.D	2.A	3.B	4.C	5.D	6.C	7.A	8.D	9.C	10.A	11.D	12.A
13.A	14.D	15.B	16.A	17.B	18.B	19.D	20.A				

綜合解析

1. 慣用語，can't help Ving。

   領隊面對緊急事件，沈著以對是必要的法則，帶團時緊急事件的處理所依靠的是經驗累積，因此面對上述困難，均應樂觀面對，積極處理。

2. 同上。

   領隊帶團可能遭遇的風險是可以事先預防的，在帶團過程中應小心；不幸遇到時，要樂觀以對，積極處理將傷害減至最低，風險的預防、分散、轉嫁與管理，都是領隊應熟悉的管理技能。

3. 被動。

   不論搭機、轉機、搭火車、輪船，都應隨時檢視告示牌為準。登機證上的時間，不見得就是最後正確的搭乘交通工具的時間點，因此，領隊要注意螢幕顯示器的即時資訊。此外英文以外的第三種語言，也是積極學習的目標。

4. make someone 過去分詞當補語。

解說的環境是很重要的，領隊從事「沿途解說（Walking Tour）」時，要注意周遭環境解說的適宜性，否則會大大減低解說的效果。

5. (A)(B)(C) 時態均不正確。

入境作業在不同國家有不同的法令限制，有些國家當地導遊可以至管制區接團，而大部分國家仍需由領隊獨自帶領團員入境，之後再由當地導遊接手，出發前應事先確認。如有導遊至管制區接待團體，領隊工作就較輕鬆，但入境書面文件應事先妥善填寫完整，以利通關順利。

6. 被動語態。

關於當地旅遊資訊應隨時蒐集，養成剪報、閱讀的好習慣。此外，當地導遊、旅行社、免稅店職員與司機，都是旅遊資訊重要的來源之一。

7. 假設語氣。

領隊辦理住宿登記分發房間時，要宣布事項中的重點工作，就是告知團員領隊自己的房間號碼；查房後與確認所有團員房間都沒問題後，也應盡量待在房間，以免團員找不到領隊；如有需要，也要告知團員緊急聯繫方式。

8. by noon 中午之前；till noon 直到中午才，(B)(C)語意不對。(A) 時態不正確。

搭機、搭船、搭火車等交通工具，領隊應事先說明搭乘時間、是否有跨時區問題、中途是否轉機等，團員一般基於好奇都會詢問領隊，此外也可以避免團員睡過頭、坐過站、中途不知下車等問題。

9. 假設語氣。

貴重物品要提醒團員勿放置遊覽車上，實務中往往許多旅遊糾紛，都是因團員將私人貴重物品留在車上，行程結束上車後發現東西不見，或遊覽車遭破壞而財物不見；因此旅客就認為都是旅行社的錯、司機的錯、領隊的

錯，也是當地政府治安不好，政府的錯。但是，領隊是第一線服務人員，必須承擔較大的責任與團員的責難，更重要是善後處理的工作全落在領隊身上。

10. 被動語態，被邀請。

領隊是團體的靈魂，除了成為團體的領袖外，也要努力促進導遊、司機與團員之間的良好互動，令外籍旅遊工作人員與台灣的遊客有良好互動，因此領隊也是民間交流重要的推手與橋梁。

11. 現在式。

領隊在團體出發前的說明會，就應將旅遊地區當地氣候說明解釋清楚，以利團員準備衣物，避免發生忘了帶、帶錯、帶不夠的窘境。如果領隊於旺季太忙碌，人未返國親自開說明會，可委由同事代勞，也應於出發前打電話至團員家，稍事問候與再次提醒，以建立第一步的好印象。

12. (B)時態錯誤，(C)(D)語法錯誤。

領隊在台灣開說明會時，就應將預計前往旅遊國家的海關規定說明清楚，出發當天在機場也應再重述一次。通關過程中，應從旁協助誠實以報，否則輕者罰款嚴重者身陷囹圄。領隊如果未說明清楚，最後還是要負擔善後處理的責任。

13. 祈使句加原形。

領隊出國除長程線團體外，一般領隊所需攜帶的現金是有限的。不論多寡，分散風險是一定要做的，不要將現金全放在同一個地方，養成置放不同重要私密之處較佳；若遭受搶劫或竊盜，也不至於全部都沒了。

14. 禁止；(B)語意錯誤，(C)語意錯且被動，(A)被動。

各國法令規定不一，身為領隊自己應先熟悉法令，不要都以台灣標準去衡量全世界，否則一不小心就容易觸法。

15. 過去分詞補語。

領隊應將長程遊覽車司機的手機號碼記下來，由於團體操作市區觀光或用餐時，有時會碰到歐洲古城區停車不方便，或當地政府對於停車有所限制等情況，因此，往往造成司機因距離太遠無法一同用餐，領隊只好事先約好一定時間、地點與司機會合；但有時餐廳客滿、團員用餐、如廁速度不一，延誤會合時間。所以，領隊與司機彼此聯絡的手機號碼於一開始接團時就應記下。

16. 慣用語 set off 出發。

提早出發是搭乘任何交通工具的基本要訣，因為司機到錯誤飯店接團、接不到團、司機會迷路、路上會塞車、路上會遇車禍、車子會壞掉等各種變數太多。因此，寧願提早出發早到，也不要遲到。

17. 司機與領隊不太可能在機場貴賓室、移民關或飛機上談話。(A)(C)(D)均錯。

長程線領隊與司機的溝通要即時且互動要佳，如此相互配合才能一路順暢；對於配合度高、專業、敬業的司機，當然小費不可少且應多給一些作為鼓勵。相對遇到金錢慾望強、路況不熟、配合度差的司機，領隊仍需耐心以對，且要主動分擔部分認路、找路與指示方向的工作。

18. ease 放鬆管制，語意正確。

身為領隊有機會也可以準備導遊考試並取得相關證照，對於領隊的歷練也是一種新的學習，且站在導遊的角度，也更能體會領隊的角色。其實導遊、領隊都是同一條船上的從業人員，「各盡其力，各取所值」。

19. 地方副詞當補語。

團體自由活動時，應清楚說明集合與解散的地點，地點的選擇是非常重要的，要選擇所有團員，不管老少都清楚的地點。「沿途解說（Walking Tour）」也應盡量走明顯的街道與易分辨的景物。小街小巷太多的地方，不

宜讓團員解散自由活動，因容易使團員迷失於古城、主題樂園或賭場之中。

20. (B)(C)(D)語意皆錯誤。

搭乘地鐵首重安全性，而掌握團體人數是其中較困難的工作，如果人數超過20人以上，通常較不易控制在同一車廂。因此要盡量避免搭乘地鐵，如果情非得已，則應分組較佳，一路上要強調私人貴重物品的留意，以及注意扒手。

歷屆試題

( ) 1. City _____ are always available at the local tourist information center.

    (A)floors   (B)streets

    (C)maps   (D)tickets　【98外語領隊】

( ) 2. _____ birds are suspected to be major carriers of avian flu.

    (A)Immigrating   (B)Migratory

    (C)Seasoning   (D)Motivating　【98外語領隊】

( ) 3. You will be _____ for littering in public places.

    (A)fined   (B)found

    (C)founded   (D)funded　【98外語領隊】

( ) 4. The time _____ is thirteen hours between Taipei and New York.

    (A)decision   (B)division

    (C)diligence   (D)difference　【98外語領隊】

( ) 5. If Scott had studied hard enough, he _____ the midterm exam. Now he has to burn the midnight oil to pass the final exam.

    (A)would pass   (B)will pass

    (C)have passed   (D)would have passed　【99外語領隊】

（　）6.　I want to make a/an _____ with Dr. Johnson tomorrow morning. I think I've

caught a cold.

(A)reservation　　　　　　　　(B)arrangement

(C)meeting　　　　　　　　　　(D)appointment　　　【99外語領隊】

（　）7.　The Department of Health urged the public to receive H1N1 flu shot as

a _____ against potential outbreaks.

(A)prohibition　　　　　　　　(B)preparation

(C)presumption　　　　　　　　(D)precaution　　　【99外語領隊】

（　）8.　Go to the office at the Tourist Information Center and they will give you a

_____ about sightseeing.

(A)destination　　　　　　　　(B)deposit

(C)baggage　　　　　　　　　　(D)brochure　　　【99外語領隊】

（　）9.　We should _____ all the possibilities when solving this problem.

(A)negate　　　　　　　　　　(B)ponder

(C)attack　　　　　　　　　　(D)project　　　【100外語領隊】

（　）10.　He runs away with the idea, and the other faculty members do not agree.

(A)They blame him for his irresponsibility.

(B)They do not accept his hasty conclusion.

(C)They turn down his unexpected invitation.

(D)They reject his application.　　　　　【100外語領隊】

（　）11.　His conclusion seems to <u>insinuate</u> that we can visit Russia very soon.

(A)report　　　　　　　　　　(B)imply

(C)deny　　　　　　　　　　　(D)affirm　　　【100外語領隊】

（　）12.　Do not be afraid to eat with your hands here. When in Rome, do _____ the

Romans do.

(A)for　　　　　　　　　　　　(B)as

(C)of   (D)since   【100外語領隊】

(   ) 13. While many couples opt for a church wedding and wedding party, a Japanese groom and a Taiwanese bride _____ in a traditional Confucian wedding in Taipei.

(A)tied the knot   (B)knocked off

(C)wore on   (D)stepped down   【101外語領隊】

(   ) 14. If the air conditioner should _____ , call this number immediately.

(A)break up   (B)break down

(C)break into   (D)break through   【101外語領隊】

(   ) 15. _____ is first to arrive in the office is responsible for checking the voice mail.

(A)The person   (B)Who

(C)Whoever   (D)Whom   【101外語領隊】

(   ) 16. Disobeying the airport security rules will _____ a civil penalty.

(A)result in   (B) make for

(C)take down   (D)bring on   【101外語領隊】

118

解答

1.C	2.B	3.A	4.D	5.D	6.D	7.D	8.D	9.B	10.B	11.B	12.B
13.A	14.B	15.C	16.A								

帶團中服務

一、工作程序（Working Procedures）

領隊帶領團員通過移民關後，應盡速帶領團員至行李提領區，領取個人行李，在等待行李的空檔，應指引團員盥洗間的位置，留置各家族成員一人等待行李，其他人員應把握時間輪流上盥洗室。確認團員人數、行李與隨身貴重物品清點無誤後，通過海關檢查至迎賓大廳，與當地導遊或司機會合。

領隊應盡速尋找當地導遊或司機，確認遊覽車位置，引導團員上車。此時應與當地導遊確認今日行程與餐食安排有無遺漏之處，如無當地導遊時，領隊此時身兼導遊工作，則必須與司機確認所有行程、餐廳與當晚飯店的位置。最高原則是中文行程表中所有行程與餐食內容，均應確認無誤，有不正確之處應盡速聯繫當地代理旅行社（Local Agent）修正。

領隊是第一線的服務者，應確實履行契約的內容，確保團員的權益，帶團中服務工作包羅萬象，不論是與司機溝通、導遊協調、餐廳用餐、飯店住宿、免稅店購物或與其他旅遊相關產業的聯繫等等，最終目標就是達成團員最高的滿意度。

二、關鍵字彙

帶團中服務領隊應熟悉的重要關鍵字彙包括下列五項：

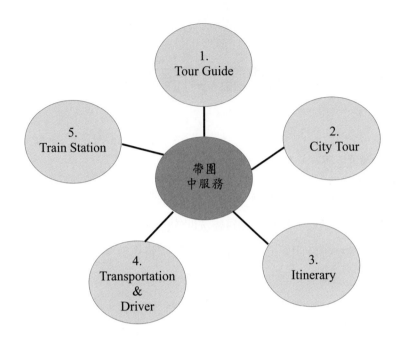

1.Tour Guide　導遊			
‧ Local Guide	當地導遊	‧ Group Size	團體大小
‧ Working Itinerary	工作日誌	‧ Conducted Tour	含導遊的行程
‧ Including	包括	‧ Driver Guide	司機兼導遊
‧ Transit Only	只接送	‧ Tour Escort	領隊
‧ Through Guide	全陪導遊	‧ Interpreter	翻譯
‧ Third Party Insurance	第三責任險	‧ Entrance Fee	門票費
‧ Passenger List	旅客名單	‧ Questionnaire	問卷
2.City Tour　市區觀光			
‧ Sightseeing	觀光	‧ Baroque Art	巴洛克藝術
‧ Square	廣場	‧ Gothic Art	哥德式藝術
‧ Palace	宮殿	‧ Rococo Art	洛可可藝術
‧ Museum	博物館	‧ Byzantine Art	拜占庭藝術
‧ Tower	塔	‧ Romanesque Art	羅馬式藝術
‧ Pagoda	中國式塔	‧ Renaissance	文藝復興
‧ Temple	廟	‧ Michelangelo	米開朗基羅
‧ Ruins	遺蹟	‧ Raphael	拉斐爾
‧ Grotto	石窟	‧ Leonardo da Vinci	李奧納多‧達文西

• Cave	洞穴	• Pyramid	三角尖頂金字塔
• City Hall	市政廳	• Mastaba	梯形平頂金字塔
• Train Station	火車站	• Pantheon	萬神殿
• Church	教堂	• Colosseum	競技場
• Baptistery	洗禮堂	• Catholicism	天主教
• Parliament Hill	國會大廈	• Christianity	基督教
• Central Park	中央公園	• Buddhism	佛教
• Opera House	歌劇院	• Hinduism	印度教
• Castle	城堡	• Islam	回教（伊斯蘭教）
• Fountain	噴泉	• Surcharge	額外費用
• Koala	無尾熊	• Platypus	鴨嘴獸

3.Itinerary　行程

• Familiarization Tour	熟悉之旅	• Package Tour	套裝行程
• Theme Park	主題樂園	• Incentive Tour	獎勵旅遊
• Amusement Park	遊樂場	• Booking Meals	訂餐
• Ocean Park	海洋公園	• Hot Spring	溫泉

4. Transportation & Driver　交通 & 司機

• Long Distance Coach	長程遊覽車	• Bus Hour	開車工作時間
• Parking Lot	停車場	• Unlimited mileage	未限制里程數
• Pull Over	開到路邊	• Intersection	十字路口
• Brakes	煞車	• Rear Wheel	後輪
• Engine	引擎	• Reflectors	反射鏡
• Battery	電池	• Front Wheel	前輪
• Windscreen	擋風鏡	• Wiper	雨刷
• Driving Wheel	驅動輪	• Turn Signal	方向燈
• Entrance Door	上下車口	• Step Plate	踏板
• Side Maker Lights	側標誌燈	• Headlights	前燈
• Windshield	擋風玻璃	• Rearview Mirror	後視鏡
• Bumper	保險桿	• Traffic Light	交通信號燈
• Berth	火車臥鋪	• Accelerator	油門
• Additional Drivers	額外駕駛	• Full Coverage	保全險
• Economy	經濟型 1,300cc-1,600cc		
• Compact	小型車 1,600cc-1,800cc		
• Mid-Size	中型車 2,200cc-2,600cc		

· Full-Size		大型車 2,600cc 以上	
5. Train Station　火車站			
· Security Officer		安全人員	
· Kiosk	車站內的零售店	· First-Class Carriage	頭等車廂
· Redcap	車站搬運工人	· Subway	地下鐵路
· Ticket Window	售票亭	· Safety Belt	安全帶
· Ticket Machine	自動售票機	· Barrier	剪票處
· Overhead Racks	頭上行李置放區	· Entrance	入口
· Brake Pedal	煞車踏板	· Gearshift Lever	齒輪
· Clutch Pedal	離合器	· Message Board	旅客留言板
· Exit	出口	· Information	詢問處
· Fare Adjustment	票價調整	· Waiting Room	等候室
· Windshield Wiper	擋風玻璃的雨刷	· Cloakroom	物品寄存處
· Limited Express	特快車	· Platform	月台
· Express	快車	· Night Train	夜車
· Underpass	地下道	· Streetcar	市內電車
· Local Train	普通車	· Luggage Storage	行李置放區
· Sleeper	臥車	· Atmosphere	氣氛

三、關鍵會話

(一)與當地導遊聯繫

【Scene：Contact the local guide】

Group member: Where is the local guide?

Tour Leader ： Please wait here. I will check the lady standing by the exit with a sign in her hand.

Local guide ： Excuse me. Are you Mr. Leo Huang from Taipei NEWS Tour?

Tour Leader ： Yes, I am. May I have your name?

Local guide ： Glad to meet you, Leo. My name is Evonne.

Tour Leader	: Thank you for coming to meet us. Glad to meet you, too.
Local guide	: How many people are there in your party?
Tour Leader	: There are 24 adults, 5 children and me.
Local guide	: How many pieces of luggage do you have?
Tour Leader	: There are 22 pieces altogether.
Local guide	: Where are your people?
Tour Leader	: Some of them are still in the restroom. They are coming soon.

圖6-1　行程中長程遊覽車

(二)與當地導遊確認行程內容

【Scene：Discussing with the local guide】

Tour Leader: May I check with you about this group itinerary?

Local guide: Certainly, Mr. Leo. Do you find anything missing in your itinerary?

Tour Leader: I think you know the location of the city is far away from city center. In such case, is it possible for us to go shopping?

Local guide: Do not worry about it. I will check with the coach driver regarding the bus hour limitation. I try my best to let you make use of the time.

Tour Leader: Thank you, Miss Evonne. It's really very thoughtful of you.

Local guide: That's all right.

Tour Leader: Please reserve a Chinese restaurant nearby the sightseeing spot for my group.

Local guide: Certainly I will do. One more thing, what are their occupations?

Tour Leader: Most of them are teachers except two newly married couple. All the members come from Taipei.

Local guide: Is there any vegetarian in your group?

Tour Leader: No, but two people are no beef.

Local guide: Do they have any special requests about the food?

Tour Leader: Most of them are senior travelers. They prefer smooth and tender food but they still like to try the local food.

Local guide: You are a very experienced tour leader. Do you agree with the adjusted itinerary?

Tour Leader: Yes, it's fine.

Local guide : I will do as you like. Mr. Leo, I believe we will have a good cooperation.

圖6-2　帶團中領隊翻譯，導遊解說內容

㈢與當地導遊溝通團員反應

【Scene：Discussing with the local guide】

Tour Leader: Miss Evonne, My group people mentioned those meals in Chinese restaurant are not so well.

Local guide : What is the problem?

Tour Leader: The quantities of meals are not enough for them to eat.

Local guide : According to the contract, and the former groups, a meal of six courses should be enough for ten people.

Tour Leader: Yes, I know, but this group maybe is special condition. Is it possible to add the quantity of each dish?

Local guide : Usually, the boss of restaurant does not add any dish unless we pay extra money.

Tour Leader: Please add the quantity of each dish, first. If they do not accept it, I will discuss you at that time.

Local guide : I am sorry to hear that and will keep it in mind.

Tour Leader: One more thing, four people complained that they had the same dishes for every meal, such as tomato soup, chicken with vegetables, scrambled eggs, and the after meal food—orange slices.

Local guide : I will tell the boss that he does not serve the same dish again. The following meals will also serve other dishes.

Tour Leader: Thank you for solving all these problems.

Local guide : No problem, Leo.

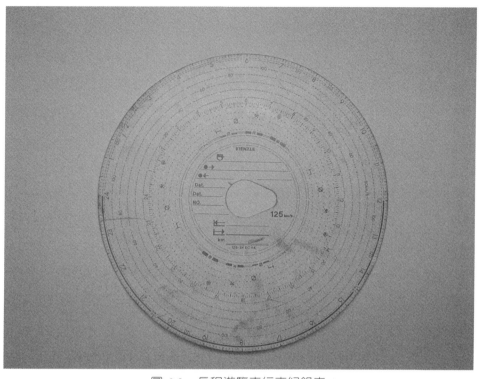

圖 6-3　長程遊覽車行車紀錄表

四、語詞測驗

1. **call in** ～　召喚 (**to summon for help**)

   Call in a doctor at once.

   立刻叫醫生來。

2. **call off** ～　取消 (**to cancel**)、或依次讀出（從名單上）

   The tour leader called off the names of his group members.

   領隊依次唸出團員名字。

3. **care for** ～　喜歡 (**to like**)

I don't really care for her new dress.

我真的不喜歡她的新衣服。

4. **carry on** ～　繼續（**to go on**）、經營、實行（**to engage in**）

Carry on your work.

繼續你的工作。

5. **carry out** ～　實行（**to accomplish; fulfill; perform**）

Tour leader tried to carry out the working itinerary.

領隊盡力實行工作日誌表（行程）。

6. **carve up** ～　平分

Tour leader will carve up the tips with local guide and driver.

領隊將小費平分給當地導遊與司機。

7. **cash in** ～　將……兌換現金（**to exchange for cash**）、死亡（**to die**）

It is a good place to cash in the travel checks in DFS.

免稅店是將旅行支票兌換成現金的好地方。

8. **catch on to** ～　了解

Some tourists seemed to can not catch on to the jokes they were telling in Las Vegas night show.

某些團員似乎無法了解拉斯維加斯夜間秀場所說的笑話。

9. **catch up with ～** 趕上（**to overtake**）

I'll catch up with local guide later.

我稍後會趕上當地導遊。

10. **chip in ～** 插嘴、湊錢、捐助

We chipped in fifty US dollars to buy her a birthday cake.

我們湊了50元美金買一個生日蛋糕幫她慶生。

11. **clear A of B ～** 清掃A中之B

I must clear all the rooms of the second floor.

我必須清掃二樓所有房間。

12. **close down ～** 完全停止（**to stop entirely**）

The driver must close down all the operations of long distance coach.

司機必須讓長程遊覽車停止運作。

13. **come about ～** 發生（**to happen; take place**）

This bus hour overtime problem has come about through tour leader's failure.

這行車時間超時的問題，完全是領隊的問題。

14. **come across ～** 橫渡、發現（**to find**）、偶然遇見（**to meet by accident**）、了解（**to be understood**）

I never came across such a problem.

我從未遇見這樣的問題。

15. **come at** 〜　到達（**to reach**）

Would you tell me how to come at the meeting point in Rome?

請你告訴我如何到達羅馬市區碰面的地方？

16. **come down with** 〜　生病（**to suffer loss in health, wealth, etc.**）

Some tourists came down with the flu.

部分團員感冒。

17. **come from** 〜　來自……（出生地、籍貫）

Where do you come from?

你來自哪裡？

18. **come in for** 〜　得到（**to get**）

Local guide came in for a lot of criticism from tourists.

團員對當地導遊有許多責難。

19. **come into** 〜　繼承（**to inherit**）、進入（**to enter into**）、得到

Tour leaders can not come into tourists' rooms without permissions.

領隊未經團員同意不可進入團員房間。

20. **come of** 〜　起因於、出身於

His illness comes of eating too much sea food.

他的病起因於吃太多海鮮。

21. **come out** 〜　出來

The moon has come out.

月亮出來了。

22. **come to** 〜 達到

The shopping sum came to ten thousand US dollars.

購物總額達到1萬美金。

23. **compensate for** 〜 補償（同 **make up for**）

I want to compensate for your loss.

我會補償你的損失。

24. **complain of** 〜 挑毛病（**to find fault with**）

Don't complain of your members of your group.

不要挑你團員的毛病。

25. **concentrate on [upon]** 〜 專注

Driver should concentrate on his driving.

司機開車要專心。

表6-1　當地代理旅行社所發服務內容卷（Voucher）

LTA Leo's Travel Agency (KHH)		
AUTOCARES BARCELONS	Tel 34-7-8060505	Issued：24/03/12
CAN OLIVA 70	8020 BARCELONA	SPAIN

Tour Ref：AAFO003904 - 25 MAR 2012　　Name：PRINCE - 18D ROM-MAD
Client：LEO TRAVEL　SERVICE　CO., LTD.
No of Adults ：23　Children：0　Tour leaders：1　LTA Escort：0

WEDNESDAY 27 MAR 2012 BARCELONA

LOCAL COACH TO MEET CLIENTS AT HOTEL FOR DINNER AND SHOW
TRANSFERS WITH SERVICES TERMINATING AT HOTEL.

五、文法測驗

本章重點：被動語態分析

第一種被動語態	This working itinerary will be finished by tour leader. 這份工作日誌將被領隊完成。
第二種被動語態	The water pipes got frozen overnight. 一夜之間水管結冰了。
S+V+IO（間接受詞）+DO（直接受詞）的被動語態	Tour leader was given the extra tips. 有人給領隊額外小費。
S+V+O+原形動詞的被動語態	The driver was made to work too hard (by him). 司機被他強迫過度工作。
表情情緒動詞的被動語態	The driver was disappointed at not being invited. 司機沒被邀請，感到很失望。
動詞片語的被動語態	By whom will the boy be taken care of? 那個男孩將由誰照顧？
They say that的被動語態	Local guide is said to have been a famous actress. 據說導遊曾是個著名的女演員。
have+受詞+過去分詞	She had her purse stolen. 她的錢包被偷了。
It+be+過去分詞+that-子句/to-不定詞	It is said that the travel agent is in financial difficulties. 據說那家旅行社陷入財務困境。

本章綜合練習

（　）1. I could not make _____ Italian.

(A) myself understand in   (B) myself understood in

(C) myself understand by   (D) myself understand with

（　）2. Tour leader needs the schedule _____ before tomorrow.

(A) done   (B) do   (C) be done   (D) be doing

（　）3. All the slot machines _____ by the end of the following week.

(A) were repaired   (B) would be repaired

(C) will have been repaired   (D) were being repaired

（　）4.　The subject of tonight show _____ by the director.

    (A) announces   (B) have been announced

    (C) announced   (D) has been announced

（　）5.　The world's supplies of oil _____.

    (A) have been gradually being exhausted

    (B) has gradually exhausted

    (C) are gradually exhausted

    (D) are being gradually exhausted

（　）6.　The crystal, _____ bought in the DFS yesterday, will be sent to you as a gift.

    (A) that was   (B) which is   (C) which was   (D) that has been

（　）7.　They considered themselves _____ superior to colored people.

    (A) be   (B) to be   (C) being   (D) been

（　）8.　Our group pictures _____ until tomorrow.

    (A) won't develop   (B) aren't developing

    (C) don't develop   (D) won't be developed

（　）9.　Things are known _____ when they unite with the oxygen of the air.

    (A) burning   (B) to burn   (C) burn   (D) being burned

（　）10.Is there anything you want from convenience store?　I am going to get _____.

    (A) those letters mailed   (B) mailed letters

    (C) to mail those letters   (D) those letters mail

（　）11.A: How's the weather in Spain?

    B: _____

    (A) Sounds like that it's a good place for a vacation.

    (B) It's quite cool, but not as cold as here in New York.

(C) It has a lot of beautiful sceneries worth seeing in Taiwan.

(D) I think most of them are good.

( ) 12. Mary joined us in American and then we _____ to Disney.

(A) exceed   (B) proceeded   (C) preceded   (D) receded

( ) 13. How often do you visit Japan?_____

(A) About every year.　　　　(B) Now it's your turn.

(C) Yes, I wan to go.　　　　(D) Twenty minutes later.

( ) 14. Sue: "_____"

Kevin: "I need to check my schedule".

(A) Do you have a date tomorrow?   (B) Could you clean your room?

(C) Do you get your master's degree?   (D) Do you finish your homework?

( ) 15. Karen: Do you want me to call local travel agency?

Kevin: _____

(A) What does it mean?　　　　(B) What do you want?

(C) I need your help?　　　　(D) I don't think we need to call.

( ) 16. Alex: Can you give me a hand with my tour schedule this weekend?

Sue: _____ because I have to go into the south of France and do some pri-

vate things.

(A) No, thank you　　　　(B) Yes, I will do it

(C) I am not sure　　　　(D) I'd like to

( ) 17. Ruth: Have you planned anything for next weekend?

Mark: _____ I'd really like to go on a trip, but I don't have extra

money.

(A) Why not?   (B) Yes or no.   (C) How come?   (D) OK!

( ) 18. California has a limited water supply _____ light rainfall.

(A) because of it's　　　　(B) because

(C) because of its　　　　　　　(D) because its

（　）19. Be sure to take your umbrella just ＿＿＿＿ case of rain.

(A) in　(B) because　(C) at　(D) on

（　）20. Allen: Oh! No, there's a police car behind us. He is signaling us to

＿＿＿＿.

Kevin: Really!　Again?　I don't want another ticket.

(A) pull side　(B) pull over　(C) pull up　(D) pull out

解答

1.B	2.A	3.C	4.D	5.D	6.C	7.B	8.D	9.B	10.A	11.B	12.B
13.A	14.A	15.D	16.C	17.B	18.C	19.A	20.B				

綜合解析

1. (C)(D)介系詞 by, with 使用錯誤，(A) understand 應改為被動。

歐洲長程線領隊，應具備的語文能力，除英文是必備溝通語言外，法文、德文、義大利文都是應多琢磨的。由於西歐部分義大利籍司機比率偏高，旺季常會遇到新手上路，因此領隊要兼做找路的工作，若語言不通，溝通時容易產生障礙，一路上就會辛苦萬分。

2. 被動。

領隊是第一線旅行業從業人員，徹底執行旅遊契約的內容，是領隊應盡最大職責。即使在非人為因素所能控制的意外下，一切仍應以契約書內容執行完畢為最大目標。縱使發生意外狀況，也應盡一切可能手段與方式，完成中文行程表中所有的內容。

3. 未來完成式。

娛樂設施的操作應向團員解說清楚，避免誤解；如遇設備故障，應盡速協調修復。賭場相關規定也要一併說明清楚，避免失禮或違法。

4. 主題the subject 為單數，被動；(B) 錯，(A)(C)皆錯。

秀場節目的歷史背景、沿革、發展與特色等，領隊應利用時間在演出前有所介紹，使團員於欣賞節目過程中有深刻的體會與了解，強化節目效果與增加滿意度。

5. 被動，(B)(D)錯誤，(A) 文法錯誤。

生態觀光與社會責任，領隊於帶團過程中，應有技巧向團員解說清楚，身為地球村的一份子，應善用資源、保護歷史遺蹟，因此領隊的解說功能，要含有教育的意義。

6. 被動且過去式，(B) (D)錯；that 前不加","。

免稅店所購買物品之提領規範各國法令規定不一，有的可以當場提貨、有的是免稅店會送貨至機場出境免稅品提領區，待旅客要出境時，再持免稅店所發給的商品交換券領取商品，應事先與團員說明清楚各國相關規定與退稅方式、金額與比率。

7. (A)雙動詞錯誤，(C)(D) 文法錯誤。

各國旅遊的禁忌，領隊應向團員解說清楚，入境隨俗，避免不必要的困擾，嚴重時更可能危及整團的安全，種族歧視更是敏感且應避免的議題。

8. 被動，(A)(C)錯誤，(B)時態錯誤。

團體照可以留下一個美好的回憶，在有些旅遊國家或地區，有時當地旅遊業者會主動邀請拍照，應先向團員說明清楚價錢與何時交件。

9. 慣用語。

領隊的誠信與誠實是基本的職業道德，特別是牽涉財務報帳，應據實以報，匯率、金額都應正確無誤。

10. 被動。

郵寄東西，可以至飯店櫃檯，若至郵局需要衡量當天行程的順路與否，因此為避免領隊自身的困擾，應事先向團員說明。

11.(A)(C)語意錯誤；(D) 文法錯誤。

天氣一般較難掌握，帶團中應天天收看當地氣象報告；前一天要跟團員說

明隔天行程內容與衣著配備，以利團員隔天的穿著。

12. 慣用語 proceed to 前往。

對於外站join客人要確認，會合地點與旅遊契約書內容，哪些是包括在團費中，哪些不包括在團費中。有時脫隊也在不同航站，須事先確認，以免送旅客至錯誤航站。如果時間無法配合，也應提供至機場的相關資訊。

13. (B)(C)(D) 語意錯誤。

日本線領隊所需語文能力當然是日文，所帶團的路線也都侷限於日本線，自2006年日本政府要求台灣領隊要加考日本當地導遊執照。因此，通過台灣日語領隊證照者，應盡早通過日本政府相關證照考試。此外，有機會也應嘗試帶領其他路線的團體，擴展視野。

14. (A)語意正確。

領隊應將重要的私人或公司行程記錄下來，否則往往因工作忙碌、人常在國外不易聯繫，導致公司、客人、親友有事常找不到人；或是公司已排帶團，臨時又要換人。

15. (A)(B)(C)語意錯誤。

帶團在國外，如有緊急事件或旅程安排不清楚時，應向當地代理旅行社洽詢或尋求支援，掌握其聯絡方式與資料是必要的。

16. (A)(B)(D)語意錯誤。

長程線領隊事先與當地導遊接洽和再確認是必要的，特別是旺季時，與導遊或司機的協調有利於行程更順暢。

17. 慣用語。

凡是有計畫、事先有規劃、過程中適度修正、事後檢討，對於下一次帶團，絕對有正面的幫助。

18. (A) 去 of；(B)缺主詞、動詞；(D)缺動詞。

愛護地球資源是你我共同的責任，現今許多飯店在浴室都會提醒所有觀光客，如非必要，浴室毛巾、盥洗用品、水都應節約使用，避免浪費水資

源；或因為清洗毛巾，產生大量清潔劑污染河川。

19.假設語。

隨時備妥必要的旅行用品，以利一路順暢，有時甚至多準備一份，提供團員不時之需。

20.慣用語 pull over 停旁邊。

行車一定要按照各國政府規定，司機工作小時（Bus Hours）也應尊重，否則不僅有罰單，更要扣交通點數，對於司機所造成的損失不易彌補，當然行程也一定要全部走完。因此，領隊時間管理的功夫就非常重要。

歷屆試題

（　）1. If you want to become a successful tour manager, you have to work _____ and learn from the seniors.

(A)hard　　　　　　　　　　(B)hardly

(C)harshly　　　　　　　　　(D)easily　　　　【98外語領隊】

（　）2. Many tourists are fascinated by the natural _____ of Taroko Gorge.

(A)sparkles　　　　　　　　(B)spectacles

(C) spectators　　　　　　　(D)sprinklers　　　【98外語領隊】

（　）3. Reservations for hotel accommodation should be made in _____ to make sure rooms are available.

(A)advance　　　　　　　　(B)advanced

(C)advances　　　　　　　　(D)advancing　　　【98外語領隊】

（　）4. This artist's _____ are on exhibition at the museum.

(A)workouts　　　　　　　　(B)presences

(C)masterminds　　　　　　(D)masterpieces　　【98外語領隊】

（　）5. It is said that there are only a few lucky days _____ for getting married in

2010.

(A)elated   (B)available

(C)elected   (D)resentful   【99外語領隊】

( ) 6. I need some _____ for taking buses around town.

(A)checks   (B)exchange

(C)change   (D)savings   【99外語領隊】

( ) 7. All the _____ on the city rail map are color-coded so that a traveler knows

which direction she/he should take.

(A)routes   (B)roads

(C)sights   (D)systems   【99外語領隊】

( ) 8. Cathedrals, mosques, and temples are all _____ buildings.

(A)religious   (B)natural

(C)political   (D)rural   【99外語領隊】

( ) 9. We all felt _____ when the manager got drunk.

(A)embarrassed   (B)embarrassing

(C)being embarrassed   (D)been embarrassed 【100外語領隊】

( ) 10. Wulai (烏來) is a famous hot-spring _____.

(A)resort   (B)mansion

(C)pivot   (D)plaque   【100外語領隊】

( ) 11. The _____ of Liberty, a gift from France, is erected in New York Harbor.

(A)Statuette   (B)Stature

(C)Status   (D)Statue   【100外語領隊】

( ) 12. I enjoyed the stay here. Thank you very much for the _____.

(A)hospital   (B)hospitality

(C)hostilities   (D)hostel   【100外語領隊】

( ) 13. _____, the applicant was not considered for the job.

(A)Due to his lack of experience　　　(B)Because his lack of experience

(C)His lack of experience　　　(D)Due to his experience lack

【101外語領隊】

(　) 14. A tour guide is _____ informing tourists about the culture and the beautiful

sites of a city or town.

(A)afraid of　　　(B)responsible for

(C)due to　　　(D)dependent on　　【101外語領隊】

(　) 15. A bus used for public transportation runs a set route; however, a _____ bus

travels at the direction of the person or organization that hires it.

(A)catering　　　(B)chatter

(C)charter　　　(D)cutter　　【101外語領隊】

(　) 16. I called to ask about the schedule of the buses _____ to Kaoshiung.

(A)leaving　　　(B)heading

(C)binding　　　(D) taking　　【101外語領隊】

解答

1.A	2.B	3.A	4.D	5.B	6.C	7.A	8.A	9.A	10.A	11.D	12.B
13.A	14.A	15.C	16.B								

表 6-2　英文行程表內容

LEO Travel Agent	
Taipei	
Taiwan	Date:　　　　23　Oct 2011
	Pages:　　　　1
	Customer-Code: LeoTAI
	ETN-Ref.:　　　402773

FINAL ITINERARY
Group Leo Travel / 402773 / Germany
25 Oct 2011 - 01 Nov 2011

Date	City	Time	Service	Details
25 Oct	Frankfurt	06:00	Arrival in FRA with flight CX289	
			Start long distance coach	Driver Mr. Jack
			Schooless-Busreisen	Mobile: 0049 177 99 10 666
			Tel. +49 [6444] 2888	
	Boppard	10:00	Rhine river cruises Boppard - Lorely - St. Goar	*Provided by LORELEY-LINIE WEINAND
			55-56 Rheinuferstr.	
			D-56341 Kamp-Bornhofen	
			Germany	
			Tel. +49 [6773] 341	
			Fax +49 [6773] 7110	
			Rhine river cruises Boppard - Lorely - St. Goar	
		11:45	Arrival St. Goar	
	St. Goar	12:00	Meal at Panorama restaurant Loreley	3 course set menu + coffee/tea
			Postfach 12 22	MENU:
			56326 St. Goar	Soup
			Germany	Grilled Knuckle of Pork
			Tel. +49 [6741] 35 6	with rice and salad
			Fax +49 [6741] 74 68	Dessert
	Boppard	13:00	Depart for Heidelberg	
	Heidelberg	Afternoon	Orientation tour Heidelberg	
		18:00	Dinner under own arrangement	
	Mannheim	19:00	Check-in Hotel Novotel Mannheim	

			Am Friedensplatz 1	
			68165 Mannheim	
			Germany	
			Tel. +49 [621] 42 34 0	
			Fax +49 [621] 41 73 43	
		Overnight	Hotel Novotel Mannheim	
26 Oct	Mannheim	08:00	Breakfast at the hotel	Hot buffet breakfast
		Morning	Check-out Hotel Novotel Mannheim	
		08:30	Depart for Baden-Baden	
	Baden-Baden	10:45	Arrival Baden-Baden / Orientation tour	
		12:30	Lunch under own arrangement	
		13:30	Depart for Titisee	
	Titisee-Neustadt	15:15	Arrival Titisee / Orientation tour	
		18:00	Dinner under own arrangement	
	Freiburg	19:00	Check-in Hotel IVB Boardhouse Best Western	
			Breisacher Strasse 84B	
			79110 Freiburg	
			Germany	
			Tel. +49 [761] 89 68 0	
			Fax +49 [761] 80 95 03 0	
			Ref. No. 14858.000	
		Overnight	Hotel IVB Boardhouse Best Western	
27 Oct	Freiburg	08:00	Breakfast at the hotel	Continental buffet breakfast
		Morning	Check-out Hotel IVB Boardhouse Best Western	
	Breitnau	08:30	Depart for Neuschwanstein via Bodensee	
	Fussen	13:00	Arrival Fussen	

Hohen-schwangau	13:15	Lunch at Schlosshotel Lisl Jägerhaus Neuschwansteinstrasse 1-3 87645 Hohenschwangau Germany Tel. +49 [8362] 8870 Fax +49 [8362] 81107	Menu: - Small salad with balsamico dressing - Pork Sausages with sauerkraut and saute potatoes - Apple strudel with cream *bread and ice-water-service
	15:30	Neuschwanstein Castle Germany Ref. No. AN00004295	*The reserved tickets have to be picked up at least one hour before the confirmed admission time. Please contact therefore a separate desk in the TICKET-CENTER. * In case of delayed arrival you have to cancel or change your reservation until two hours before the confirmed admission time via phone:0049 (0) 8362/93083-0
Fussen	19:00	Check-in Treff Luitpoldpark Hotel Luitpoldstrasse D-87629 Fussen Germany Tel. +49 [83] 62 90 40 Fax +49 [83] 62 90 46 78	
	19:30	Dinner at the hotel	3-course meal with coffee and/or tea
	Overnight	Treff Luitpoldpark Hotel	

28 Oct Fussen	08:00	Breakfast at the hotel	Hot buffet breakfast
	Morning	Check-out Treff Luitpoldpark Hotel	
	08:30	Depart for Munich via Linderof	
Munich	18:45	Transfer by coach to Pschoor Keller	
	19:00	Check-in Hotel to be advised	
	19:30	Dinner show at Pschorr-Keller Restaurant	MENU 58
			Consommé with Egg Drops
		Menu 58 + half a litre of beer	Genuine Munich Grilled Sausage
		United Kingdom	with mashed potatoes and
		Tel. +44 [89] 50 03 666	sauerkraut
		Fax +44 [89] 50 47 77	Layered Chocolate-Vanilla-Strawberry ice cream
			+ half a litre of beer!
	20:30	Return transfer by coach from Pschorr Keller to the hotel	
	Overnight	Hotel to be advised	
29 Oct Munich	08:00	Breakfast at the hotel	Hot buffet breakfast
	08:30	Depart for Rothenburg	
Rothen-burg	11:00	Arrival in Rothenburg / Orientation tour	
	12:30	Lunch under own arrangement	
	14:00	Continue to Wurzburg	
Wurzburg	19:00	Check-in Hotel to be advised	
	Overnight	Hotel to be advised	
30 Oct Wurzburg	08:00	Breakfast at the hotel	Hot buffet breakfast
	08:30	Depart for Eisenach via Bad Hersfeld	
	12:30	Lunch under own arrangement	
Eisenach	19:00	Check-in Hotel Courtyard	

			Weinbergstr. 5	
			99817 Eisenach	
			Germany	
			Tel. +49 [369] 18150	
			Fax +49 [369] 1815100	
		Overnight	Hotel Courtyard	
31 Oct	Eisenach	08:00	Breakfast at the hotel	Hot buffet breakfast
		Morning	Check-out Hotel Courtyard	
		08:30	Depart via Alsfeld and Marburg to Frankfurt	
	Marburg	12:30	Lunch under own arrangement	
	Frankfurt	19:00	Finish long distance coach	Drop-Off Hotel in Mannheim area (name to be confirmed!)
			Check-in City Hotel Bad Vilbel or similar	
			Alte Frankfurter Str. 13	
			61118 Bad Vilbel	
			Germany	
			Tel. +49 [6101] 588 152	
			Fax +49 [6101] 588 488	
		Overnight	City Hotel Bad Vilbel or similar	
01 Nov	Frankfurt	08:00	Breakfast at the hotel	Hot buffet breakfast
		Morning	Check-out City Hotel Bad Vilbel or similar	
		09:30	Private coach for transfer from Airport Frankfurt to Frankfurt Hotel	Pick-Up Hotel in Frankfurt (name to be confirmed)
			Eschbach Reisen	
			Tel. +49 [69] 5 07 29 59	
		11:30	Arrival Frankfurt APT - CX288 @ 14:00 uhr	

*** END OF OUR SERVICES ***

In emergencies please contact LTA under the following Free phone numbers:

Germany   [0800] 956 956

It is the responsibility of the group/ tour leader to advice passengers to use seat belts and ask the driver for the location of first-aid kits, fire extinguishers and emergency exits.

第七章

餐廳作業

一、工作程序（Working Procedures）

　　團體訂餐短線團體，例如：東南亞、大陸；長程線團體，例如：美西、美東、加拿大、紐西蘭、澳洲、南非等；多數都由當地代理旅行社所訂妥，領隊角色與功能主要在監督餐食品質與協助服務的工作。領隊最後只有交付簽單（Voucher），並無訂餐的主動權，只有例外狀況領隊才可以調整餐食。

　　相反的，歐洲團或日本團領隊則有訂餐的任務，此時，與司機、導遊的協調工作，搭配司機的路況熟悉度、導遊行程操作的順暢度，在不能超過公司預算的前提下，領隊應做最適當的訂餐工作。使團員吃得滿意、司機開車／停車方便、導遊帶團順利，是領隊所必須達成的餐廳作業。

　　抵達餐廳後，應主動協助餐廳做必要的服務工作，盡速令團員有位子座、有佳餚享用，而非站著指揮吆喝餐廳工作人員。用餐結束後，應提醒團員個人的貴重物品需攜帶，且上車前應先上盥洗室，避免上車後發現東西未帶或急於找廁所，而耽誤團體旅遊行程。

二、關鍵字彙

　　領隊應熟悉的重要關鍵字彙包括下列六項：

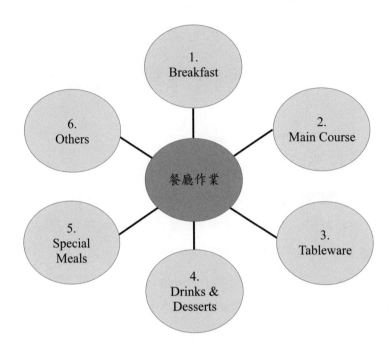

1.Breakfast　早餐

· American Breakfast	美式早餐
· Continental Breakfast	歐陸式早餐
· English Breakfast	英式早餐

2.Main Course　主餐

· A La Carte	單點	· Bar-B-Q	烤肉
· Set Menu= Table D' Hote	套餐	· Buffet	自助餐
· Specialty	招牌菜	· Scrambled Egg	炒蛋
· Appetizers	前菜	· Fried Egg	煎蛋
· Main Dish	主菜	· Sunny Side Up	荷包蛋
· Desserts	甜點	· Turn Over	煎兩面
· Pork	豬肉	· Over Easy	輕煎兩面
· Chicken	雞肉	· Over Hard	熟煎兩面
· Beef	牛肉	· Boiled Egg	水煮蛋
· Fish	魚	· Poached Egg	水煮荷包蛋
· Seafood	海鮮	· Vegetable	蔬菜
· Ostrich Eggs	鴕鳥蛋	· Bean	豆子
· Scallop	干貝	· Carrot	胡蘿蔔

· Oyster	生蠔	· Cabbage	包心菜
· Escargot	田螺	· Cereal	穀類
· Steak	牛排	· Noodle	麵
· Rare	一分熟	· Baked Potato	烤馬鈴薯
· Medium Rare	三分熟	· Refreshment	茶點
· Medium	五分熟	· Roast Beef	烤牛肉
· Medium Well	七分熟	· Western Food	西餐
· Well Done	九分熟	· Calculation	計算

3.Tableware　餐具

· Dining Table	餐桌	· Teapot	茶壺
· Tablecloth	桌布	· Saucer	茶碟
· Knife	刀	· Chopsticks	筷子
· Fork	叉	· Vinegar Bottle	醋瓶
· Spoon	匙	· Salt Shaker	鹽罐
· Fish Knife	魚刀	· Pepper Shaker	胡椒罐
· Snail Fork	田螺叉	· Soy Sauce Bottle	醬油瓶
· Paper Napkin	紙巾	· Toothpick Holder	牙籤盒
· Ashtray	菸灰缸	· Lobster Pick	龍蝦叉
· Snail Tongs	田螺夾	· Lobster Clacker	龍蝦鉗
· Jigger	盎司杯	· Finger Bowel	洗手碗

4.Drinks & Desserts　飲料 & 甜點

· Pub	酒吧	· Orange Juice	柳橙汁
· Alcoholic	含酒精的	· Apple Juice	蘋果汁
· Aperitif	飯前酒	· Tea	茶
· Brandy	白蘭地	· Coffee	咖啡
· Sparkling Wine	汽泡酒	· Black Coffee	不加糖咖啡
· Spirit	烈酒	· Aspartame	代糖（阿斯巴甜）
· Cocktail	雞尾酒	· Coke	可樂
· Red Wine	紅酒	· Diet Coke	無糖可樂
· White Wine	白酒	· Black Tea	紅茶
· Champagne	香檳	· Milkshake	奶昔
· Beer	啤酒	· Ice Cream	冰淇淋
· Whisky on the Rocks	威士忌加冰塊	· Pudding	布丁
· Whisky Straight	威士忌加不冰塊	· Corkage	開瓶費

· Mineral Water	礦泉水	· Ginger Ale	薑汁汽水
· Tequila	龍舌蘭酒	· Armagnac	（Armagnac區）白蘭地
· Beaujolais	薄酒萊	· Cognac	（Cognac區）白蘭地
· Cointreau	君度橙酒	· Calvados	蘋果白蘭地

5.Special meals　風味餐

· Cheese Fondue	瑞士起司火鍋	· Chocolate Fondue	瑞士巧克力火鍋
· Beef Fondue	瑞士牛肉火鍋	· Sausage	香腸
· Spaghetti	義大利麵	· Macaroni	義大利通心麵
· Irish Stew	愛爾蘭燉肉	· Mussel	（比利時）淡菜
· Pasta	千層麵	· Smoked Salmon	煙燻鮭魚
· Oyster	生蠔	· Crayfish	（澳洲）螯蝦
· Foie Gras	鵝肝醬	· Couscous	北非小米飯（羊／雞）
· Chicken in Champagne	香檳雞	· Haggis	蘇格蘭羊胃餐
· Sherbet	義式冰淇淋	· Lasagna	薄的千層麵
· Risotto Milanese	米蘭燴飯	· Paella	西班牙海鮮飯

6.Others　其他

· Waiter	服務生	· Take Away	外帶
· Waitress	女服務生	· Banqueting Hall	宴會廳
· Bartender	酒保	· Cover Charge	最低消費
· Chef	主廚	· Dressing	吃沙拉的調味醬
· Head Waiter	領班	· Sauce	吃肉類的調味醬
· Room Service	客房服務	· Calorie	卡路里
· Club Catering	俱樂部餐飲服務	· Vending Machine	自動販賣機
· Bill	帳單	· Open Charge	開瓶費

三、關鍵會話

(一)安排團體用餐

【Scene：On tour】

Tour Leader:　Hello! Miss Evonne, I am very happy to have you as the guide of our Paris Tour tomorrow. Last time, you offered very good service for my group.

Local guide : It is my pleasure to serve you. I hope we will have a good cooperation as well this time.

Tour Leader: What will be the meal arrangement for this group tomorrow?

Local guide : After we visit the Versailles Palace, we will have Chinese food lunch in Paris downtown.

Tour Leader: Go back to Paris city for lunch?

Local guide : Yes, because we have a half-day city tour in the afternoon.

Tour Leader: I got it. Is it far from the Eiffel Tower?

Local guide : No. It will only take us about 5 minutes by walk to get there.

Tour Leader: What can we have for lunch in the Chinese restaurant?

Local guide : It depends on your budgets.

Tour Leader: As you know, I have budget limits.

Local guide : No problems, I will arrange six courses of Chinese meal and meet your budget.

Tour Leader: That sounds good. We will try that.

Local guide : All right. See you tomorrow. Have a good sleep, Mr. Leo.

(二)帶領至餐廳用餐

【Scene：Restaurant】

Restaurant waiters: Good evening, sir. May I have your tour name?

Tour Leader　　　: Good evening. Leo Tour. There are 30 people in my group.

Restaurant waiters: Yes, I got your reservation number. There are three tables for your group.

Tour Leader　　　: We order six courses of meal for lunch. May I see the menu?

圖7-1　葡萄牙烤乳豬風味餐

Restaurant waiters: Sure. May we serve your people, now?

Tour Leader : Yes, please.

Restaurant waiters: How is everything here?

Tour Leader : Please give some more rice to the second table and one pot of tea to the first table.

Restaurant waiters: No problem, sir. Did you enjoy your lunch?

Tour Leader : Yes, very much. Thank you.

Restaurant waiters: Excuse me, sir. May I have your voucher for this group?

Tour Leader : Of course, here you are.

Restaurant waiters: Please sign here.

Tour Leader : Oh, I forget that. Thank you.

圖7-2 標準三道式西餐餐桌擺設

㈢協商早餐供應時間

【Scene：Front office】

Tour Leader ： Excuse me, sir. We are going to leave early tomorrow morning for our flight schedule. Shall we have an early breakfast arrangement for my group.

Duty manager: When is the departure time of this flight?

Tour Leader ： It's 9:00 a.m.. We should be at the airport two hours before the plane takes off.

Duty manager: Yes. I think so.

Tour Leader ： How long does it take from the hotel to the airport?

Duty manager: It takes one hour by coach unless there is a traffic jam.

Tour Leader : You mean that it also needs to take one hour driving from hotel to airport. In other words, we must leave at 6:00 a.m.

Duty manager: Yes. What time do you want to eat breakfast?

Tour Leader : 5:00 a.m..

Duty manager: It is not easy for me. Our restaurant normally will be open at 7:00 a.m..

Tour Leader : I know, but please prepare 30 plus 2 breakfast boxes for my group. We will enjoy the breakfast in the coach on the way to airport.

Duty manager: Sure. It sounds a good way.

圖7-3　歐洲火車上的餐車

Tour Leader　：Thank you for your cooperation and help.

Duty manager: You are welcome. We appreciate your staying in our hotel very much.

四、語詞測驗

1. **consist of** 〜　（由……）組成（**to be composed of**）

The tour group consists of twenty members.

這一旅遊團由20人所組成。

2. **contribute to** 〜　促成、有助於

The tourism industry contributed to the economic growth.

觀光產業有助於經濟成長。

3. **convince** 人 **of** 〜　使相信（**to make feel sure**）

I couldn't convince tour guide of his mistake.

我無法使導遊相信這都是他的錯。

4. **correspond to** 〜　符合、相配

Tour leader's standard of living doesn't correspond to his incomes.

領隊的生活水準與他的收入不相符合。

5. **correspond with** 〜　一致

Tour leader's words correspond with his actions.

這位領隊言行一致。

6. count [rely] on [upon] ～　指望

Don't count on local agent for any help.

不要指望當地旅行社的任何協助。

7. creep into ～　悄悄地進行

She crept into bed.

她悄悄地上床睡覺。

8. crowd out ～　被擠出來（**to exclude because of insufficient space or time**）

Our groups tried to get on the train but some tourists were crowded out.

我們整團試著要擠上火車，但是有部分團員被擠出車廂。

9. cry for ～　要求、渴望得到

The tourists are crying for tour leader's help.

團員渴望得到領隊的協助。

10. cry off ～　取消（**to withdraw from an agreement**）

Tour leader will cry off the optional tour at the last moment.

領隊在最後一刻取消自費活動。

11. cure A of B ～　治療A的B

Good tips cured tour leader of the exhaustion after the long journey.

豐富的小費可以治療領隊長途旅行後的身心疲憊。

12. deal with ～　對待、面對、討論

Tour leaders should deal fairly with their members of tour group.

領隊對於所有團員應公平對待。

13. **depend on [upon]** ～ 信賴

Tour leader is a man to be depended on.

領隊是值得信賴的人。

14. **deprive [rob] A of B** ～ 從A剝奪了B

They deprived the king of his power.

他們剝奪了國王的權利。

15. **derive A from B** ～ 從B得到A

He derives pleasure from being tour leader.

他從當領隊中得到滿足。

16. **do for** ～ 照料、代替

I'll do for members of tour group these days.

這幾天我會好好照顧團員。

17. **do with** ～ 處置（**to make use of**）

What have you done with our luggage?

你如何處理我們的行李？

18. **do without** ～ 不用（**to get along without**）

I can't do city tour without a local guide in Rome.

沒有當地導遊，我無法操作羅馬市區觀光。

19. draw off ～　脱下

You had better draw off your hat entering the Notre Dame.

進入聖母院時要脫下帽子。

20. draw out ～　拉長

Tour guide tried to draw out the visiting time in Duty-free Shop.

導遊試圖拉長免稅店參觀時間。

21. dread to ～　非常害怕（to be very fearful）

I dread to think of overbooking in tonight hotel.

想到今晚飯店超賣我就非常害怕。

22. dress up ～　盛裝（to dress in formal clothes）

I dressed up when I went to that Craze Horse Show in Paris.

我盛裝去欣賞巴黎瘋馬秀。

23. drop [look] in at ＋ 場所　順道拜訪

I'll drop in at local agent office on my way to hotel.

回飯店的路上，我去當地旅行社一下。

24. drop off ～　睡著

Some tourists dropped off during tour leader's speech on the coach.

當領隊在遊覽車上解說時，一些團員睡著了。

25. emerge from ～　出現

The sun emerged from behind the cloud.

太陽從雲後出現。

五、文法測驗

本章重點：假設法分析

與現在或未來事實相反的假設	If I were rich, I would travel around the world. 如果我很富有，我會去環遊世界。
與過去事實相反的假設	If tour leader had left earlier, he would have missed the evening rush hour. 如果領隊當時早點離開，就能避開傍晚的尖峰時間。
wish	We wish local guide didn't live so far away. 我們真希望當地導遊不是住那麼遠。
假設法的混合	If tour group had missed this train, tourists would now be waiting there. 如果這一團錯過這班火車，團員現在可能還在那裡等。
If的省略	Were it not for the sun, no creature could live. 如果沒有太陽，就沒有生物。
假設法的慣用語	But for the wind, it might be a warm day. 要不是有風，應該是個暖和的日子。
If only, Would that假設法	If only I know the answer now! 要是我現在知道答案就好了。
假設法條件句的省略	Tour leader could easily do it. 領隊可以簡單地將它完成。

本章綜合練習

（　）1. If the phone rings again, I _____ it.

    (A) ignore   (B) will ignore

    (C) will have ignored   (D) would have ignored

（　）2. If you _____ quiet, I'll tell you what happened.

    (A) are   (B) will be   (C) are to be   (D) be

（　）3. I would have told him the answer had it been possible, but I _____ so busy then.

    (A) had been   (B) were   (C) would be   (D) was

( ) 4. You may not go out _____ your work is done.

(A) before　(B) until　(C) where　(D) as

( ) 5. Take an umbrella _____ it should rain.

(A) in time　(B) in case　(C) fearing　(D) even if

( ) 6. _____ much effort, they still failed to win the match.

(A) Despite　(B) Against　(C) Though　(D) With

( ) 7. I don't think tour leader will be upset, but I'll see her in case _____.

(A) she'll　(B) she is　(C) she does　(D) she would

( ) 8. _____ we hurry, we will be late.

(A) Without　(B) If not　(C) Unless　(D) But

( ) 9. _____ anti-trust laws did not exist in Taiwan, there would not be as much

competition in travel industry.

(A) So　(B) If　(C) For　(D) Also

領隊英文

160

( ) 10. _____ of the seven groups were checked in the hotel in different time,

there would still be space left for tourist seating in hotel lobby.

(A) Each　(B) If each　(C) Were each　(D) Since each

( ) 11. The host will want the total amount _____ before paying the bill.

(A) checking　(B) check　(C) checked　(D) be checked

( ) 12. He was made _____ the contract though he was unwilling to.

(A) signing　(B) signed　(C) to sign　(D) sign

( ) 13. _____ you give me the money, I cannot let you take the tickets with you.

(A) If　(B) Because　(C) When　(D) Unless

( ) 14. Get the invoice _____ upon receipt.

(A) signed　(B) paid　(C) got　(D) sign

( ) 15. Karen: Did you get to eat breakfast on time this morning?

Tom: _____.

(A) The stock market crashed yesterday.

(B) No, I did.

(C) I barely made it.

(D) I always late for it.

（　）16. The table was big enough to _____ two couples.

(A) serve　(B) account　(C) valuable　(D) accumulate

（　）17. If your _____ is poor, you don't want to eat anything.

(A) attitude　(B) temper　(C) appetite　(D) pressure

（　）18. Why are you so_____? I'm only 35 minutes late!

(A) break down　(B) put off　(C) work out　(D) steamed up

（　）19. Steak that is just barely cooked is _____.

(A) rare　(B) raw　(C) medium　(D) fresh

（　）20. The waiter spilled the juice by accident, it is not his _____.

(A) error　(B) fault　(C) mistake　(D) problem

解答

1.B	2.A	3.D	4.B	5.B	6.A	7.B	8.C	9.B	10.B	11.C	12.C
13.D	14.A	15.C	16.A	17.C	18.D	19.A	20.B				

綜合解析

1. 與未來的假設。

接電話的禮節是必要的，人在國外手機應開機以利聯繫。如果固定帶領某一條線的行程，也應早日申請該國的手機門號，方便又便宜。

2. 與未來的假設。

團員中的意見領袖是領隊獲悉團體意見的良好來源之一，對於這一類型團員應心存感激，往往愛說話者所提供的意見是領隊自我檢討的依歸。

3. 過去的事實。

「今日事、今日畢」是領隊要落實的名言，不僅如此，最好提早做完，否則，旅遊產業所處變數太多、不確定性也太高，隨時應準備好突發事件的發生；萬一發生，也早已在預料之中。

4. 慣用語否定加until；肯定加till。

領隊既然是第一線服務人員，事情當然必須按計畫、時程完成，儘管部分工作非直接屬於領隊份內工作，也應積極協調處理，而非放著不管，使其到了不可收拾的地步。

5. 假設語氣。

事先多一份準備，意外發生時就少一份損失與不便。

6. 儘管 despite 語意正確。

領隊應戮力完成帶團工作，即使得不到所有團員的掌聲，也應朝此目標邁進，即使不是所有人都百分百滿意，至少也應有大多數人認同你的努力。

7. 現在式代替未來。

遇到難以解決的事情，應樂觀以對，積極處理，自我心情的調適與心理建設是平時就應養成的，更要以笑臉迎人之方式面對團員。

8. unless 除非，其他語意錯誤。

通知團員集合時間應明確，且要每一位團員都清楚。如遇不同語言別的團員，若能分別用團員所熟悉的語言，再一次說明清楚，則能避免少數團員「有聽沒有懂」。跨時區的旅遊地點，也應即時調整手錶時間，領隊不僅不可遲到，更應提早5-10分鐘到較佳。

9. 假設語氣。

旅遊業競爭激烈是全世界發展之趨勢，而領隊從某一個角度而言，也是一位旅遊銷售人員，因此對於旅遊產品成本、設計、包裝與行銷方式也應有所涉獵。往往團員「出國前比較價錢、出國後卻比較品質」，領隊應有相關旅遊成品基本分析與回應的能力。

10. 假設語氣。

旺季時，一路上都可以遇到同業的團體，領隊應主動聯繫，協調相互避開同一時間進同一餐廳、同一免稅店、同一飯店，否則令團員等待時間過長，當然旅遊滿意度也會不佳。

11. 被動。

帳單要清楚之外，並且當場要點清所購買貨品，特別是團員購買的東西，一定要告知團員金額、匯率、找錢及所購商品是否都正確。不僅如此，打包、裝箱一定要委請團員親眼在旁確認，並於外包裝上簽名，避免同團拿錯，或返國後才發現裝錯、少裝等窘境。

12. 慣用語。(A) 時態錯誤，(B)(D) 雙動詞錯。

領隊在外代表公司，一言一行一舉，都是代表所服務的旅行社，當然要注意自己的言行。對於書面文件簽署，當然要有公司授權，領隊與團員之間善意的契約也最好要書面訂定；不要只是以口頭或默默不表達意見的方式，團員不說話，不代表他或她同意。切記，當場不表達反對意見，返國後卻申訴的事件，也時有所聞。

13. 假設語氣，Unless 除非。

銷售自費活動，要預訂秀場位置，應先向團員說明清楚，是否有訂位費用（reservation fee），取消是否有取消費用（cancellation charge）；國人對於這些費用的觀念並未完全建立，事先應說明且建立正確觀念，避免臨時取消時，衍生出相關費用時，團員又無法接受扣款的事實。

14. 被動。

領隊帶團的所有收據應合法，如有無法取得單據的特例，也應請當事人簽名，例如：司機誤餐費、發給團員現金作為自我餐費時，都應簽名。

15. (A)(D)語意錯誤；(B) 否定才對。

團體用餐時間應按預訂時間，否則，許多團體擠在一起，不僅用餐品質不佳，有時也可能位置不夠。少數領隊有不吃早餐習慣，也應準時至餐廳招

呼團員，不然團員往往找不到領隊，語言溝通時遇到困難，抱怨也就因此產生。

16. 慣用語 serve people。

餐廳位置的安排當然要夠，除此之外，有素食者也應於訂餐時，提早告知餐廳準備，如有特殊需求也一定盡量符合團員需求，不幸遇到同一團有團員不吃牛肉、又同時有人不吃豬肉、羊肉等，領隊也要想盡辦法解決。

17. 專有名詞，appetite 胃口。

各地餐食安排，當然口味也不盡相同，更不能用台灣的餐廳口味來比較，應適度教育團員各地風味餐，或許「不適合」國人口味，但不是「不好吃」，意義是不同的。

18. (A)(B)(C)語意不對，Steamed up 火大。

領隊、導遊、司機遲到是團員較不能接受的事情，因此，提早是最佳的法則。

19. rare 三分熟。

團體旅遊也應有個性化的服務，應事先徵詢不同團員的個別需求，提供不同的服務。

20. 語意正確，his fault 他的錯。

領隊應從旁協助餐廳服務生，點飲料、點餐、說明工作，甚至必要的翻譯，而非完全由服務生處理，領隊是最清楚團員個別屬性之不同。因此，領隊從旁協助能強化用餐的滿意度。

歷屆試題

（　）1.　This is a non-smoking restaurant. Please _____ your cigarette at once.

(A)put in 　　　　　　　　　　(B)put on

(C)put out 　　　　　　　　　　(D)put up 　　　　【98外語領隊】

( ) 2. The _____ cake appears so _____.

    (A)flash...inviting   (B)flesh...invited

    (C)fresh...inviting   (D)flush...invited   【98外語領隊】

( ) 3. Many people have put on some pounds during the New Year vacation.

    (A)dressed up   (B)gained

    (C)gambled   (D)turned into   【98外語領隊】

( ) 4. You will need to brush up on your Spanish if you want to do business with people from South American countries.

    (A)improve   (B)learn painting

    (C)pretend to master   (D)withdraw   【98外語領隊】

( ) 5. If you're looking for Greek food in this area, sorry to say, there is very _____ choice.

    (A)few   (B)any

    (C)much   (D)little   【99外語領隊】

( ) 6. Many restaurants in Paris offer a _____ of snails for guests to taste.

    (A)plate   (B)group

    (C)chunk   (D)loaf   【99外語領隊】

( ) 7. Waiter: Are you ready to order, sir? Guest: _____

    (A)Your food looks tasty.

    (B)OK, I'll have that!

    (C)I don't eat meat.

    (D)I think so. But what is your specialty?   【99外語領隊】

( ) 8. The guest is given a _____ after he makes a complaint to the restaurant.

    (A)change   (B)profit

    (C)refund   (D)bonus   【99外語領隊】

( ) 9. It is not my cup of tea!

(A)I must obey the instructions. (B)I don't like it.

(C)I am not good at making tea. (D) It is not my imagination.

【100外語領隊】

( ) 10. Our _____ wants to reserve a table for dinner tomorrow.

(A)alcoholic (B)client

(C)gambler (D)retailer 【100外語領隊】

( ) 11. Would you like to order a/an _____ or refer to the a la carte menu?

(A)complex meal (B)singular meal

(C)set meal (D)united meal 【100外語領隊】

( ) 12. Please don't order so much food! _____ for the last two months.

(A)Earned much weight was I (B)I have been putting on weight

(C)My weight has put on (D)My weight was gaining

【100外語領隊】

( ) 13. _____ the offer is, the more pressure we will have to bear.

(A)The greatest (B)The greater

(C)More of (D)Most of 【101外語領隊】

( ) 14. _____ the father came into the bedroom did the two little brothers stopped

fighting.

(A)Only when (B)Only if

(C)If only (D)While 【101外語領隊】

( ) 15. The non-smoking policy will apply to any person working for the company

_____ of their status or position.

(A)regardless (B)regarding

(C)in regard (D)as regards 【101外語領隊】

( ) 16. _____ unemployed for almost one year, Henry has little chance of getting a job.

(A)Having been (B)Be

(C)Maybe (D)Since having 【101外語領隊】

解答

1.C	2.C	3.B	4.A	5.D	6.A	7.D	8.C	9.B	10.B	11.C	12.B
13.B	14.A	15.A	16.A								

第八章

飯店作業

一、工作程序（Working Procedures）

經過一天的行程結束後，團員也都累了，領隊除事先確定飯店的位置外，應按時間辦理住宿登記。抵達飯店後，領隊應盡速分發房間、說明隔天早餐時間、地點、下行李時間、團體出發時間等。隨即發放房間的鑰匙，協助行李員加速分送行李，讓團員有必備用品進行盥洗。

通常在分房後10-20分鐘，可以用電話確認所有團員房間設施是否正常運作，有必要時，在團員同意下，也可以親自至團員房間說明房間設施與協助調整必要的設施。確認所有團員行李與房間都沒問題時，領隊才可以處理個人事務；當然領隊房間號碼與打電話的方式所有團員也都要很清楚，如有急事才可以隨時找到隨團領隊。

隔天早上，領隊要提早30分鐘起床，事先確認餐廳是否備妥團體位置，應於團體用餐時間前至餐廳招呼團員用餐，隨時提供必要的服務與溝通飯店餐廳人員即時補充供應餐食。最後，協助辦理飯店遷出手續，並提醒團員上車前應要上洗手間。

二、關鍵字彙

領隊應熟悉的重要關鍵字彙包括下列六項：

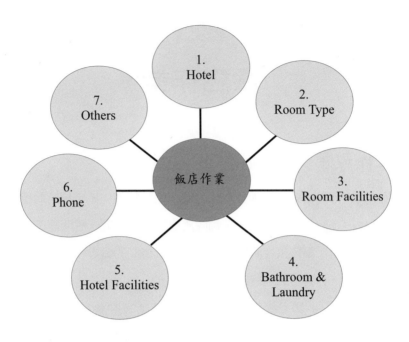

1.Hotel　飯店			
・Commercial Hotel	商務旅館	・Floating Hotel	水上飯店
・Resort Hotel	休閒旅館	・Safaris Lodge	狩獵木屋
・Tree Top Hotel	樹屋旅館	・Bed & Breakfast (B&B)	民宿
・Motel	汽車旅館	・Hostel	青年旅舍
・Boatel	船屋旅館	・Overnight Train	過夜火車
・Airtel	由航空公司直營的機場飯店	・Inside Cabin	無窗內艙
・Airport Hotel	機場飯店	・Outside Cabin	海景外艙
・American Plan= Full Pension		美式計價方式（住宿含三餐）	
・Modified American Plan=Half Pension		修正美式計價（住宿含兩餐）	
・Continental Plan		歐陸式計價方式（住宿含歐式早餐）	
・European Plan		歐式計價方式（住宿不含早餐）	
2.Room Type　房間類型			
・Single Room	單人房	・Extra Bed	加床
・Double Room	雙人房（一張大床）	・Baby Cot	嬰兒床
・Twin Room	雙人房（二張小床）	・Inside Room	無窗房
・Triple Room	三人房	・Balcony Room	附有陽台房

· Quad= Group Chamber	四人房	· Outside Room	有窗房
· Connecting Room	連通房 （兩房間內有門）	· Adjoining Room	緊鄰房（兩房間 外有共同房門）
· Corner Room	轉角房	· Room Status	房間狀況
· Suite	套房	· Courtesy Room	招待房

3.Room Facilities　房間設施

· Twin-Size　　99×190 Centimeters		雙人床	
· Full-Size　　137×190 Centimeters		加大雙人房	
· Queen-Size　152×203 Centimeters		皇后式雙人房	
· King-Size　　193×203 Centimeters		國王式雙人房	
· Complimentary Fruit Basket		迎賓水果籃	
· Complimentary Newspaper		免費當天日報	
· ADSL Internet Connection		高速上網連結	
· Bedcover	床罩	· Wall Lamp	壁燈
· Linen	床單	· Lamp	檯燈
· Blanket	毯子	· Air Conditioner	冷氣
· Pillow	枕頭	· Key Card	鑰匙卡
· Pillowcase	枕頭套	· Mini Bar	迷你吧檯
· Television	電視	· Refrigerator	冰箱
· Pay-TV	付費電視	· Dressing Table	化妝檯
· Television Remote Control	電視遙控器	· Drawer	抽屜
· Closet	壁櫥	· Toilet Paper	衛生紙
· Chest Of Drawers	衣櫃	· Sofa Bed	沙發床
· Safety Box	保險箱	· Don't Disturb	勿打擾
· Slippers	室內用拖鞋	· Shoe Shining Machine	擦鞋機
· Clothes Hanger	衣架	· Electronic Kettle	電水壺

4.Bathroom & Laundry　浴室 & 洗衣房

· Bathtub	浴缸	· Laundry Service	洗衣服務
· Jacuzzi	按摩浴缸	· Laundry List	洗衣單
· Shower Curtain	浴簾	· Laundry Bag	送洗衣袋
· Shower head	蓮蓬頭	· Laundry Charge	洗衣費用
· Shower Cap	浴帽	· Dry Cleaning	乾洗

‧ Shampoo	洗髮乳	‧ Press	燙衣服
‧ Lotion	乳液	‧ Jacket	外套
‧ Towel Rack	毛巾架	‧ Business Suit	西裝
‧ Towel	毛巾	‧ Vest	背心
‧ Hair Dryer	吹風機	‧ Shirt	襯衫
‧ Wash basin	洗手檯	‧ Trouser	長褲
‧ Basin	洗臉盆	‧ Skirt	裙子
‧ Soap Stand	肥皂盒	‧ Bidet	淨身盆
‧ Tooth Paste	牙膏	‧ Pot	坐式馬桶
‧ Toothbrush	牙刷	‧ Razor	刮鬍刀

5.Hotel Facilities 飯店設施

‧ Front Desk	櫃檯	‧ Night Club	夜總會
‧ Elevator	電梯	‧ Gym Room	健身房
‧ Lobby	大廳	‧ Business Center	商務中心
‧ Banquet Room	宴會廳	‧ Sauna	三溫暖
‧ Restaurant	餐廳	‧ Massage	按摩
‧ Coffee Shop	咖啡店	‧ Beauty Parlor	美容院
‧ Cafeteria	自助餐館	‧ Tennis Court	網球場
‧ Health Center	健康中心	‧ Bowling Alley	保齡球場
‧ Chess Room	下棋間	‧ Mahjong Room	麻將間
‧ Billiard Room	撞球間	‧ Toilet	廁所
‧ Lounge	休息室	‧ Casino	賭場

6.Phone 電話

‧ International Direct Dial (IDD)		國際直撥電話	
‧ Station-to-Station Call		叫號電話	
‧ Person-to-Person Call		叫人電話	
‧ Collect Call	對方付費電話	‧ Mobile Phone	手機
‧ Room to Room Dial	房間互通電話	‧ Extension	分機
‧ House phone	館內電話	‧ Message	留言
‧ Country Code	國家代碼	‧ Area Code	區域代碼

7.Others 其他

‧ Duty Manager	值班經理	‧ Room Rate	房價
‧ Supervisor	主管	‧ Hotel Voucher	住宿券
‧ Foreman	領班	‧ Extra Charge	額外付費

· Cashier	出納	· Discount	折扣
· Receptionist	櫃檯接待員	· Service Charge	服務費
· Concierge	資深櫃檯服務員	· Registration Form	住宿登記表
· Floor Attendant	樓層服務員	· Morning Call	叫醒服務
· Room Maid	房務員	· Souvenir Shop	紀念品店
· Bellman	行李員	· Food & Beverage	餐飲
· Housekeeping	房務	· Master Key	萬能鑰匙
· Check-out Time	遷出時間	· Hotel Card	飯店卡
· Check-in Time	遷入時間	· Decoration	裝飾
· Fully Booked	客滿	· Oversleep	睡過頭
· Sold Out	賣光	· Rack Rate	牌價
· Vacancy	空房	· Reception	接待
· Advance Reservations	事先訂位	· Available	可利用／可行的
· Method of Payment	付費方式	· Room and Board	食宿
· Allocation of Accommodation　分房			

三、關鍵會話

(一)辦理住宿登記

【Scene：Front desk】

Receptionist: Good evening, sir. What can I do for you?

Tour Leader：I am the tour leader of Leo Travel. My tour reference number is 0800-956-956.

Receptionist: Just a minute, please. I am checking the reservation records. I got a reservation for 2 double rooms and 13 twin rooms.

Tour Leader：Yes, it is correct for my group.

Receptionist: Can I see your passports, please, sir?

Tour Leader：Certainly, miss. Here is the room list and my passport.

Receptionist: Thank you, sir. And fill in the registration forms and give me your voucher, please.

Tour Leader : All right.

Receptionist: Here are the keys to your rooms. Please make sure that you have them with you all the time.

Tour Leader : Ok. I will tell my members.

Receptionist: Here are your 29 plus one vouchers for American breakfast. You will be required to give voucher to the waiter for your meals in the restaurant.

Tour Leader : When could we eat breakfast tomorrow morning?

Receptionist: The restaurant will be open from 7:00 to 10:00.

Tour Leader : Thank you.

Receptionist: How many pieces of luggage do you have?

Tour Leader : There are twenty pieces of luggage altogether. Please copy another room list for the bell captain and send these 20 pieces to the rooms.

Receptionist: Is there anything valuable or breakable in them?

Tour Leader : No, nothing at all.

Receptionist: Don't worry. Your luggage will be sent to your rooms immediately.

Tour Leader : Thank you.

Receptionist: Your check-out time is at 8:30 tomorrow morning. Has there been any change in your schedule?

Tour Leader : No. We will be on schedule.

Receptionist: May I have your room number, tour leader?

Tour Leader : 888.

Receptionist: Is everything all right for your group?

Tour Leader: Yes. Thank you.

Receptionist: My pleasure. Have a good time at our hotel.

圖8-1　飯店櫃檯

(二)領隊查房後協調櫃檯服務

【Scene：In tour leader's room】

Tour Leader: Good evening. I am Leo, the tour leader of Leo Travel. Could you send someone to fix shower head in Room 866, please? There is no water coming out.

Receptionist: I am sorry for that. I will send someone to take care of it, immediately.

Tour Leader : One more thing, the room 877 is not ready to sell. Maybe you make a mistake. Please change another clean room for this couple.

Receptionist: I am terribly sorry for that. I will arrange Room 878 for them.

Tour Leader : Thank you, miss.

Receptionist: Anything else, Mr. Leo.

Tour Leader : The people next door are very noisy. Would you tell them keep quiet, please?

Receptionist: You mean Room 889.

Tour Leader : Yes.

Receptionist: I am sorry about the noise, sir. I will tell them.

Tour Leader : Fine, appreciate.

Receptionist: It is our pleasure to serve you. Have a good night.

圖8-2 飯店等級告示牌

(三)房間設施故障處置

【Scene：In tour leader's room】

Receptionist: Reception. May I help you?

Tour Leader : Yes. I am Leo, the tour leader of Leo Travel. There are some problems in Room 833. Can you get someone up here?

Receptionist: What's wrong?

Tour Leader : The TV and air conditioner do not work. Besides, the tap is broken, too. It won't stop running.

Receptionist: I am terribly sorry about it, sir. We will send a repairman there immediately.

Tour Leader : May I change room for my tour member?

Receptionist: I'm sorry, but we have no vacant room tonight.

Tour Leader : OK. Please fix it as soon as possible.

Receptionist: No problem.

Tour Leader : One more thing, one of our tour members wants to deposit valuables.

Receptionist: Certainly, sir. Please tell him to take them to the reception and I will take care of it.

Tour Leader : I see. Thank you very much.

圖8-3　歐洲常見衛浴設備（右為淨身盆）

表8-1　住宿登記表

GUEST REGISTRATION					
				GUEST SIGNATURE_____	
ACCOUNT NO.			ARRIVAL DATE		DEPARTURE DATE
DATE	ROOM NO.	RATE	NO. OF GUEST		ROOM TYPE
REMARK					
RESERVATION BY					

FUL NAME_____

PASSPORT NO._____NATIONALITY_____SEX_____

DATE OF BIRTH_____TELEPHONE NO._____

ADDRESS_____

RECEPTIONIST_____TIME_____

四、語詞測驗

1. **face up to** ～　沉著應付

   We faced up to that long distance coach accident.

   我們沉著應付長程遊覽車意外事件。

2. **figure out** ～　想出（**to understand**）、解決（**to solve**）、計算

   Tour leader figured out the cost of all meals in this group.

   領隊計算出團體行程中所有的餐費。

3. **fill out [in]** ～　填寫（**to make complete by inserting information**）

   Tour leader filled out the hotel registration form.

   領隊填寫飯店住宿表。

4. **fill up** ～　裝滿（**to make completely full**）

   Please fill up my glass.

   請裝滿我的杯子。

5. **find out** ～　發現（**to discover; learn**）

   How did you find out the driver?

   你如何發現司機的？

6. **freeze（on）to** ～　抓緊（**to cling to**）

   Tour leader will freeze on to her when she needs to help.

   當她需要幫忙時，領隊抓緊她。

7. **gaze at** ～　注視

What are you gazing at?

你在看什麼？

8. **get after** ～　跟著某人之後

Tourists got after tour leader.

團員跟著領隊。

9. **get back** ～　回來（**to return**）、收回（**to recover**）

When will you get back to the hotel?

你何時回飯店？

10. **get over** ～　克服（**to overcome**）、康復（**to recover from**）

Everyone got over the earthquake shock soon.

每一個人很快地克服地震的內心衝擊。

11. **get through** ～　設法活下去、完成（**to finish**）

Tour leader has to get through all missions in working itinerary on the tour.

領隊必須在行程中完成所有工作日誌內的任務。

12. **go about** ～　四處走動（**to move from place to place**）

I often go about in the London Hyde Park.

我常去倫敦海德公園。

13. **go on** ～　繼續（**to continue**）、發生（**to take place**）

Without tour guide, nothing is going on well in Paris.

在巴黎沒有導遊，一切都無法順利進行。

14. **go through with** ～ 履行（**to pursue to the end**）

Being tour leader should go through with the promise.

當一位領隊要履行諾言。

15. **go with** ～ 配合、陪伴

This tie doesn't go with your suit.

這條領帶和你的西裝不配。

16. **grumble at** ～ 喃喃地抱怨（**to complain of**）

Some tour leaders are always grumbling at Italian drivers.

一些領隊常常抱怨義大利司機。

17. **hand in** ～ 提出（**to submit**）、交出

We handed in the passports as requested on border.

在邊界時，我們應交出護照查驗。

18. **hang on** 緊握（**to keep hold**）、（電話）請稍候（**to hold the line**）

Hang on, please.

請稍候。

19. **hang [lean] out** ～ 伸出身體

Don't hang out of the window in the train.

搭火車時，頭手請勿伸出窗外。

20. **hang up**　掛起來（**to put on a hanger**）、中止（**to suspend**）、掛斷電話（**to put a telephone receiver back**）

Don't hang up, please.

請別掛斷電話。

21. **hear from** ∼　接到某人的信（**to get a letter**）

I haven't hear from since he telephoned.

自從那次他來電話後，我就一直沒有收到他的來信。

22. **hunt after [for]** ∼　尋找

What are you hunting for in the Louvre？

你在羅浮宮內尋找什麼？

23. **intend to** ∼　意欲

What do you intend to do in free time？

在空閒時間，你打算做什麼？

24. **keep out**　使不進入

Danger！Keep out！

危險！不准進入！

25. **keep up with** ∼　趕得上

You should keep up with the TGV.

你應該趕得上法國子彈列車。

五、文法測驗

本章重點：不定詞分析

名詞用法	To know is one thing, to guiding is another. 知道是一回事，帶團又是另一回事。
形容詞用法	Tour guide was the only man to know the secret. 導遊是唯一知道祕密的人。
副詞用法	I've come to have a talk with you. 我來和你談一談。
完成式不定詞	The driver seems to have been homesick for a long time. 司機似乎已經患有思鄉病很久了。
hope, etc. ＋完成式不定詞	I hoped to have seen this tour guide. 我真希望見過這位導遊。
不定詞	You can come with tour guide if you'd like to. 如果你願意，可以跟導遊一起走。
原形不定詞	They do nothing but complain. 他們只是抱怨。

本章綜合練習

（　）1. Who allowed you _____ my coach?

   (A) driving   (B) to drive   (C) riding   (D)to ride

（　）2. Local guide advised us to withdraw _____.

   (A) so as to get not involved   (B) so as not to get involved

   (C) as not to get involved   (D) as to get not involved

（　）3. I cannot come to your dinner party tonight. I really would be _____, but I

   have a previous engagement.

   (A) glad   (B) glad to have   (C) glad to   (D) glad to do it

（　）4. "Have you gone to see the drama?" "No, but _____."

(A) I go   (B) I'm going to see

(C) I go to see   (D) I'm going to

( ) 5. The following statements could be things that tour members asked tour leader to correct in their room, except:

(A) taking off the old bed sheets and putting on new ones;

(B) rebuilding the floor and carpet;

(C) changing a larger bed;

(D) washing the bathroom.

( ) 6. Local guide said to me, "How long did it take to build the church?"

= Local guide asked me how long _____ to build the church.

(A) it was taken   (B) did it take   (C) it had taken   (D) does it take

( ) 7. Obviously, the duty manager did not handle the complaint very well. The manager should _____

(A) apologize appropriately.

(B) showing his/her sympathy and politeness.

(C) call the guest by his/her name.

(D) sending the guest to another lodging establishment.

( ) 8. "You ought to have called local guide yesterday." "Yes. I know I _____."

(A) ought to   (B) have to   (C) should have   (D) must have

( ) 9. You _____ yesterday if you were really serious about this exhibition.

(A) ought to come   (B) ought to be coming

(C) ought to have come   (D) ought have come

( ) 10. When the tour member said "this room is absolutely filthy", she most likely meant _____.

(A) the room was very dirty   (B) all things were pleasant

(C) most things were clean   (D) she requested upgrade her room

( ) 11. "Local driver says he won't help us."

"Oh, perhaps I can persuade him _____."

(A) to help   (B) for helping   (C) helping   (D) that he helps

( ) 12. After seeing the drama, _____.

(A) the book was read by him

(B) the book made him want to read it

(C) he wanted to read the book

(D) the reading of the book interested him

( ) 13. I really appreciate _____ to help me, but I am sure that I will be able to

manage by myself.

(A) you to offer   (B) your offering

(C) that you offer   (D) that you are offering

( ) 14. _____ time and money, most tour operators use local coach for airport

transit.

(A) Saved   (B) Saves   (C) To save   (D) The saving

( ) 15. Aspirin is used _____ a constriction of the blood vessels.

(A) the counteraction   (B) to counteract

(C) counteract   (D) counteracting

( ) 16. I _____ a tour leader some day.

(A) dream to become   (B) dream to becoming

(C) dream of becoming   (D) dream for becoming

( ) 17. The newspaper exclaimed that three hotels _____ last night.

(A) was buring down   (B) burn down

(C) burned down   (D) have burend

( ) 18. Your room has been reserved _____ two days.

(A) in   (B) for   (C) with   (D) at

（　）19. The hotel offers guests a continental breakfast in the lobby _____ a full

breakfast in the restaurant.

(A) with　(B) since　(C) either　(D) or

（　）20. The _____ is inside the cabinet.

(A) laundry bag　(B) mobile phone　(C) morning call　(D) maid

解答

1.B	2.B	3.C	4.D	5.B	6.C	7.A	8.C	9.C	10.A	11.A	12.C
13.B	14.C	15.B	16.C	17.C	18.B	19.D	20.A				

綜合解析

1. allow someone to V（原形）。

司機車上的設備是嚴禁其他人員操作，即使是領隊也不例外。因此，通常要放影片、CD或傳統卡帶都需經司機同意，或委請司機代為播放。麥克風的操作也是如此，避免司機不悅。

2. so as not to 為否定；(A)錯，(C) as 錯，(D) 語法錯誤。

當地導遊的建議，當然要尊重，行程內容的優先順序是要衡量當地當天的狀況。此外，司機的意見也要參考，畢竟停車開車是司機。

3. 慣用語be glad to。

領隊帶團要起帶頭作用，誘導團員參與任何社交活動與遊樂節目，特別是長天數的郵輪。如果團員每天只有吃飯、睡覺，不出5天就會深感無聊，因為該吃也吃了、該看也看了、該睡也睡夠了，最後搭乘郵輪的整體滿意度就會有所缺憾。因此領隊要激發團員參與社交活動，增強與其他國籍觀光客互動的機會，留下特別的印象與美麗記憶。

4. 現在進行式代表「未來」。

領隊對不同的戲劇、歌劇與音樂劇都應該有所涉獵，因為如果自己都未曾

去過、看過、聽過，又如何去說服團員參與相關活動。

5. (B)語意錯誤，重建不可能的事。

從事服務業的最高原則「客人永遠是對的，即使是錯，也不與之爭對錯」，上述可能改變的，都應盡力符合團員的期待；但切記推諉、欺騙。

6. 合併句，前半部過去式，過去的過去，為過去完成式。

有導遊帶團時，領隊也應仔細聽，記筆記。因為有天可能中文導遊不夠，派遣英文導遊或甚至導遊臨時出狀況、No Show，此時身為領隊就可以告訴自己I am ready to...。

7. (A)語意正確，其他語意錯誤。

「值班經理」是飯店小夜班或大夜班最高職務的主管，也是領隊最需要配合與互動的對象，換房間、升等、加房、隔天早餐的安排等許多事情最後決定者，就是Duty Manager。

8. (A)(B)時態錯誤，(D) 少to。

領隊更應信守承諾，因為旅遊業是無形產品，團員無法事先看貨，且出發前3天或說明會時要把團費繳清。如果領隊與團員間相處無「信任」存在，則一切旅程就會在猜忌中度過。因此，領隊敢說的就要敢做到，答應出現的就應該要出現。

9. (C)我有（已經做了），正確。

即早聯繫，避免延誤行程，萬一無法聯繫上，也應盡速聯絡當地代理旅行社聯繫，或留言請導遊主動與領隊聯繫。

10. filthy 髒亂之意，(A) 語意正確。

飯店有時管理缺失，將未整理好房間就賣出或重複出售，團員至房間後發現房間竟然未整理，當然心情會受影響。因此，對於此情形應盡速協調換房間與表達歉意。如果常有此情況發生，就應向當地代理旅行社反應，應修改飯店；返國後也應向當線「線控」說明事實，作為改進的參考。

11. 慣用語 persuade someone to V（原形）。

合法、合理與合情的事，司機一定會配合，歐美紐澳司機最忌諱的是超時工作與違法。這一點是國人並未建立的觀念，領隊應灌輸正確的服務觀念，任何服務都是有價值且應尊重服務從業人員。

12. (A)(B)(D)主詞錯誤。

著名戲劇、歌劇相關周邊產品，往往也是團員爭相購買作紀念的商品。身為領隊相關書籍都應詳閱過，以利帶團工作的開展。

13. (A) (C)語法錯誤，(D) 時態錯誤。

時時抱著感恩的心，感謝所有旅遊同業的協助，有了同業的樂心幫忙，當有偶發事件發生時，都可以透過這些友人的協助，而獲得相對較好的結果。因此，平時做人的功夫要多磨練。

14. to V（原形）代表「目的」。

旅遊價格競爭激烈，因此旅行社、國外代理旅行社都想盡方法要節省成本。因此，機場接送都是以當地遊覽車為主，計價方式是以點對點的報價（Transit Only）。

15. is used to 用來。

團員有不適，應先在尋求團員同意下將其送醫。如情況不嚴重，也應多加照料，提供團員必要的協助。但切記不要給團員口服藥品，因為領隊不是醫生，此舉是違法且危險的行為。

16. 慣用語 dream of Ving動名詞。

領隊工作是多彩多姿，但風險也相對較高，完全看個人是否適合做領隊工作。如果個性或態度不適合，但願意修正自己的態度、行為與價值觀，也是能成為一位優秀的領隊。

17. 過去式。

飯店著火，當然要先喚醒團員起床，趕緊從樓梯逃生。因此領隊在查房時也應先確認逃生方向，以備不時之需。

18. 慣用語，reserved for。

長程線領隊帶團往往都是帶Voucher辦理住宿登記，領隊要確定最後使用房間數，才可以簽名。如遇加床或另有要求時，應請團員當場付清，有時也會遇到團員有當地朋友，臨時取消房間，但應跟團員解釋清楚，無法退房或退費，其理由應詳盡告知。

19. 對等連接詞，or。

不同旅遊國家或地區，所提供的早餐也有所不同。一般國人消費水準已無法接受大陸式早餐，美式早餐是一般國人可以接受的餐飲品質，但歐洲地區有些只提供Cold Buffet。所以於出發前應向團員說明清楚，何謂「大陸式早餐」？何謂「美式早餐」？避免客訴。

20. (A)語意正確。

洗衣應注意安全性與是否會危及房間的設備，因為曾經發生有人將盥洗衣物掛在燈罩上導致起火。因此，要事先提醒團員必要的禮節，也應注意在飯店內的穿著。

歷屆試題

（　）1. The police officer needs to ＿＿＿ the traffic during the rush hours.

(A)assign　　　　　　　　(B)break

(C)compete　　　　　　　(D)direct　　　　　【98外語領隊】

（　）2. We look forward to ＿＿＿ from you soon.

(A)seeing　　　　　　　　(B)hear

(C)hearing　　　　　　　(D)listen　　　　　【98外語領隊】

（　）3. The hotel services are far from satisfactory. I need to ＿＿＿ a complaint with the manager.

(A)pay　　　　　　　　　(B)claim

(C)file   (D)add   【98外語領隊】

( ) 4. The news was _____ good _____ true.

    (A)to...is   (B)two...to be

    (C)too...to be   (D)so...that is   【98外語領隊】

( ) 5. Our hotel provides free _____ service to the airport every day.

    (A)accommodation   (B)communication

    (C)transmission   (D)shuttle   【99外語領隊】

( ) 6. Guest: What _____ do you have in your hotel?

Hotel clerk: We have a fitness center, a swimming pool, two restaurants, a

beauty parlor, and a boutique.

    (A)facilities   (B)benefits

    (C)itineraries   (D)details   【99外語領隊】

( ) 7. Guest: _____

Hotel clerk: Our standard room costs NT$3,500 per night.

    (A)Is room service included in your price?

    (B)What is your room rate?

    (C)How much do you charge for a luxury room?

    (D)Do I have to pay for an extra bed?   【99外語領隊】

( ) 8. Guest: Hello, this is room 205. The faucet in our bathroom is dripping and I

can't turn it off.

Hotel clerk: _____

    (A)I'm terribly sorry about that. I'll get it cleaned for you right away.

    (B)OK, I'll have it changed by the electrician.

    (C)Is it? I'm sorry, I'll get it fixed by a plumber.

    (D)I do apologize. If you tell me which one, I'll send someone to open it.

【99外語領隊】

( ) 9. The waiters will show you where to bed down.

(A)The waiters will tell you the place that you may put your beddings.

(B)The waiters will ask for your assistance later.

(C)The waiters will tell you where you may stay tonight.

(D)The waiters will provide everything you need. 【100外語領隊】

( ) 10. This group of people would like to stay in _____ hotels. They need to be

five star hotels.

(A)convenient　　　　　　　(B)leisure

(C)luxurious　　　　　　　　(D)public 【100外語領隊】

( ) 11. Hotel clerk: I'm sorry, could you spell that for me, please?

Guest: Yes, certainly. _____.

(A)It's three days counting from today

(B)It's S-M-Y-T-H

(C)It's Sunday next week

(D)It's 100 US dollars 【100外語領隊】

( ) 12. Guest: You have answered my questions thoroughly. Thank you very much.

Hotel clerk: You are welcome._____

(A)It's been my address.　　　(B)It's been my intention.

(C)It's been my pleasure.　　　(D)It's been my thinking.

【100外語領隊】

( ) 13. Client: What are this hotel's _____?

Agent: It includes a great restaurant, a fitness center, an outdoor pool, and

much more, such as in-room Internet access, 24-hour room service,

and trustworthy babysitting, etc..

(A)installations　　　　　　(B)utilities

(C)amenities　　　　　　　(D)surroundings 【101外語領隊】

( ) 14. Working as a hotel _____ means that your focus is to ensure that the needs and requests of hotel guests are met, and that each guest has a memorable stay.

(A)commander (B)celebrity

(C)concierge (D)candidat 【101外語領隊】

( ) 15. If you have to extend your stay at the hotel room, you should inform the front desk at least one day _____ your original departure time.

(A)ahead to (B)forward to

(C)prior to (D)in front of 【101外語領隊】

( ) 16. As for the delivery service of our hotel, FedEx and UPS can make _____ at the front desk Monday through Friday, excluding holidays.

(A)posts (B)pickups

(C)picnics (D)practices 【101外語領隊】

解答

1.D	2.C	3.C	4.C	5.D	6.A	7.B	8.C	9.C	10.C	11.B	12.C
13.C	14.C	15.C	16.B								

第九章

推銷自費行程

一、工作程序（Working Procedures）

　　團體套裝行程的價格競爭激烈，有時不得不將部分不適合老少咸宜的行程或旅遊節目挪至「自費活動」（Optional Tour），一方面降低售價更具競爭力，另一方面也令團員能有部分自主選擇行程內容的權利；讓真正有需求的團員，選擇所愛、花其所願。

　　但從旅行業者的角度而言，自費活動也是公司重要收入的來源之一，領隊是第一線的服務人員與銷售者，銷售自費活動的成果也是領隊績效評估的項目之一。身為領隊第一要務是確保參加團員的「旅遊安全」與「滿意度」，如果上述兩項未能達成，即使賺到了應有利潤，也失去領隊應有的職業道德。

二、關鍵字彙

　　領隊應熟悉的重要關鍵字彙包括下列四項：

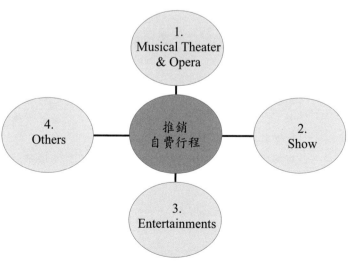

1. Musical Theater & Opera　音樂劇 & 歌劇			
·Melodrama	劇情劇	·Operetta	輕歌劇
·Balled Opera	民謠歌劇	·Comedy	喜劇
·Score	樂譜	·Broadway	百老匯
·Lyrics	歌詞	·Puppetry	木偶劇
·Book=Script	劇本	·Black Theater	黑光劇
·Libretto	曲本	·Concert Hall	音樂廳
·Beauty and the Beast		美女與野獸	
·Cats		貓	
·Chicago		芝加哥	
·Les Miserables		孤星淚=悲慘世界	
·Miss Saigon		西貢小姐	
·My Fair Lady		窈窕淑女	
·Notre Dame de Paris		鐘樓怪人	
·Romeo & Juliette		羅蜜歐與茱麗葉	
·The Phantom of the Opera		歌劇魅影	
·West Side Story		西城故事	
2.Show　秀			
·Crazy Horse	瘋馬秀	·Lido de Paris	麗都秀
·Moulin Rouge	紅磨坊秀	·Gender-Bender	人妖
·Folk Dance	民族舞蹈	·Guarantee	保證
3.Entertainments　娛樂			
·Casino	賭場	·Aquatic Activities	水域活動
·Player	玩家	·Skin Diving	浮潛
·Wager	賭注	·Surfing	衝浪運動
·Dealer	莊家	·Windsurfing	風帆運動
·Black Jack	21點	·Scuba	水肺
·Roulette	輪盤	·Canoe	輕艇運動
·Dice	骰子	·Rafting	泛舟活動
·Poker	撲克牌	·Sailboat	帆船
·Keno/Bingo	賓果	·Water Safety	水域安全
·Baccarat	百家樂	·Parasoaring	拖曳傘
·Crap shooting	美式擲骰子	·Banana Boat	香蕉船
·Slot Machine	吃角子老虎	·Wet Bike	水上摩托車

· Lever	手桿	· Gondola	鳳尾船（貢多拉）
· Chip	籌碼	· Diving	潛水
· Line Up	排隊	· Bus Tour	巴士旅遊
· Golf Course	高爾夫球場	· City Tour	市區觀光
· Helicopter	直升機	· Night Tour	夜遊
· Hydroplane	水上飛機	· Spa	美容美體療程
· Amphibian	水陸兩用飛機	· Optional Tour	自費活動
· Aquarium	水族館	· Accelerated	加速

4.Others　其他

· Exchange Rate	匯率	· Peak Season	旅遊旺季
· Traveler's Check	旅行支票	· Low Season	旅遊淡季
· Cash	現金	· On Season	旺季
· Credit Card	信用卡	· Off Season	淡季
· Buying Rate	買入匯率	· Surcharge	額外付費
· Selling Rate	賣出匯率	· Free lance	自由領隊／導遊
· Ren Min Bi (RMB)	人民幣	· Backpacker	自助旅行者
· British Pound	英鎊	· Department Store	百貨公司
· Euro	歐元	· Business Hours	營業時間
· Rebate	回扣	· Fruit Store	水果店
· Escort Perdiem	出差費	· Pharmacy	藥房
· Tour Fare	團費	· Convenience Store	便利商店
· Calculate	計算	· Box Office	賣票亭
· Push	推	· Taxi Stand	計程車招呼站
· Restriction	限制	· Capacity	容納量
· To Insure Prompt Service (Tips)	確保迅速快捷服務（小費）		

三、關鍵會話

㈠確認自費活動相關事項

【Scene：In hotel lobby】

Tourists ：Tour Leader, How much money do I need to pay for tomorrow optional tour?

Tour Leader: It depends on what you join.

Tourists : I prefer to join Optional Tour 1. Those two meals are included, isn't it?

Tour Leader: Yes. The optional tour fees include the entry fees, meals, transportation fees, and tips.

Tourists : How long does it take the optional tour journey?

Tour Leader: It's an eight-hour journey.

Tourists : Well, we are two adults and one 8-year-old child. Is there any reduction for us?

Tour Leader: Yes. Your lovely child is free of charge.

Tourists : And what about reservations? Do we have to book well in advance?

Tour Leader: Well, if you can pay now, I reserve three seats for you.

Tourists : No problem. May I pay by credit card?

Tour Leader: Sorry. I only accept cash.

Tourists : OK. What time will we have to leave the hotel and come back to the hotel?

Tour Leader: We will leave at 8:30 and come back about 8:00 p.m.

Tourists : Thank you. See you tomorrow.

Tour Leader: Certainly. Thank you.

圖9-1　西班牙佛郎明哥舞秀

四、語詞測驗

1. **lay off** ～　暫時解催、中止

I will lay off smoking.

我會停止抽菸。

2. **lead A to B** ～　把A帶到B

This street will lead you to the post office.

這條街直走會到郵局。

3. **lean against** 〜　靠著

Tour guide stood leaning against the wall.

導遊靠著牆站著。

4. **leave ~ behind** 〜　忘了帶某物

I left my purse behind at the restaurant.

我把包包忘了放在餐廳。

5. **let by** 〜　通過

Please let me by.

請讓我通過。

6. **let down** 〜　使失望

We are counting on tour leader. Don't let us down.

我們依賴領隊，不要令我們失望。

7. **lie in** 〜　在於

All my hopes lie in tour leader.

我所有的希望都在領隊身上。

8. **live on** 〜　以……爲食

The European are used to live on potatoes.

歐洲人習慣以馬鈴薯為主要食物。

9. **live through** 〜　經歷……而未死

His grandfather has lived through two World Wars.

他的祖父經歷過兩次世界大戰。

10. **long for** 〜　渴望

We have been longing for an opportunity of seeing the king.

我們渴望有機會見到國王。

11. **look after** 〜　照顧（**to take care of; watch over**）

Tour leader looks after his members of group.

領隊會照顧他的團員。

12. **look for** 〜　尋找

The driver is looking for parking lot to drop off tourists.

司機尋找停車位，以便客人下車。

13. **look on** 〜　看作（**to regard**）

Tour leader is looked on as a good scholar.

這位領隊像一位學者。

14. **look over** 〜　檢查

Tour leader wants driver to look over the coach.

領隊要求司機檢查遊覽車。

15. **make up** 〜　捏造（**to arrange**）、化妝、形成（**to compose**）

She makes up carefully for attending dinner show.

為了參加表演晚宴，她妝化得很仔細。

16. **mark down** 〜　減價

Would you mark down the price, please?

請你減價可以嗎？

17. **mean by** 〜　意指

What do you mean by that？

你是什麼意思？

18. **mistake A for B** 〜　誤把**A**當成**B**

Everyone mistakes interpreter for official tour guide in Rome.

在羅馬時每個人都把翻譯者當成正式導遊。

19. **mix up** 〜　混淆

Tour leader always mixes up the members' names of tour group.

領隊常常混淆團員的名字。

20. **muddle up** 〜　弄亂

The driver has muddled up my schedules.

司機弄亂我的行程。

21. **object to** 〜　反對

I don't object to your proposal.

我不反對你的提議。

22. **occur to** 〜　使想到（**to come into one's mind**）

A good idea occurred to me.

我想到一個好點子。

23. **open up** 〜　打開

I opened up the package at once.

我立刻打開包裹。

24. **originate in** ～ 發生

The airport strike originated in the demand for higher wages.

機場罷工發生原因在於要求提高工資。

25. **part from** ～ 跟……分手

I parted from local guide at five o'clock.

我5點與當地導遊分開。

五、文法測驗

本章重點：分詞分析

現在分詞作修飾語	An escalator is a moving staircase. 電扶梯是活動的梯子。
過去分詞當修補語	I got a fax written in Spanish. 我收到一封用西班牙文寫的傳真。
補語	Tour leader sat surrounded by all members of his group. 領隊坐著，身旁圍繞著所有團員。
Go +V-ing	Do you often go shopping in the DFS? 你常去免稅店購物嗎?
分詞構句	The man, playing the cards, is our driver. 玩橋牌的那個人是我們的司機。 Arriving at the Paris station, tour leader found his train gone. 到了巴黎車站，領隊發現火車開走了。
被動態分詞構句	Compared with London local guide, she is less beautiful. 和倫敦的導遊相比，她比較不美。
獨立分詞構句	The driver hesitating, tour leader made the decision herself. 因為司機猶豫不決，領隊自己做決定。
慣用句	Generally speaking, Italy has a good climate in fall. 一般來說，義大利秋天的氣候還不錯。
分詞構句的位置	The cruise will start business in May, weather permitting. 天氣許可的話，郵輪將在五月開始營運。

分詞構句+as one does	Staying as groups do far from town, tourists seldom have night markets for shopping. 團體住的地方離城鎮很遠，所以觀光客很少有夜市可逛。
完成式分詞構句和 not	Not having seen the local guide for a long time, I did not recognize him at first sight. 有很長一段時間沒見過那一位導遊，我第一眼認不出來是他。

本章綜合練習

(　) 1. When I returned hotel room, I found the window open and something _____.

(A) to steal　(B) stealing　(C) stolen　(D) missed

(　) 2. _____ she went back to her room.

(A) There is no cause for alarm,　　(B) There being no cause for alarm,

(C) Without has cause for alarm,　　(D) Being no cause of alarm,

(　) 3. Digital television is another major instrument of communication, _____ us to see as well as to hear the performer.

(A) permitted　　　　　　(B) permitting

(C) to permit　　　　　　(D) being permitted

(　) 4. _____ all his travel reports, tour leader went to bed.

(A) Doing　　　　　　(B) He has been doing

(C) He had done　　　　(D) Having done

(　) 5. _____ in the fog, we were compelled to spend two hours in the forest.

(A) To lose　(B) Losing　(C) Lost　(D) Having lost

(　) 6. Alice, ____ where to find the guide book, asked her colleague where the book was?

(A) not to know　　　　(B) never to know

(C) with no knowledge　　(D) not knowing

( ) 7. _____ health, I could have gone to England.

      (A) Granted (B) Granting (C) Having granted (D) Be granting

( ) 8. _____ a fine day, we decided to go out on a picnic.

      (A) Having been (B) Being (C) What (D) It being

( ) 9. Weather _____, the city tour will be held as scheduled.

      (A) permits (B) should permit (C) will permit (D) permitting

( ) 10. There are four hotels in our institute _____.

      (A) with each having over 100 workers

      (B) each having over 100 workers

      (C) which there are over 100 workers

      (D) with each that has over 100 workers

( ) 11. Excuse me, but it is time to have your temperature _____.

      (A) taking (B) to take (C) take (D) taken

( ) 12. I don't like _____ at my members of group.

      (A) them shouting (B) them shout (C) their shout (D) that they shout

( ) 13. He said he saw Italian driver _____ in the front of hotel the night before.

      (A) working (B) to work (C) worked (D) works

( ) 14. _____ we went swimming.

      (A) Being a hot day,   (B) It a hot day,

      (C) The day being hot,   (D) The day to be hot,

( ) 15. The room door remained _____.

      (A) locking (B) locked (C) lock (D) to lock

( ) 16. Most cruise passengers will _____ the ship between 4:00 and 5:00.

      (A) board (B) arrive (C) deliver (D) keep

( ) 17. The ticket said "_____ adult" on it.

      (A) allow (B) admit (C) limit (D) adjust

（　）18. _____ the gift and give it to the birthday child.

(A) Drop　(B) Wipe　(C) Take　(D) Wrap

（　）19. I bought a coke out of the _____.

(A) vending machine　　　　　　(B) fax machine

(C) automatic teller machine　　　(D) casino machine

（　）20. This skirt is so _____, I cannot breathe.

(A) big　(B) tight　(C) small　(D) tie

解答

1.C	2.B	3.B	4.D	5.C	6.D	7.A	8.D	9.D	10.B	11.D	12.A
13.A	14.C	15.B	16.A	17.B	18.D	19.A	20.B				

綜合解析

1. 被動，被偷。

貴重物品應於住宿同時辦理寄放在保險箱，離開房間時窗戶與落地窗均應鎖上，避免歹徒入侵，即使是洗澡時也應將貴重物品攜入浴室並上鎖。

2. (A) (C) 缺連接詞，(D) no cause of 錯誤。

警鈴響起應盡速喚醒團員起床為優先，需確認安全無虞，才可通知團員返回房間就寢。如有狀況應依照緊急事件處理程序辦理，迅速於24小時內通知公司、觀光局。

3. (A)過去式錯誤，(C)不定詞錯誤，(D)要省略being。

飯店房間相關設備系統的操作方式應向團員說明清楚，特別是付費電視的使用方式、計價都應說明，如有小孩更應向家長再三強調，勿亂按開關，避免小孩觀賞不適合的節目，或事後團員對於觀看電視要付費一事，而感到無法接受。

4. (A)時態錯誤，(B)(C)缺連接詞。

領隊應養成每天記帳的好習慣，今日事今日畢，特別是天數過長的團體，每天浮動匯率、所經國家貨幣不同，都會影響報帳的準確性，返國後又無暇整理，日子愈拖愈無法真實寫下完整報告。

5. 過去分詞；(A)錯誤，(B) 現在分詞錯誤，(D) having 去掉。

容易迷路的旅遊區域、遊樂場、博物館，領隊應不要安排自由活動時間，如不得已，也要找一處明確且顯著的目標物，當作最後集合地點，並將緊急聯絡方式告知所有團員。

6. (D) 補語，正確。

旅遊資料的蒐集，要靠平常下功夫，並非接到帶團通知時，才開始準備，多與前輩、同事、同業相互切磋，彼此教學相長，更要不恥下問。

7. 假設語氣省略 If。

領隊的職業病最常見包括：痛風、胃病、腰受傷、肝病等，因此，平時就應多注意飲食，搬運行李應注意姿勢是否正確，否則事後遺憾終身。

8. (A)(B)缺虛主詞，(C)缺動詞。

帶團要天天遇到好天氣是可遇而不可求的，如果遇到天氣不佳、下大雨、下大雪、颱風等，應以安全為最主要考量，在不影響安全情況下，把行程走完。此時因為外在不利的旅遊環境對團員情緒的影響，就需靠領隊的帶團技巧來加以彌補。

9. (A)(B)(C)雙動詞，錯誤。

即使當天天氣狀況不佳，應想盡辦法在不違反旅遊安全的前提下，試圖找出隔天完成的可行機會，或者如果是單點進出的旅遊行程，也可以回程時將行程做完。總之，百分百實踐旅遊行程內容是領隊的天職。

10.(A) 錯誤，缺連接詞；(B)(D)語法錯誤。

連鎖經營的飯店，例如：Holiday Inns、Hilton等，有時同一個城市有數家飯店，領隊要先確認入住飯店是位於哪一區，因為有時連司機也會跑錯飯

店，因此領隊事先應了解清楚是哪一家飯店。

11. 量體溫，被動。

　　於說明會時要向團員說明清楚應隨身攜帶個人藥品或是處方簽，否則出國就醫較不方便，因為國外就醫，如果沒有醫療保險，則費用更高。

12. (B) 雙動詞，(C) their 錯誤。

　　團員的行為，如有不適宜或不禮貌，領隊應負一定的責任，事先將各國國際禮儀與禁忌事項包括：用餐禮節、欣賞戲劇禮節、飯店住宿禮節等告知團員，是領隊應盡的工作。

13. 動名詞當受詞補語，working。

　　司機通常於晚間抵達飯店後，仍需做初步車廂清潔工作，因此在遊覽車上要告知團員注意清潔，通常車上避免享用薯條、瓜子、冰淇淋等易掉落、黏性高的食品，當然更禁止吸菸。

14. (B) 缺連接詞，(D)缺動詞，(A)語意錯誤。

　　團員從事水上活動應事先作安全性說明，依標準作業流程規範實行，如已超過服務時間，設施並無相關安全人員時，應勸阻團員作違法行為，且勸阻時一定要有第三人在場較佳。

15. 過去分詞當補語。

　　房間一定要上鎖，領隊有時必須要與團員共宿一間，更應注意安全，否則私人財物甚至公司機密資料外洩，對自己與公司都是損失。目前大多數旅行業者並未提供領隊單人房的福利，往往有時領隊自己要負擔「單間差」（Single Supplement）才有單人房住宿。付費或與團員同宿之間的取捨，領隊自行衡量。

16. 慣用語，board 登船。

　　登船除應注意安全外，行李有貴重東西應隨身攜帶，領隊要確認所有團員的房間位置，可事先調整安排盡量在同一艙層，以利彼此聯繫。事後要一一查房，確認所有房間設施是否正常。搭乘夜渡輪，女性團員應要優先

給予有盥洗室的房間，較安全。

17. 慣用語。

票券使用應按規定，且要清點清楚。年齡限制或免費規定都依旅遊地區有所不同，應站在公司角度與利益考量，購買相對優惠的票券。

18. wrap 包裝。

領隊帶團要用心，遇到團員於行程中生日、結婚紀念日或其他重要紀念日，理應為團員慶祝，儘管人在國外，無法像在台灣可以提供生日蛋糕，但至少心意要令團員感受到。

19. vending machine 自動販賣機。

領隊隨身要有當地零錢，團員有時上廁所要小費、投幣要零錢，領隊應有隨時提供必要服務的功能，換錢甚至代墊小錢。

20. tight 緊。

領隊穿著除必要的一套正式西裝外，穿著應輕鬆，以利帶團工作，不必花太多時間整理的服裝、髮式與鞋子等是優先之考量。否則天天整理上述個人用品，耽誤集合時間是得不償失。

歷屆試題

（　）1. Tourists are advised to _____ traveling to areas with landslides.

(A)avoid (B)assume

(C)assist (D)accompany 【98外語領隊】

（　）2. He likes to travel. He is very _____ in learning foreign languages and cultures.

(A)interest (B)interested

(C)interesting (D)interestingly 【98外語領隊】

（　）3. You will pay a _____ of fifty dollars for your ferry ride.

(A)fan   (B)fate

(C)fair   (D)fare   【98外語領隊】

(   ) 4. The airplane is <u>cruising</u> at an altitude of 30,000 feet at 700 kilometers per hour.

(A)detecting   (B) moving

(C)showing   (D)speeding   【98外語領隊】

(   ) 5. Tourists enjoy visiting night markets around the island to taste _____ local snacks.

(A)authentic   (B)blend

(C)inclusive   (D)invisible   【99外語領隊】

(   ) 6. Living in a highly _____ society, some Taiwanese children are forced by their parents to learn many skills at a very young age.

(A)compatible   (B)prospective

(C)threatened   (D)competitive   【99外語領隊】

(   ) 7. Our company has been on a very tight _____ since 2008.

(A)deficit   (B)management

(C)budget   (D)debt   【99外語領隊】

(   ) 8. The _____ at the information desk in a hotel provides traveling information to guests.

(A)bellhop   (B)concierge

(C)butler   (D)bartender   【99外語領隊】

(   ) 9. The mobs were <u>mollified</u> when he gave a speech.

(A)wiped out   (B)attended

(C)pacified   (D)angry   【100外語領隊】

(   ) 10. He devoted himself to _____ poor children.

(A)be taught   (B)teaching

(C)teach   (D)teaching with   【100外語領隊】

( ) 11. The wedding anniversary is worth _____.

(A) being celebrated   (B)celebrating

(C)of celebrating   (D)celebrated   【100外語領隊】

( ) 12. Is there any problem _____ my reservation?

(A)in   (B)of

(C)to   (D)with   【100外語領隊】

( ) 13. The downtown bed-and-breakfast agency has _____.

(A)a two-night minimum reservation policy

(B)a policy two-night minimum reservation

(C)a reservation two-night policy minimum

(D)a minimum policy two-night reservation   【101外語領隊】

( ) 14. Ecotourism is not only entertaining and exotic; it is also highly educational

and _____.

(A)rewarded   (B)rewards

(C)reward   (D)rewarding   【101外語領隊】

( ) 15. Palm Beach is a coastline _____ where thousands of tourists from all over

the world spend their summer vacation.

(A)airport   (B)resort

(C)pavement   (D)passage   【101外語領隊】

( ) 16. Mount Fuji is considered _____; therefore, many people pay special visits

to it, wishing to bring good luck to themselves and their loved ones.

(A)horrifying   (B)scared

(C)sacred   (D)superficial   【101外語領隊】

解答

1.A	2.B	3.D	4.B	5.A	6.D	7.C	8.B	9.C	10.B	11.B	12.D
13.A	14.D	15.B	16.C								

第十章

操作團體購物

一、工作程序（Working Procedures）

　　領隊的收入來源包括：出差費、小費、自費活動與購物佣金，所以購物不僅對團員能實踐購物的願景，也能達成親友委託購買之商品；相對於旅行業者、領隊、導遊或司機，也是收入的一小部分。

　　但是，如何操作避免客訴，當然第一線領隊要負起最大責任。首先要確定旅遊契約書的內容，按照契約內容安排購物，不可臨時增加購物點。有時當地導遊或司機會建議增加購物點，此時領隊應按公司規定處理。如果是團員自行前往，也應事先告知注意事項與退稅規定。

二、關鍵字彙

　　領隊應熟悉的重要關鍵字彙包括下列三項：

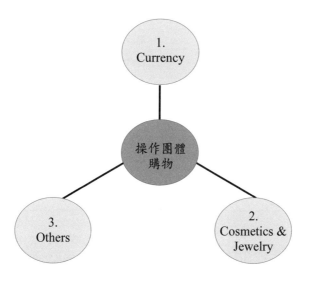

1.Currency　貨幣

・Bank	銀行	・Bank Note	紙幣
・Rate	匯率	・Check	支票
・Coin	硬幣	・Moneychanger	換錢機
・Cash	現金	・Promissory Note	期票
・Bank Clerk	銀行服務員		
・Bill of Exchange	匯票		
・Safe-Deposit Box	出租保險箱		
・Cash Transport Car	現金輸送車		
・Security Service	保安部門		

2.Cosmetics & Jewelry　化妝品 & 珠寶

・Perfume	香水	・Necklace	項鍊
・Lipstick	口紅	・Diamond Ring	鑽戒
・Pearl	珍珠	・Crystal	水晶

3.Others　其他

・Key Ring	鑰匙圈	・Brand	品牌
・Replica	複製品	・Recommend	推薦
・Sculpture	雕刻品	・Gift-Wrap	包裝禮物
・Handicraft	手工藝品	・Pack	包裝
・Boots	靴子	・Supermarket	超市
・Leather	皮件	・Shopping Mall	購物中心
・Bouquet	花束	・Shopping Bag	購物袋
・Sandals	拖鞋	・Basket	籃子
・Price Tag	價格標籤	・Bazaar	市集
・Special Price	特別價	・Handbag	手提包
・Retail Price	零售價	・Flea Market	跳蚤市場
・On Sale	特價	・Scalp	賣黃牛票
・Bargain	議價	・Pickup Time	上車時間
・Cheap	便宜	・Fade	褪色
・Fake	贗品	・Jack-in-a-Box	魔術箱
・VAT (Value Added Tax)	加值稅		
・Miscellaneous Charge	雜費		

三、關鍵會話

(一)帶領至免稅店購物

【Scene：Duty-free shop】

Tourist　　　: I would like to buy some cigarettes. Tour leader, how many cigarettes can we bring back home without duty? Do you know the dutyfree limit?

Tour Leader: Mr. John, you can bring two cartons of cigarettes with you.

Tourist　　　: Thank you, Tour leader.

Salesman　　: Welcome, may I help you?

Tourist　　　: Please give me one carton of Mild Seven, the other one carton of Davidoff.

Salesman　　: Fine. Would you like anything else?

Tourist　　　: By the way, give me one bottle of Scotch whisky, please.

Salesman　　: Fine, it totals 48 Euros.

Tourist　　　: I only have 25 Euros. Can I pay in some cash and the rest will be paid by credit card?

Salesman　　: Certainly, you can do that.

Tourist　　　: Thank you.

Salesman　　: Please give me your passport and boarding pass.

Tourist　　　: Here you are.

Salesman　　: Thank you. Here is the receipt, boarding pass, and passport. Have a nice fly.

Tourist　　　: Thank you.

Tour Leader: Please take all your belongings. It is time to go to boarding gate.

圖 10-1　埃及開羅香精油免稅店

(二)帶領至藝品店購物

【Scene：Souvenir shop】

Salesman　　: Good afternoon. Welcome to Australia. Do you need some souvenirs with you?

Tour Leader: Yes, Miss. This lady of our Leo Tour wants to buy some deep-sea fish oil and lanolin cream.

Salesman　　: Deepsea fish oil is available at the counter by the entrance, and we offer all kinds of products of sheep lanolin including skin care items.

Tourist　　　: Do you know the duty-free limit for these products, Miss?

Salesman   : There is no limit.

Tourist   : It sounds good. I want to take 30 bottles as gifts for my relatives and friends.

Salesman   : We will give you 10% discount totally.

Tourist   : Do you accept US dollars?

Salesman   : Of course. Today's exchange rate is 1 US dollar for 1.28 Australian dollars.

Tour Leader: It seems to be reasonable to pay with Australian dollar. The rest will be paid by your credit card.

Tourist   : It sounds a good idea. Thank you, tour leader.

Salesman   : It is OK for me. Thank you. Enjoy your stay in Australia.

圖10-2　馬來西亞錫器工廠

(三)詢問如何退稅

【Scene：Souvenir shop】

Tour Leader: Excuse me, Miss. We are foreign tourists. May we get a tax refund form for the diamond we just bought?

Salesman ： Of course, sir. May I see each of your group members' passports?

Tour Leader: Here you are.

Salesman ： All right, sir. I will write out a tax refund form for each of you.

Tour Leader: Thank you. After we get the forms, what should we do?

Salesman ： First, please check your name, passport number, nationality, home address, purchasing items, and signature on the form. Secondly, when you are leaving the European Union countries, please remember to take this tax refund form with all items you bought to the Customs Certification at the airport for stamping. The customs officer will check your passport, boarding pass, receipt, VAT refund form, and the merchandise you have bought.

Tour Leader: Will the customs officer check everything we buy?

Salesman ： It depends on their decisions. They normally spot check them. Then you must get your VAT refund form, and show your items. When you got the stamped VAT refund form from the customs officer. You may go to the Cash Refund counter nearby the Emigration for getting your money back.

Tour Leader: If I do not want to get the payment in cash, do I have any other options?

Salesman   : Yes, your refund will be transferred into your credit card account.

Tour Leader: I prefer the cash. May I change those Euros into US dollars?

Salesman   : Yes.

Tour Leader: Thank you for your considerate service.

Salesman   : It is my pleasure. Have a good time.

圖10-3　機場免稅店

四、語詞測驗

1. participate [join] in ～　參與（to take part in）

Some tourists participated in the casino games.

一些觀光客參與賭博遊戲。

2. pass away ～　死亡（to die）

The king passed away in peace last night.

國王昨晚平靜地去世。

3. pass by ～　過去

The years quickly passed by.

歲月很快消逝。

4. pass on ～　傳遞

Please read the paper and pass it on.

請閱讀報紙且傳閱。

5. pass through ～　經過、經驗

I passed through the Rhine River last night.

我昨晚經過萊茵河。

6. pay A for B ～　花費A買B

I paid 10 Euros for the map.

我花10歐元買地圖。

7. **persist in** ～ 堅持

I persisted in going my own way.

我堅持自己的作法。

8. **persuade A of B** ～ 說服A相信B

How can you persuade long distance coach driver of your plan?

你如何說服長程遊覽車司機接受你的計畫？

9. **pick up** ～ 拾起（**to take up; lift**）、舉起、順路搭載

The long distance coach picks up passengers in the airport.

長程遊覽車司機在機場接客人。

10. **plunge into** ～ 跳進

Tour guide took off his coat at once and plunged into the Tiber River in Rome.

導遊立刻脫掉他的外套，跳入羅馬台伯河。

11. **point out** ～ 指出（**to show**）

He pointed out the local guide to me.

他指出當地導遊讓我知道。

12. **prepare for** ～ 做心理準備

Tour leader must prepare for an emergency.

領隊應隨時準備好應付緊急事件。

13. **pretend to** ～ 假裝

I pretended to be indifferent.

我假裝一點都不在乎。

14. **protect A from [against] B** 〜　保護A以防備B

Protect your eyes from the sun on the summit of Mountain Cook.

在庫克山頂上要保護眼睛避免直視太陽。

15. **prove to** 〜　證明

My good tips from tourists have proved to be a good service of leading tour.

我從團員收到的小費如此好，可以證明我帶團時提供非常好的服務。

16. **pull out** 〜　拔（瓶塞、牙等）

You must have the cork pulled out from the bottle of wine.

你必須將葡萄酒瓶上的軟木塞拔出。

17. **put down to** 〜　記下

Tour leader should put each meal bill down to daily account files.

領隊要記下每一餐的餐費到每天的帳簿中。

18. **put forward** 〜　提出

I put forward some suggestions for driver in Amsterdam city tour.

我提出一些關於阿姆斯特丹市區觀光的意見給司機。

19. **put off** 〜　延期（**to postpone**）出發、妨礙、脫衣

Don't put off till tomorrow what you can do today.

今日事今日畢。

20. **put on** 〜　穿（**to clothe**）、欺騙（**to hoax**）、增加（**to add**）

He put on his coat and went out.

他穿上外套然後出去。

21. **put out** 〜　熄滅（**to extinguish**）

Put out the light before you go to bed.

上床前請熄燈。

22. **put up at** 〜　投宿

The travelers put up at a seaside hotel.

旅行者投宿於海濱飯店。

23. **put up with** 〜　忍耐（**to bear; stand; suffer; tolerate**）

Tour leader can't put up with such bad working conditions any more.

領隊無法再忍耐如此惡劣的工作環境。

24. **puzzle out** 〜　找出……的解答

I can't succeed in puzzling out this problem.

我無法成功找出這個問題的解答。

25. **recover from** 〜　復原（**to regain**）

Some tourists have recovered from their bad cold.

一些觀光客已從重感冒中復原。

五、文法測驗

本章重點：動名詞分析

主詞、受詞	Doing nothing means doing ill. 無所事事就是為惡。
補語	The driver's chief fault is wasting too much time for parking. 司機最大的缺點就是浪費太多時間找停車位。
完成式動名詞	He denied having been there. 他否認去過那裡。
慣用語	It is no use crying over spilt milk. 覆水難收。

( ) 1. Tour guide is going to the photographer's _____.

    (A) to take her photograph   (B) to have taken her photograph

    (C) to have her photograph taken   (D) that he takes her photograph

( ) 2. We went _____ with tour leader yesterday.

    (A) to swimming   (B) swimming   (C) by swimming   (D) on swim

( ) 3. All the tour leaders were busy _____ their various tasks on tour.

    (A) doing   (B) to do   (C) done   (D) of doing

( ) 4. "Will the child recover?" "Right now, there's no way _____".

    (A) for knowing   (B) to have known   (C) of knowing   (D) to be known

( ) 5. In ancient times soldiers sent messages at a distance by _____.

    (A) having beaten drums   (B) to beat drums

    (C) beating drums   (D) beat drums

( ) 6. In a duty-free shop, _____ customers.

    (A) it is important pleasing   (B) it is important to please

    (C) there is important pleasing   (D) there is important to please

( ) 7. I _____ American breakfast every morning.

    (A) am used to eat   (B) used to eating

    (C) can used to eating   (D) use to eat

( ) 8. Tour leader must be used to _____ early.

    (A) get up   (B) be getting up   (C) the getting up   (D) getting up

( ) 9. Mark gambled his money away _____ Kathy spent hers all on shopping.

    (A) while   (B) if   (C) however   (D) unless

( ) 10. It is no use crying _____ spilt milk.

    (A) for   (B) in   (C) of   (D) over

( ) 11. He has an _____ at that bank.

(A) statement (B) schedule (C) account (D) accident

( ) 12. Tour leader cashes the _____ at the bank.

(A) ticket (B) check (C) diploma (D) credit card

( ) 13. She spent the last day of vacation giving gifts and _____ the Darling harbor.

(A) took a look finally around (B) taking around a look at

(C) taking a finally look around (D) taking a final look around

( ) 14. My recent journey to Turkey has left a _____ impression on me.

(A) forever (B) long (C) lasting (D) fine

( ) 15. _____ speaking, the European loves to drink wine.

(A) General (B) In general (C) In regular (D) Generally

( ) 16. A: How much did you new Rolex cost?

B: _____

(A) I paid it by credit card. (B) I paid an arm and a leg.

(C) It took me three hours. (D) I bought it yesterday.

( ) 17. I wonder how long ago this store _____.

(A) has begun (B) begins (C) began (D) had started

( ) 18. The delicious cheese is a wonderful _____.

(A) appetizer (B) app (C) appendix (D) approach

( ) 19. The i-Phone may be the most important _____ of the 21th century.

(A) atmosphere (B) invention (C) problem (D) research

( ) 20. I think you should eat less, or you may gain some _____ quickly.

(A) popularity (B) power (C) wealth (D) weight

解答

1.C	2.B	3.A	4.C	5.C	6.B	7.C	8.D	9.A	10.D	11.C	12.B
13.D	14.C	15.D	16.B	17.C	18.A	19.B	20.D				

綜合解析

1. 被動語態。

   某些旅遊地區有拍攝團體照片的活動，要入境隨俗，領隊應說明是否需要費用，或可以自由選購。事先說明過程要態度大方，不必閃躲。事後可以自由審視照片品質，自主性決定購買與否。

2. 慣用語 go swimming。

   團員從事水上活動時，貴重東西應寄放保險箱，領隊切勿基於好意幫忙保管團員貴重東西，自己卻無法脫身，連上個廁所都不方便。萬一有狀況需要離開，卻又走不開，又要委託其他人代為看管，假如不幸東西遺失，到底誰要負責賠償呢？

3. 慣用語，be busy 加 Ving。

   領隊的工作是多重性的功能與角色，有時又要扮演導遊的角色；遇到司機不熟，又要像司機一樣的專業；遇到餐廳忙碌時，又要扮演跑堂的工作；到了免稅店，又要扮演業務員的角色。因此，領隊在不同的地點，扮演不同的角色，而且要成功的演出。

4. 慣用語 no way of Ving。

   團員身體不適要適時送醫；事後要多關心，表達關切之意。

5. by 加 Ving。

   外國歷史與地理，領隊平常就應下功夫，不僅是教科書的熟記，更要比較中國歷史與西洋史的差異性，以國人熟悉的人、事、物來做比較，才能使團員較具深刻印象。

6. 慣用語 it is important to V（原形）。

   至免稅店購物當然環境及氣氛都要有一定水準，此外貨品品質、價格也具一定競爭力，特別是有退稅的國家或旅遊地區，應向團員說明清楚退稅比率及方式。

7. used to Ving 習慣於。

　　美式早餐，內容包括：培根、蛋、水果、優酪乳與熱食，較符合國人的消費水準。但歐洲幅員廣大，各地早餐有所不同，尚有英式早餐、斯堪地納維亞式早餐，領隊應了解其中差異性。

8. used to Ving習慣於。

　　領隊應凡事提早作業，因此個人習慣應即早修正，以符合領隊工作的特性。例如：睡覺會認床、認枕頭、上廁所會認馬桶、坐車會暈車、搭船會暈船、搭飛機會暈機等都應有所調整。

9. (B)(C)(D)語意不順。

　　領隊不涉入賭博，更不能與團員有私人借貸行為，懂得理財規劃的領隊，才能在面對領隊工作不確定性時，有所準備，以防不時之需。國外賭場小賭宜情，大賭傷心且傷身。

10. 諺語 It is no use crying over spilt milk 覆水難收。

　　領隊是第一線服務者，當下要做出正確的判斷與決策，否則事後客訴所導致的理賠是覆水難收。

11. account 帳戶。

　　領隊工作壓力大、賺的是辛苦錢，所賺的多數屬於外幣，因此，領隊個人財務管理也相當重要，如何讓1+1大於2是領隊應思考的議題。不同理財組合，不僅分散風險，更可以創造更大的財富。

12. check 支票。

　　長程線領隊有時需要攜帶零用金或餐費，一般公司會讓領隊帶旅行支票出國支付必要之費用，除了匯率較佳外，具有一定的安全性，但如果領隊不事先簽名旅行支票，掉了也無濟於事。旅行支票部分商家並不樂於接受，因此領隊要事先找空檔，至銀行兌換成現金。

13. (D) 語意正確。

　　旅遊業是令人實現夢想的行業，而領隊正是圓夢的推手，試著令每一團

員、每一團都有一個美好的回憶，是領隊首要的職業道德。

14. (C)語意正確。

領隊帶團盡量要客觀，太過主觀、負面的解說會對團員產生不良的印象。特別是政治問題，最好少提國內部分，否則容易讓自己陷入窘境。

15. 慣用語。

葡萄酒是歐洲人慣用的主餐飲料，領隊當然要熟悉各種葡萄酒的製造過程、如何飲用，甚至如何選購。

16. 慣用語，(B)花大錢。

購買貴重的商品時，應向團員強調財不露白，特別是在治安不佳、宵小多的國家或旅遊地區。

17. 過去式。

具有特色及歷史意義的商店、咖啡店，領隊應記錄並了解其背景故事；對於導覽解說時，如能親自蒞臨或品嚐，必能使團員留下深刻印象。

18. 正確用字，appetizer開胃菜。

每一道風味餐、當地特殊小吃，試著努力了解其製造過程與如何享用，更重要的是當地居民為何食用此風味餐的背景意義，才是旅遊解說的重點。

19. (B)正確選字，invention 發明。

領隊也要跟上時代，了解新的資訊設備與操作方式，因為團員來自不同的年齡層、教育背景、財務能力。因此，領隊要能符合不同背景團員的專業期待並給予所需的服務。

20. 正確用字，gain weight增重。

注重自身健康與職業病的預防是領隊應隨時警惕自己的，否則出國帶領團體時，自己卻帶了一堆藥品，並可能隨時身體不適，如何帶給團員健康、安全與快樂的旅行，特別是領隊的喉嚨，如果失聲，解說工作就無法進行，當然就是一趟沒有靈魂的旅行。

( ) 1. May I have two hundred U.S. dollars in small _____?

(A)accounts (B)balance

(C)numbers (D)denominations 【98外語領隊】

( ) 2. I would like to _____ $500 from my savings account.

(A)give in (B)put out

(C)withdraw (D)reject 【98外語領隊】

( ) 3. My boss is very _____; he keeps asking us to complete assigned tasks within the limited time span.

(A)luxurious (B)demanding

(C)obvious (D)relaxing 【98外語領隊】

( ) 4. The airline company finally broke even last year.

(A)was highly profitable (B)went bankrupt

(C)stopped losing money (D)had an accident 【98外語領隊】

( ) 5. Many customers complained that they had difficulty assembling the M-20 mountain bicycle, because the instructions in the manual were not _____.

(A)implicit (B)explicit

(C)complex (D)exquisite 【99外語領隊】

( ) 6. To use a TravelPass, you have to insert it _____ the automatic stamping machine when you get off.

(A)through (B)between

(C)off (D)into 【99外語領隊】

( ) 7. If you want to work in tourism, you need to know how to work as part of a team. But sometimes, you also need to know how to work _____.

(A)separately (B)confidently

(C)creatively   (D)independently   【99外語領隊】

( ) 8. I'm afraid your credit card has already _____. Would you like to pay in cash

instead?

(A)cancelled   (B)booked

(C)expired   (D)exposed   【99外語領隊】

( ) 9. The tour guide _____ him into buying some expensive souvenirs.

(A)persuaded   (B)dissuaded

(C)suggested   (D)purified   【100外語領隊】

( ) 10. Bonnie signed up _____ dancing classes in the Extension Program.

(A)on   (B)in

(C)for   (D)about   【100外語領隊】

( ) 11. Do not draw attention to yourself by _____ large amounts of cash or expen-

sive jewelry.

(A)display   (B)displayed

(C)displays   (D)displaying   【100外語領隊】

( ) 12. Client: I would like to change 500 US dollars into NT dollars.

Bank clerk: Certainly, sir. Please complete this form and make sure _____.

(A)you jot down the capital appreciation

(B)you put the full name in capitals

(C)you visited the capitals of other countries

(D)you vote against capital punishment   【100外語領隊】

( ) 13. If the tapes do not meet your satisfaction, you can return them within thirty

days for a full _____.

(A)fund   (B)refund

(C)funding   (D)fundraising   【101外語領隊】

( ) 14. Readers _____ to the magazine pay less per issue than those buying it at a newsstand.

(A)subscribe   (B)subscribing

(C)subscribed   (D)are subscribing 　【101外語領隊】

(　) 15. If I had called to reserve a table at Royal House one week earlier, we _____

a gourmet reunion dinner last night.

(A)can have   (B)will have had

(C)would have had   (D)would have eating 　【101外語領隊】

(　) 16. The school boys stopped _____ the stray dog when their teacher went up to

them.

(A)bully   (B)bullied

(C)to be bullying   (D)bullying 　　　　　【101外語領隊】

解答

1.D	2.C	3.B	4.C	5.B	6.D	7.D	8.C	9.A	10.C	11.D	12.B
13.B	14.B	15.C	16.D								

第十一章

返國前辦理出境手續

一、工作程序（Working Procedures）

經過辛苦的帶團工作，最完美的結局就是將團員平安的帶領返國，必要的程序是：按時到機場，辦理登機與離境手續。最重要是如果團員有退稅的稅單，領隊應協助完成必備程序，讓所有團員將退稅金額「落袋為安」。長程線領隊特別要注意，時間的掌握，有時司機路況不熟、遲到、跑錯飯店、往機場公路塞車、甚至跑錯機場或航站。「國內線」轉機「國際線」，因為氣候、罷工或機械故障而導致班機延誤，嚴重情形如轉接不到國際航班；輕者導致團員來不及退稅，嚴重是趕不上搭機時間，延遲返國。返國後必定導致團員「客訴」、「要求賠償」，身為領隊最後一個帶團流程不可輕忽

二、關鍵字彙

此階段應熟悉的重要關鍵字彙包括如下：

1.Tax Refund 退稅			
・Stamp	蓋章	・Monitor	螢幕
・Disembarkation Card	出境卡	・Procedures	手續
・Local Agent	當地代理旅行社	・On Schedule	按時
・Souvenirs	紀念品	・X Ray Check	X光檢查
・Cash Refund Counter	退現金服務台	・Money Exchange	換錢
・Availability	可行性	・Label	標籤
・Announce	宣告	・Wallet	皮夾
2.Spot Check 抽查			
・Exceed	超過	・Bail	保釋金
・Wallet	皮夾	・Preference	偏好
・Green Channel	免報稅通關	・Stuff	雜物
・Red Channel	需報稅通關	・Attention	注意
・Overhead Bin	上方行李箱	・Tobacco	菸草製品
・Compensate	補償	・Daily Necessities	日常用品
・Foreign Currency	外國貨幣	・Deport	驅逐出境
・Confiscate	沒收		

三、關鍵會話

㈠辦理出境手續狀況一

【Scene：Immigration】

Immigration officer: May I have your passport and departure card, please?

Tour Leader ：Certainly, sir. Here you are.

Immigration officer: It's all right. Please go to the customs.

Customs inspector ：Please show me your Customs Declaration, sir. Do you have anything to declare?

Tour Leader ：No, I don't think so.

Customs inspector ：Well, would you mind opening this bag?

Tour Leader ：I guess not.

Customs inspector : Let me examine your luggage and check it with your declaration form. Please show me the valuable articles you brought in.

Tour Leader　　　 : Certainly, officer.

Customs inspector : Do you still have this article?

Tour Leader　　　 : I am sorry. It has been lost.

Customs inspector : Do you have a certificate for the loss?

Tour Leader　　　 : Yes. This is the certificate for the loss.

Customs inspector : All right. Everything is fine. Your luggage is passed.

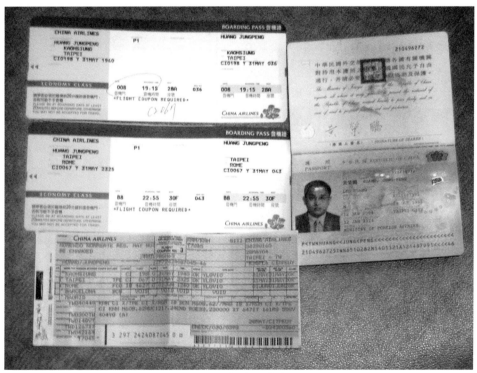

圖11-1　出境必備文件

(二)辦理出境手續狀況二

【Scene：Immigration counter】

Immigration officer: May I see your passport, boarding card, and departure card, please?

Tour Leader　　　 : Here you are.

Immigration officer: Are you a tour leader?

Tour Leader　　　 : Yes, I am.

Immigration officer: How many people are there in your group?

Tour Leader　　　 : There are 30 people in this tour group and include me.

Immigration officer: Please tell your people to wait on a line.

Tour Leader　　　 : OK.

Immigration officer: Have a nice trip.

Tour Leader　　　 : Thanks, officer.

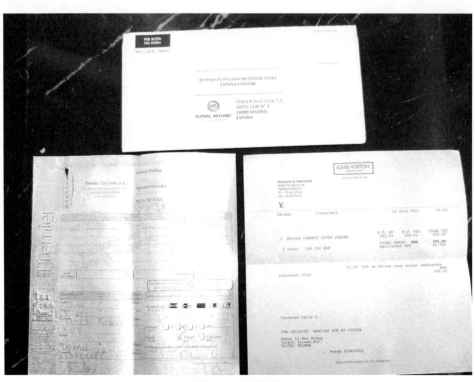

圖11-2　退稅單

㈢辦理退稅手續狀況一

【Scene：Customs & Refund】

Customs official: Good afternoon, sir. May I help you?

Tour Leader ：Yes. Is this the place where I can draw back the tax paid for the watch I bought in Italy? I would like to have my tax refund form stamped.

Customs official: Certainly, sir. May I have your passport, boarding pass, tax refund form and the merchandise you've bought, please?

Tour Leader ：Here you are.

Customs official: Ok. Here is your refund form. Please go to get your tax refund at the Cash Refund Counter at the Emigration.

Tour Leader ：I see. Thank you, officer.

圖11-3　退稅海關

㈣辦理退稅手續狀況二

Tour Leader	: Excuse me, sir. May I get my tax refund, here?
Official of the Cash Refund:	Certainly, sir. Can I have your stamped refund form, please?
Tour Leader	: Here you are, and my passport and boarding pass.
Official of the Cash Refund:	Thank you. You've paid 510 Euros for the watch. The tax is 17%. So you'll get a refund of 86.7 Euros. How would you like to have it, get it in cash or send it to your credit account?
Tour Leader	: Cash, please.
Official of the Cash Refund:	All right. Here are your passport, boarding pass and 86.7 Euros tax refund.
Tour Leader	: Thank you very much.

圖11-4　機場退稅單寄回郵筒

圖11-5　返國入境移民關

圖11-6　行李提領區與入境海關

四 、 語詞測驗

1. refrain from ～ 抑制（to forbear）

Please refrain from smoking.

請不要吸菸。

2. remind A of B ～ 使A想起B

He reminds me of my tour leader.

他令我想起我的領隊。

3. repent of ～ 後悔

I have nothing at all to repent of.

我未曾後悔過。

4. result from ～ （作爲結果而）發生（to happen as an effect）

That accident resulted from tour leader's carelessness.

這件意外事件起因於領隊的粗心。

5. rob A of B ～ 搶了A的B

The gangsters robbed the purse of the tourist.

這幫歹徒搶走觀光客的皮包。

6. rub up ～ 擦亮、重溫

Try to rub up your memory.

試著重溫記憶。

7. **run across** ～　偶遇

I ran across my tour guide while shopping in the department store.

當我在百貨公司購物時，巧遇導遊。

8. **run into** ～　偶然遇見（**to encounter by chance**）

I'm glad I ran into you today.

我很高興今天遇見你。

9. **search for** ～　調查

What have you been searching for？

你在調查什麼？

10. **see about** ～　處理（**to attend to**）

Tour leader will see about it as soon as possible.

領隊會盡速處理這件事。

11. **see off** ～　為（某人）送行

Tour guide saw us off at the airport.

導遊至機場為我們送行。

12. **seem to** ～　似乎

Tour guide seems to have been sick.

導遊似乎生病了。

13. **stand by** ～　支持、站在旁邊（**to be near**）、援助（**to support**）

I am willing to stand by tour leader.

我願意支持領隊。

14. share A with B 〜　將A與B共享。

Tour leader wanted to share the room with the local guide.

領隊希望與當地導遊住同一個房間。

15. shout at 〜　大聲喊叫

Don't shout at me.

不要對我大聲喊叫。

16. show off 〜　炫耀（to display）

Do not show off your money on the street.

不要在街上炫耀你的錢。

17. skim through 〜　略讀

Tour guide skimmed through his schedule quickly.

導遊迅速地略讀完行程。

18. sleep in 〜　睡過頭（to sleep later in the morning than usual）

Tour guide was late for our tour because he slept in this morning.

導遊因為今早睡過頭了而遲到。

19. smell out 〜　嗅出（to look for by smelling）

The dog smells out the drug.

這條狗嗅出毒品。

20. sneer at 〜　嘲笑

Don't sneer at others' religion.

不要嘲笑別人的宗教信仰。

21. **speak out** ～　開誠布公地說

I tried to speak out my viewpoint.

我試著說出我的觀點。

22. **spout out** ～　噴出

Blood spouted out from the wound.

血從傷口處噴出。

23. **spring from** ～　湧出、發源、出身（貴族等）

Errors always spring from carelessness.

錯誤往往源自粗心。

24. **spring up** ～　產生、發生

A good idea sprang up in my mind.

好主意浮現在我心中。

25. **set off** ～　爆發、動身、襯托（**to cause to explode**），（**to start; leave**）

We set off for New York.

我們動身前往紐約。

五、文法測驗

本章重點：關係詞分析

關係代名詞

who	I have three children who came from Kaohsiung in my group. 我這一團有三個來自高雄的小孩子。
whose	I know a local guide whose wife is a Taiwanese. 我認識一位他老婆是台灣人的當地導遊。
whom	The local guide (whom) you saw at the party is my colleague. 你在宴會上看到的當地導遊是我的同事。
which	Nobody wants to have a coach which has been used for years. 沒有人想要用了好幾年的遊覽車。 Tour guide received a plan from tour leader, which surprised her. 領隊向導遊提出令導遊感到很驚訝的計畫。
of which	I visited Malaysia the capital of which is Kuala Lumpur. 我遊覽馬來西亞的首都吉隆坡。
受格which的省略	He offered me an insult I couldn't put up with. 他對我的汙辱，我無法忍受。
that	He is the tour leader that solved the problem. 他是把問題解開的那個領隊。
what	Listen to what tour guide is saying. 注意聽導遊說些什麼。
關係代名詞的雙重限制	Is there anything you want that you don't have? 有沒有什麼東西是你想要卻沒有的?
as	The driver was not such a smart guy as we thought. 司機並不是我們想像中的聰明。
but	There is no rule but has exceptions. 沒有一個規則會沒有例外。
than	Don't give impolite drivers more tips than is needed. 不要給無禮的司機超出必須給的小費。

複合關係代名詞

whoever	Whoever comes will be welcome. 凡是來的人都會受到歡迎。
whatever	She looks pretty whatever she wears. 無論穿什麼，她看起來都很漂亮。
whichever	The extra tips will be given whichever of them serves the best hospitality to tourists. 這份額外小費將給他們之中服務觀光客最殷勤的人。

關係形容詞

what	I gave her what little money I had. 我把我所有的一點錢都給了她。
which	The driver spoke French, which language I didn't understand. 司機講法文，那種語言我不懂。
複合關係形容詞	Whichever way you go, you'll have to cross the Rhone River. 無論你走那一條路，都必須渡過隆河。

關係副詞

when	The day will come when your dream come true. 你夢想實現的日子一定會來臨。
關係副詞when和連接詞when的比較	It was a time when GPS on the long distance coach were rare. 當時衛星導航系統在長程遊覽車上還很少見。
where	Marseille is the city where the streets are not planned. 馬賽的街道未經規劃。
關係副詞的限定用法語補述用法	This is the village where Napoleon was born. 這是拿破崙出生的村莊。
why	The reason why tour leader did it is obscure. 領隊做那件事的理由並不清楚。
how	This is how it happened. 事情就是這樣發生的。
the+比較級	The more you earn, the more you spend. 賺得愈多，花得愈多。

複合關係副詞

whenever	Come whenever you like. 你喜歡什麼時候來都可以。
wherever	I'll sit wherever I can find a seat. 有座位的地方，我就坐下來。
however	However hard I try, I can never catch up with him. 無論我怎麼努力，都不可能趕上他。

本章綜合練習

( ) 1. I had scarcely left Rome downtown _____ it began to rain.

(A) than (B) when (C) just (D) then

( ) 2. The reason for his success is _____ he worked hard.

(A) why (B) that (C) because (D) for

( ) 3. The town _____ our driver grew up in is not far from here.

(A) what (B) where (C) wherever (D) which

( ) 4. I tried to get out of the travel industry business, _____ I found impossible.

(A) who (B) which (C) that (D) what

( ) 5. This guide book is for tourists _____ native language is not English.

(A) of whom (B) that (C) which (D) whose

( ) 6. Young _____ he was, he was equal to the task.

(A) as (B) because (C) if (D) unless

( ) 7. I wouldn't go abroad for sightseeing _____ who recommends it.

(A) regardless (B) since (C) no matter (D) for

( ) 8. I'll buy one Rolex _____ it costs.

(A) every (B) whatever (C) when (D) as

( ) 9. Make a message of it _____ you should forget.

(A) so (B) to (C) how (D) lest

( ) 10. You can stay hotel _____ you are quiet.

　　(A) but　(B) however　(C) so long as　(D) if not

( ) 11. All _____ is a continuous supply of friendly smile.

　　(A) what is needed　　　　　(B) that is needed

　　(C) the thing is needed　　　(D) for their needs

( ) 12. He has lots of travel books, _____ that he is still a tour leader.

　　(A) considering　　　　　(B) considered

　　(C) being considered　　　(D) our considering

( ) 13. The reason _____ I can't come is that I have to work late.

　　(A) because　(B) for　(C) as　(D) why

( ) 14. You can fly to London this evening _____ you don't mind changing planes in Paris.

　　(A) provided　(B) except　(C) unless　(D) so far as

( ) 15. _____ entering the hall, tour leader found everyone waiting for him.

　　(A) At　(B) While　(C) On　(D) In

( ) 16. You'll have to _____ at Taxes airport.

　　(A) change　(B) transfer　(C) exchange　(D) translate

( ) 17. How long will we take to get to New York?

　　(A) You're right. It's New York.　　(B) It is about 10 o'clock now.

　　(C) It takes 17 hours from here.　　(D) We can go there by train.

( ) 18. I checked the _____ to see when the fly would be here.

　　(A) timetable　(B) schedule　(C) ticket　(D) clock

( ) 19. Could you _____ at 10:00a.m. to the Kaohsiung International Airport?

　　(A) wake me up　(B) draw me up　(C) pick me up　(D) take me off

( ) 20. Emily: Hello, Steven. When did you get home last night?

　　Steven: I arrived at the airport around 10:00p.m. _____.

(A) I wanted to come along.　　(B) I saw a lot of new stuff there.

(C) My wife picked me up.　　(D) I ate so much.

解答

1.B	2.B	3.D	4.B	5.D	6.A	7.C	8.B	9.D	10.C	11.B	12.A
13.D	14.A	15.C	16.B	17.C	18.A	19.C	20.C				

綜合解析

1. (B)連接詞，且語意正確。

   當我一離開羅馬市區就開始下雨，這是可遇而不可求的事。行程中，當然會期待天氣良好，但下雨時更應注意團員行走安全。

2. (A)(C)重複語意，(D) 缺連接詞。

   努力、全力以赴，把團帶好，當然會得到團員的掌聲與公司主管的肯定。遇到挫折更應積極反省，尋求改進之道，重點是不要犯同樣的錯誤。

3. 關係詞，表地方前有the town用which。

   歐洲長程線司機有時於旺季中，連續三個月未回家者時有所聞。有時相互體諒司機，加強團員與司機的互動，也能減緩司機思鄉之苦。

4. 關係代名詞。(C) that 前不加「，」，錯誤。(A)who是人非business，錯誤。

   旅遊業儘管辛苦至極，但也相對多彩多姿，時時充滿挑戰，是其他行業所無法比擬的，「開闊你的胸襟、拓展你的視野」是領隊工作應有的期許。

5. 關係代名詞。

   旅遊書籍現在是團員出國時人手一本，因此領隊不僅要熟悉書坊相關旅遊書籍，更應蒐集更深入的旅遊資訊，強化專業性，對其解說的正確性更形重要。

6. (B)(C)(D)語意錯誤。

   領隊的年紀與帶團績效不見得成正比，但對於某一旅遊路線的深耕程度，

是會影響帶團的效果，因為「聞道有先後，術業有專攻」。

7. (C) no matter 不論。

旅遊的障礙因素分為許多類，因人而異。身為領隊可分析團員參團旅遊的
動機，如此就能提供不同服務，給不同的團員，滿足不同的期待。

8. 複合關係代名詞 whatever。

一生珍愛有限，如果有機會遇到，應該勇敢買下，往往過了，才後悔沒
買、沒買夠。

9. (D) 假設語氣 lest 除非。

重要的訊息或領隊的蹤跡，應隨時讓團員、公司與家人知道。不要整天帶
團，賺了錢，失去親情、友情與愛情。

10. (C) so long as 只要。

旅館是國際觀光客住宿的地方，出國代表台灣，團員的一言一行，都代表
台灣國家整體形象，領隊如沒有適度教育團員國際禮儀，當場又不適當規
勸，最後整體國家形象也會毀於一旦，領隊是旅遊者之友、之師，應言教
也要身教。

11. (C) 雙動詞，(D) 語意錯誤，(A)關係代名詞。

「笑是最好的化妝品」，笑也是不分國籍、不分男女，是世界共同的友善
語言，特別是服務業。因此，領隊態度要積極、表情要親切，適度的笑，
有利於整團氣氛的營造。

12 .(A) 補語。

養成閱讀的好習慣，至國外有機會也要閱讀當地報紙與書籍，試著以不同
角度看事情，所得的解說也更多元、更客觀。切忌永遠以台灣角度看世
界，那就太狹隘。

13. the reason why (D)正確。

遇到事件推諉責任，為自己找台階下，無所不用其極找出行為合理化的藉
口，是一般人的通病。但身為領隊，應將帶團視為一種責任，以「麻煩的

解決者」自許，即便不是領隊的錯，領隊也能克服。最後，令團員高高興興的返國是努力的目標。

14.(A) Provided假如。

轉機對領隊帶團是較具風險性，特別是不同航空公司或轉機超過三個中轉站，必須重新取得登機證，行李要再一次電腦確認，否則往往人到目的地，行李總是會掉幾件，如果又碰到機場或航空公司罷工，那領隊就有許多後續工作要處理。

15.(C) on entering the hall一進入。

領隊事事要提前完成，千萬不要遲到是基本帶團的要領。台灣人習慣，遲到5-10分鐘是正常的行為，但領隊是沒有這項權利。此外德語系國家，通常民族性較嚴謹，碰到此類型司機，最好與司機約的時間比團體集合時間晚5分鐘較佳，否則，當習慣遲到的台灣團員，碰上準時如勞力士手錶的德國裔司機，那司機避免不了數落領隊一句「You are always late.」，領隊只能回應說「Customers are always right.」。

16.(B) 正確選字。

轉機有時是不同的航站大廈，甚至國際線要轉國內線，國際線要轉歐盟境內，又要先入境再辦轉機手續。因此，領隊應事先向前輩或剛回國的領隊確認一下相關程序。

17.(C) 語意正確。

搭機時間、機上用幾餐、中間要不要轉機，通常是團員常問領隊的問題。因此，最好在辦理登機手續時，就應事先向航空公司地勤人員洽詢清楚上述問題。

18.(A) 選字正確。

飛機時刻表，最好是透過電腦訂位系統（Computer Reservation System, CRS）較正確，資訊較即時，Timetable只能當參考時用。

19.(C) 載我。

機場接團或接人，首先要搞清楚哪一個機場，像巴黎有兩個主要機場、倫敦也有兩個主要機場、紐約有三個主要機場、東京也有二個主要機場。就算弄對機場，有時司機或領隊經驗不足，司機會停錯航站、停錯樓層、停錯停車場，領隊如果也是新手，當然就「牛郎碰織女」，很難會找到。

20.(C) 語意正確。

返國後請家人接機，最怕是飛機延誤抵達，甚至因航班故障、颱風或氣候因素而延遲許久才返國。在國外應爭取航空公司，給團員打電話報平安的基本權益；如果不行，至少領隊應要求打一通電話至公司，請公司一一通知在台家屬，目前團體狀況與預定抵台時間。

歷屆試題

( ) 1. I missed the early morning train because I _____.

(A)overbooked   (B)overcooked

(C)overtook   (D)overslept   【98外語領隊】

( ) 2. Beware of strangers at the airport and do not leave your luggage _____.

(A)unanswered   (B)uninterested

(C)unimportant   (D)unattended   【98外語領隊】

( ) 3. If you have the receipts for the goods you have purchased, you can claim a tax _____ at the airport upon departure.

(A)relief   (B)rebate

(C)involve   (D)reply   【98外語領隊】

( ) 4. I came across my high school classmate when I traveled to Los Angeles.

(A)met by chance   (B)planned to visit

(C)moved to see   (D)was glad to find   【98外語領隊】

(　) 5. ＿＿＿＿ has become a very serious problem in the modern world. It's esti-

mated that there are more than 1 billion overweight adults globally.

(A)Depression (B)Obesity

(C)Malnutrition (D)Starvation 【99外語領隊】

(　) 6. There is clear ＿＿＿＿ that the defendant committed the murder of the rich

old man.

(A)research (B)evidence

(C)statistics (D)vision 【99外語領隊】

(　) 7. All my friends are recommending the movie, *Avatar*; ＿＿＿＿, I am too busy

to see it.

(A)but (B)therefore

(C)so (D)however 【99外語領隊】

(　) 8. A kimono is a kind of clothing ＿＿＿＿ the Japanese wear during special cer-

emonies.

(A)where (B)who

(C)when (D)that 【99外語領隊】

(　) 9. He will tell you as soon as he ＿＿＿＿.

(A)knows (B)has known

(C)will know (D)is knowing 【100外語領隊】

(　) 10. Neither you, nor I, nor he ＿＿＿＿ in Mr. Brown's class.

(A)am (B)is

(C)are (D)be 【100外語領隊】

(　) 11. ＿＿＿＿ there is a holiday, we always go hiking.

(A)During (B)Whatever

(C)Whenever (D)While 【100外語領隊】

(　) 12. ＿＿＿＿ there is more than one Paris in the world, there's really only one Paris in the world. It is the capital of France.

    (A)Although   (B)Already

    (C)However   (D)And   【100外語領隊】

(   ) 13. The hotel _____ for the conference featured a nine-hole golf course.

    (A)that he selected   (B)that he selected it

    (C)that selected   (D)he selected it   【100外語領隊】

(   ) 14. Each country has its own regulations _____ fruit and vegetable imports.

    (A)pertaining   (B)edible

    (C)allowable   (D)regarding   【100外語領隊】

(   ) 15. The convenience store _____ owner just won the grand lottery will be

closed next month.

    (A)which   (B)who

    (C)whose   (D)that   【100外語領隊】

(   ) 16. After disembarking the flight, I went directly to the _____ to pick up my

bags and trunks.

    (A)airport lounge   (B)cockpit

    (C)runway   (D)baggage claim   【100外語領隊】

解答

1.D	2.D	3.B	4.A	5.B	6.B	7.D	8.D	9.A	10.B	11.C	12.A
13.A	14.D	15.C	16.D								

第十二章

突發狀況處理

一、工作程序（Working Procedures）

旅行產業是一個高度不穩定性的行業，旅行業（Travel Agent）是代理（Agent）的角色與功能，而組成旅行商品的所有上游供應商，例如：航空公司、飯店、主題樂園、餐廳、遊樂場所等，皆非完全可直接由旅行業者直接掌握旅遊品質，唯有透過「訂位」（Reservation）、「確認」（Confirm）與「再確認」（Reconfirm），或許能掌控部分的變數與不可預測性。而身為領隊是第一線的工作人員，領隊人員要以身為「麻煩的處理者」（Trouble Dealers）自許，於第一時間、突發事件發生的地點，迅速處理；如果做不到、做不好，那你這位領隊的角色，將變成為「麻煩的製造者」（Trouble Makers）之一，更不好的是將此「麻煩」帶回台灣，公司還需花許多時間與成本處理「客訴事件」，這一團的「領隊」不僅令「團員」搖頭，也令「公司」遺憾。

二、關鍵字彙

領隊應熟悉的重要關鍵字彙包括下列三項：

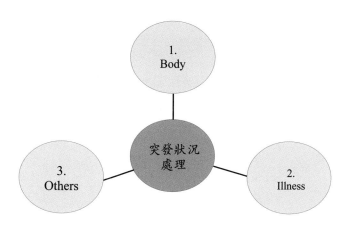

1.Body　身體

• Neck	脖子	• Shoulder	肩膀
• Chest	胸部	• Breast	乳房
• Abdomen	腹部	• Elbow	肘
• Waist	腰部	• Navel	肚臍
• Hip	臀部	• Thigh	大腿
• Knee	膝蓋	• Shank	小腿
• Stomach	胃	• Appendix	盲腸
• Heart	心臟	• Urinary Ladder	膀胱
• Anus	肛門	• Urethra	尿道

2.Illness　身體不適

• Fracture	骨折	• Sprain	扭傷
• Sprained Finger	手指扭傷	• Pregnancy	懷孕
• Asthma	氣喘	• Chicken Pox	水痘
• Pneumonia	肺炎	• High Blood Pressure	高血壓
• Gastric Cancer	胃癌	• Cough	咳嗽
• Headache	頭痛	• Dizzy	頭暈
• Sore Throat	喉嚨痛	• Plague	鼠疫
• Runny Nose	流鼻涕	• Bellyache	腹痛
• Fever	發燒	• Chest Pain	胸痛
• Gout	痛風	• Dull Pain	悶痛
• Catch Cold	感冒	• Throbbing Pain	抽痛
• Rash	發疹	• Backache	背痛
• Vomit	嘔吐物	• Sharp Pain	劇痛
• Appendicitis	盲腸炎	• Prescription	處方
• Stomachache	胃痛	• Cold	感冒
• Stroke	中風	• Chill	風寒
• Shortness of Breath	呼吸急促	• Heart Disease	心臟病
• Paralysis	麻痺	• Throw Up	嘔吐
• Flu	流行性感冒	• Melatonin	褪黑激素
• Lung Cancer	肺癌	• Ointment	軟膏
• Burn	燒傷	• Tumidity	腫脹
• Seasickness	暈船	• Phlegm	痰
• Ambulance	救護車	• Tablet	藥片

領隊英文

· Symptoms	症狀	· First-aid kit	急救箱
· Physician	內科醫生	· Anodyne	止痛劑
· Loose	鬆的	· Pill	藥丸
· Surgeon	外科醫生	· Antibiotic	抗生素
· Sleeping Pill	安眠藥	· Dentist	牙科醫生
· Bandage	繃帶	· Pain-Killer	止痛藥
· Suffocate	使窒息	· Injection	注射
· Medicine	藥品	· Emergency Form	緊急事件表
· Shoot	注射	· Scald	燙傷

3.Others　其他

· Restriction	限制	· Permanently	長期
· Prohibit	禁止	· Temporary	暫時
· Drugs	毒品	· Combine	合併
· Illegal	非法	· Fine	罰款
· Weapon	武器	· Cigarette	香煙
· Spirits	酒類	· Fruit	水果
· Cigar	雪茄	· Tourism Appliances	旅遊用品類
· Animals	動物	· Spirituous Drinks	含酒精類飲料
· Wildlife	野生動物	· Inflammable	易燃品類
· Soil	土壤	· Compressed Gases	高壓縮罐
· Plant	植物	· Corrosive	腐蝕性物質
· False	錯誤	· Nail Scissors	指甲剪
· Explosives	爆炸物	· Radioactive Materials	放射性物質
· Articles not hand carried but checked in		禁止手提但可托運	
· Articles prohibited on the aircraft		禁止攜帶上機物品	

三、關鍵會話

(一)登機證遺失

【Scene：Boarding gate】

Tour Leader：Ladies and gentlemen. It's time for us to get aboard the plane.
Please get your boarding passes ready and follow me to the

boarding gate one by one. Please don't leave any personal belongings behind.

Tour member: Oh, my goodness! What shall I do?

Tour Leader : What's wrong? May I help you?

Tour member: I can not find my boarding pass. I put it right here in my pocket when you gave it to me in the waiting room.

Tour Leader : Have you checked your coat or anywhere else?

Tour member: Let me see. Oh, perhaps I left it in the gift shop when I bought some souvenirs for my family.

Tour Leader : Let's go to look for it in the gift shop. What's the seat number on your boarding pass?

Tour member: It says 12B.

（To the ticket inspector）

Tour Leader : Inspector, a tourist of our group, Tsai, Ming-Hsin, has lost her boarding pass. The seat number is 12B. I will look for it with her.

（In the gift shop）

Sales girl　　: Good morning. May I help you?

Tour Leader : Yes. The lady bought some gifts here this morning and probably left her boarding pass here. Have you found it?

Sales girl　　: Which counter has she been to?

Tour Leader : She bought three necklaces at that counter.

Sales girl　　: What is the seat number on the boarding card?

Tour Leader : It says 12B.

Sales girl　　: That's right. Here you are. Your boarding card has been left on our counter.

Tour member: Oh, I am so careless. Thank you so much.

Sales girl ：With pleasure.

Tour Leader ：Now let's go to catch the plane. Come on.

圖12-1　登機證

(二)航班延誤

【Scene：Airline counter】

Tour Leader	：Excuse me, madam. I just heard an announcement that our flight has been delayed.
Clerk of the Airline counter:	What's your flight number?
Tour Leader	：Flight KA437 bound for Hong Kong.
Clerk of the Airline counter:	Oh, yes, the delay is due to Mechanical difficulties.
Tour Leader	：Do you know how long it will be delayed?
Clerk of the Airline counter:	Probably not more than two hours.
Tour Leader	：I am the tour leader of a tour group. There are some aged people and children in my group.

Clerk of the Airline counter: We will provide free lunch and drinks for the passengers. Please take your group to the coffee shop next to the departure lounge. You can have some food and have a rest there with your boarding passes. I'm terribly sorry to cause inconvenience to you.

Tour Leader : But I' m afraid we'll miss our connecting flight. We are supposed to catch a Best Airline flight to Paris at 11:10p.m. Is there another flight available?

Clerk of the Airline counter: Just a minute. Let me check.... Yes, there is a flight leaving for Paris in thirty minutes. But there are only 19 seats available. How many persons are there in your group?

Tour Leader : There are 17 people including me.

Clerk of the Airline counter: That's all right. Please give me your passports and boarding passes. I'll get you on Flight OS 642 to Paris.

Tour Leader : Which airline does this flight belong to?

Clerk of the Airline counter: Oh, it's an Austrian Airlines flight.

Tour Leader : Thank you very much for your help, madam.

Clerk of the Airline counter: It's our pleasure to serve you.

圖 12-2　登機閘口顯示螢幕

㈢行李遺失

【Scene：Airline counter】

Tour Leader	: Excuse me, where is the counter for lost baggage?
Ground Service Agent	: It is at the far end of the baggage claim area.
Tour Leader	: Thank you.
Clerk of the Airline counter:	Good afternoon. May I help you?
Tour Leader	: We've been waiting in the baggage claim area for one hour, but some of our group members still can't find their luggage.

Clerk of the Airline counter: What kind of luggage?

Tour Leader : One big blue suitcase and two green back-packs.

Clerk of the Airline counter: May I know your airline company and the flight number?

Tour Leader : It is Best Airline. The flight number is 316.

Clerk of the Airline counter: Do you have the baggage claim tags?

Tour Leader : Yes. Here you are.

Clerk of the Airline counter: Just a minute, please. Let me check.... I am sorry. Your luggage was probably misplaced on Flight KA 317 in Hong Kong.

Tour Leader : What should I do now?

Clerk of the Airline counter: Would you please fill out this form and leave your address and phone number that we can contact you.

Tour Leader : When can we get the information?

Clerk of the Airline counter: About 9 o'clock tonight. Once we find your luggage, we'll contact you as soon as possible.

Tour Leader : Do we have to come here again?

Clerk of the Airline counter: No. We will deliver them to where you are staying.

Tour Leader : Ok. We will be in the downtown for two days. But what if our luggage was damaged?

Clerk of the Airline counter: Then, we will give you reasonable compen-sation for it.

Tour Leader   : So, that's it?

Clerk of the Airline counter: Yes, that's it. We are terribly sorry for the inconvenience.

圖12-3　航空公司行李遺失登記櫃檯

㈣旅客搭機不適

【Scene：In flight】

Tour Leader   : Excuse me, one of our group members is not feeling well.

Airline Attendant: I am sorry for that. What can I do for her?

Tourist   : I think I got a cold.

Tour Leader	: Could she stretch out on those two empty seats?
Airline Attendant:	Of course, would you like a pillow and a blanket for her?
Tour Leader	: Yes, please. Do you have any medicine for her?
Airline Attendant:	Sorry, we can not offer any medicine for our passengers.
Tourist	: I will be fine. Thank you very much.
Tour Leader	: We will arrive in one hour. I will call a doctor for you at that time.
Tourist	: Thanks.

圖 12-4　機場保險銷售櫃檯

四 、語詞測驗

1. **stand up for** 〜 　支持（**to take the side of; support**）

   Will you stand up for tour guide？

   你會支持導遊嗎？

2. **stand for** 〜 　代表、忍耐（**to represent**）,（**to put up with; endure**）

   What does "FOC" stand for？

   FOC代表什麼意思？

3. **stay [sit] up** 〜 　熬夜

   Don't stay up late watching television.

   不要熬夜看電視。

4. **stem from** 〜 　發生

   Tour guide's failure stems from his laziness.

   導遊的錯誤是由於他的懶惰。

5. **stop off** 〜 　中途停車

   Tour group stopped off at a restaurant to eat lunch.

   旅行團途中停車去餐廳用餐。

6. **submit to** 〜 　使服從

   I was forced to submit to my fate.

   我被迫向我的命運投降。

7. **substitute A for B** ～ 以A代B

We substitute white wine for sparkling wine.

我用白酒取代氣泡酒。

8. **succeed to** ～ 繼承（**to follow another into office, possession, ect.**）

The prince succeeded to the throne.

王子繼承王位。

9. **suffer from** ～ 患病

I'm suffering from the fever.

我正發燒中。

10. **suspect A of B** ～ 懷疑A做了B

The tour leader suspected the driver of stealing the purse.

領隊懷疑司機偷了皮包。

11. **take after** ～ 相似、長得像（**to resemble**）

The new watch really takes after Swatch.

這支新錶很像瑞士帥氣錶。

12. **take A for B** ～ 把A誤認為B

At first I took her for my local guide.

我第一眼看見她，以為她是我們的當地導遊。

13. **take out** ～ 取出、護送

Tour guide went to the bank to take out some money.

導遊去銀行領錢。

14. **take over** ～ 接管

Tour leader took over local guide's role.

領隊接管當地導遊的角色。

15. **take A to B** ～ 送A至B處

Tour leader takes her members of group to the Craze Horse show.

領隊帶團員去欣賞瘋馬秀。

16. **talk over** ～ 討論（**to discuss**）

Tourists came to talk over the optional tour.

觀光客討論自費活動。

17. **tell against** ～ 不利於……

Everything told against tour leader.

每一件事皆不利於領隊。

18. **tell off** ～ 申斥（**to rebuke severely**）

Tour guide was told off for being late.

導遊被斥責遲到。

19. **thing [regard] of A as B** ～ 把A當作B

I think of you as our tour guide.

我以為你是我們的導遊。

20. **think over** ～ 考慮（**to ponder**）

You must think it over.

你必須考慮。

21. **turn down** ～ 拒絕（**to refuse; reject**）

The driver turned down tour leader's proposal.

司機拒絕領隊的提議。

22. **turn in** ～ 交出

You must turn in tour reports by Friday.

你必須星期五以前交出旅遊報告書。

23. **turn up** ～ 出現（**to show up**）

Tour guide promised to come but he hasn't turned up yet.

導遊答應要來，但卻未出現。

24. **use up** ～ 用光、耗盡

Most tourists used up a whole roll of film.

大多數觀光客用光底片。

25. **walk away** ～ 走開

Tour guide walked away without saying a word.

導遊離開時一句話也沒說。

五、文法測驗

本章重點：特殊構句分析

否定詞放在句首的倒裝	Never will I forget local guide's kindness. 我永遠不會忘記導遊的善意。
only+副詞放在句首的倒裝	Only then did I understand what tour guide meant. 到那個時候我才知道導遊是什麼意思。

副詞片語放在句首的倒裝	Next came David. 下一個來的是大衛。
表次數片語放在句首的倒裝	Twice in my life have I climbed the summit of Alpes. 我這輩子爬過阿爾卑斯山山頂兩次。
well, etc.放在句首的倒裝	Well did I know the Italian driver. 我很了解那位義大利司機。
as, than子句的倒裝	Tour leader spend less than do most tourists in my group. 領隊花的錢比大部分團員少。
假設法條件子句的倒裝	Were she my local guide, I would ask for her advice. 如果她是我的當地導遊，我會請她給我建議。
讓步子句的倒裝	Child as he is, he is brave. 雖然他是小孩，卻很勇敢。
受詞放在句首的倒裝	Such a stupid thing I will not do. 我不會做這麼笨的事。
補語放在句首的倒裝	Handsome is tour leader who handsome does. 領隊心美、貌亦美。
nor, neither, so放在句首的倒裝	I can speak Italian, so can tour leader. 我會說義大利文，領隊也會。
避免重複而省略	Tour leader is more thoughtful than I (am). 領隊比我更深思熟慮。
主詞與動詞的省略	I'll take a chance, if (it is) necessary. 如果有必要，我會冒險。
關係代名詞的省略	Here is the local guide (who) wants to see you. 這位當地導遊想見你。
連接詞that的省略	I don't think (that) tour guide is mistaken. 我不認為導遊被誤解。

本章綜合練習

( ) 1. _____ 1988 did Taiwan government begin to open policy for setting up
travel agencies.

(A) Not until　(B) Not since　(C) Until　(D) In

( ) 2. No sooner _____ tour leader arrived at the airport than the fly started to check in.

(A) was (B) did (C) has (D) had

( ) 3. _____, I would have told you.

(A) If I would have know it   (B) If I had have know it

(C) Had I know it   (D) Should I know it

( ) 4. Rarely _____ acorns until the trees are more than twenty years old.

(A) do oak trees bear   (B) when oak trees bear

(C) oak trees are bear   (D) oak trees bear

( ) 5. Only in the nineteenth century _____ carefully and systematically.

(A) were dreams first scrutinized   (B) that dreams first were scrutinized

(C) scrutinized were dream first   (D) and dream were first scrutinized

( ) 6. Under the guidance of choreographers Martha Graham and Jerome Robbins, American dance _____ new levels of artistic achievement.

(A) reaching (B) has reached (C) reach (D) have reached

( ) 7. _____ begun to understand how the deal with overbooking situations.

(A) In the past decade have only tourists

(B) Only in the past decade have tourists

(C) The only tourists in the past decade

(D) Only in the past decade tourists

( ) 8. _____ the history of the touch, strong-willed Netherlands farmer.

(A) Not only is much of the history of Netherlands

(B) Although it is much of the history of Netherlands that is

(C) It is as much the history of Netherlands ' being

(D) Much of the history of Netherlands is

( ) 9. _____I saw the Grand Canyon, I was speechless.

(A) Until　(B) The first time　(C) Before　(D) Because

( ) 10. Our long distance coach got caught in the _____.

(A) air traffic　(B) traffic jam　(C) traffic jet　(D) traffic light

( ) 11. The weather is _____, perfect for diving.

(A) terrific　(B) horrible　(C) terrible　(D) tumor

( ) 12. The last time that you _____ Rome was in 1976.

(A) had visited　(B) see　(C) had been saw　(D) visited

( ) 13. Michelle enjoys his trip _____ the snow.

(A) although　(B) despite　(C) because　(D) unless

( ) 14. Even though Kevin would like to visit Sherry, she never invites him, _____?

(A) doesn't he　(B) would he　(C) does he　(D) does she

( ) 15. Is that snake in this house? I hate snakes!

No, it just looks like an old house, _____.

(A) take it hard　(B) take it slow　(C) take it easy　(D) take it quickly

( ) 16. Mary: I got another _____ for speeding.

Mark: It's your own fault.

(A) ticket　(B) book　(C) stopping　(D) paper

( ) 17. A: What do you have in your long distance coach?

B: _____.

(A) I have anything.　　　(B) Nothing special!

(C) What do you need?　　(D) We have all kinds of stuff.

( ) 18. If we get up early tomorrow, we shall _____ the train.

(A) catch　(B) contain　(C) go　(D) pick

（　）19. Do you think _____ should be more respected?

(A) old　(B) an old　(C) the old　(D) a old

（　）20. We can't walk fast because the road is _____.

(A) slippery　(B) clean　(C) flat　(D) safe

解答

1.A	2.D	3.C	4.A	5.A	6.B	7.B	8.D	9.B	10.B	11.A	12.D
13.B	14.D	15.C	16.A	17.D	18.A	19.C	20.A				

綜合解析

1. 否定詞放在句首的倒裝句，(B)語意錯誤。

   1988年政府開放旅行業執照申請後，旅行業已屬於完全競爭的市場，領隊的工作機會是大幅增加，但是帶團收入卻不可同日而語。

2. (D)正確，否定詞放在句首的倒裝句。

   應提早到較佳，以備不時之需。此外有退稅國家，至少要預留1小時至30分鐘，辦理退稅手續。

3. (C)假設法條件子句的倒裝。

   事關公司機密，即使知道也不需跟團員、導遊或司機提及，領隊應替公司、團員保守相關個人或公司隱私。

4. Rarely，否定詞放在句首的倒裝。

   領隊應努力充實自己，有上知天文、下知地理，且動物、植物、地質等都應有所涉獵。

5. only+副詞放在句首的倒裝。

   團員的旅遊夢想是要靠領隊來實踐，領隊的夢想是要靠努力去完成，而非坐著空想。

6. 補語放在句首的倒裝。

每位領隊應有的期許是「領隊的一小步，卻是台灣人的一大步」。因此，領隊帶領團員出國應做好國民外交的工作，保持國家正面的形象與領隊專業形象。

7. only+副詞放在句首的倒裝。

旅遊行業的特性，overbooking是旺季時偶爾會造成不便之處，領隊應適時、適宜向團員解釋其背後原因與處理的原則。如果不幸碰上飯店、航空公司、娛樂秀場，及其他交通工具的overbooking，團員也大多可以勉強接受。

8. 表次數片語放在句首的倒裝。

荷蘭國家人口比台灣少，土地原本也比台灣小，但藉由荷蘭人的努力，國土現今比台灣大、國力也比台灣強，值得國人深思，特別是政治人物。領隊帶團出國不是比誰購物，哪一團買得多？Optional Tour 誰做得好？小費誰收得高？而是團員是否能藉由出國機會，學習旅遊地區或國家人民的優點、改善自身的缺點，最後改變國人外顯的行為，更符合先進國家、泱泱大國的國民風範，才是領隊的重責大任。

9. (A)錯，till 正確；(C)(D)語意錯誤。

世界何其大、世人何其多，世界有七大奇景，都等著領隊一一實踐，常常要告訴自己，「Open your mind, broaden your eyes.」，團員偶爾超出常理的要求、公司主管有時不合理的待遇、OP或業務員往往無心的犯錯、旅行同業跟團又嫌東嫌西、分東分西，卻什麼都不做也不會，司機整天想錢、超時開車不高興、團員遲到又要唸領隊、車子又爆胎、導遊按表操課、下班時間準得像瑞士手錶一樣、小費收的像子彈列車一樣快、餐廳沒位子、菜色都一樣，飛機罷工、位子被拉掉、飯店超額訂房，被迫分兩團分住不同飯店。如果上述事件都在同一團、同一時間碰上，那領隊「你」，離成功的日子也不遠了。

10. 塞車，正確(B)。

　　塞車是所有大都會的惡瘤，領隊時間掌握就更形重要。此外車上解說能力與團員互動更加重要，當然長程線歐洲領隊對於司機也不要期待太高，領隊要試著早日認清事實，找路並非只是司機的任務也是領隊工作之一。否則有一天司機會「惱羞成怒」的回答你「You are tour leader. You should tell me.」。領隊只剩沒上駕駛座開車而已，其他都要會處理，且親自去做。

11. 口語意思是「好得不得了」，(A)。

　　天氣好，是可遇而不可求的，好天氣就有好的條件，可創造好的旅遊總體驗；天氣不好，也是不同的感受與體驗，完全取決於領隊帶團技巧。

12. (D) 過去式。

　　往事往往值得細細回味，特別是領隊工作，有苦有樂，凡走過一定留下痕跡。因此，領隊帶團一定沿途蒐集旅遊資料、明信片、照片、紀念品等，都是一生美好的回憶。此外，帶團相關資料攜帶返國，也有利於晚輩、公司線控、主管修正行程或教育訓練的教材。

13. despite 儘管，(B)正確；(A)連接詞錯誤；(C)(D)語意錯誤。

　　下雪對於多數國人是興奮的，但是少數人卻習慣手插口袋，一時不小心就滑倒，更嚴重的導致骨折。出國前說明會應告知團員，準備一雙防滑的鞋子、手套等必備用品，以防萬一。

14. 附加問句，根據 never 故為肯定，invites 故為does，所以(C)正確。

　　領隊帶團要一視同仁，不要二分法切割團員。更不要將自己偏好寫在臉上，造成一個團體分兩小組，領隊試想帶團時若天天有人反對你，又如何一路順暢。

15. (C) 放心。

　　參觀具危險性的野生動物園、鱷魚園、獅子園等，應事先解說園區規範，要求團員切實遵守。如有專業解說員陪同，一定要尊重他的指示，領隊也要從頭至尾陪同團體。

16. (A)罰單，正確。

超時、超速、超載都是違法，不僅影響整團旅遊安全，所產生的罰款應由誰買單？就算有人願意買單，有時團員會很自負說：「大不了我付錢」，但是，交通違規的扣點是無法用錢衡量，且不能因為一個人的利益，就危及整體的安全性。

17. (D) 語意正確，stuff 統稱「一切物品」。

秉持財不露白之原則，提醒旅客貴重的私人物品，不要隨意放置在車上，特別不要放在椅子上，引起歹徒的覬覦，事先向團員說清楚，領隊麻煩事就比較少。一般當地代理旅行社不會事先向領隊宣導，車上貴重物品遺失是無法理賠。

18. (A) 語意正確，趕上火車。

交通工具一般不等團體，在歐美大城火車站往往有一個以上，前往不同的地方，要從不同車站搭乘，領隊事先應確認正確火車站，接下來就是哪一個月台，跑錯火車站、上錯月台、搭錯車，行程就延誤，接著客訴就在你身旁。

19. (C) 統稱「銀髮族」的集合名詞the old。

「分齡旅遊」是旅遊的趨勢之一，銀髮族是其中特殊屬性的團體，講究特殊餐食安排、養生行程、住宿要求與更具人性化呵護和關懷，領隊應具備可塑性與彈性，可以勝任不同屬性的團體。

20. (A)slippery滑，語意正確。

領隊行進速度要考量不同團體的屬性。銀髮族較多的團體，要選擇較為平順的路徑以符合此類型團員需求，年輕人則應選具挑戰性的Walking Tour路徑，給予最深刻的印象，當然一切以旅遊安全為第一。

歷居試題

( ) 1. The American government has decided to provide financial assistance to _____ the automobile industry. Car makers are relieved at the news.

(A)accommodate   (B)bail out

(C)cash in on   (D)detect   【98外語領隊】

( ) 2. All transportation vehicles should be well- _____ and kept in good running

condition.

(A)retrained   (B)maintained

(C)entertained   (D)suspended   【98外語領隊】

( ) 3. The company is _____ the new products now, so you can buy one and get

the second one free.

(A)forwarding   (B)progressing

(C)promoting   (D)pretending   【98外語領隊】

( ) 4. _____ a fire, the heritage building _____.

(A)It is because...burned down

(B)Because...burned down

(C)Because of...was burned down

(D)That because of...had burned down   【98外語領隊】

( ) 5. Remember to _____ some sunscreen before you go to the beach.

(A)drink   (B)scrub

(C)wear   (D)move   【99外語領隊】

( ) 6. These ancient porcelains are very _____ and might break easily, so please

handle them carefully.

(A)wicked   (B)infirm

(C)fragile   (D)stout   【99外語領隊】

( ) 7. The Ministry of the Interior has decided to _____ telephone fraud.

(A)dismiss   (B)discharge

(C)eliminate   (D)execute   【99外語領隊】

( ) 8. It's difficult to find a hotel with a/an _____ room in high season.

(A)occupied   (B)vacant

(C)lank   (D)unattended   【99外語領隊】

( ) 9. I like those stamps, but _____.

(A)I would not like to cost lots on money to buy them

(B)I would rather buy something else

(C)they would spend much money

(D)they would waste much money   【100外語領隊】

( ) 10. Due to the impending disaster, we have to _____ our flight to Bangkok.

(A)provide   (B)cancel

(C)resume   (D)tailor   【100外語領隊】

( ) 11. If I cancel the trip, will I _____?

(A)be refunded   (B)refund

(C)refunded   (D)refunding   【100外語領隊】

( ) 12. A: Have you seen my iPod? I can't find it anywhere.

B: Don't worry. _____.

(A)It will approach eventually   (B)It will come out eventually

(C)It will turn up eventually   (D)It will turn out eventually

【100外語領隊】

( ) 13. My father always asks everyone in the car to _____ for safety, no matter

how short the ride is.

(A)tight up   (B)fast up

(C)buckle up   (D)stay up   【101外語領隊】

( ) 14. The manager gave a copy of his _____ to his secretary and asked her to ar-

range some business meetings for him during his stay in Sydney.

(A)visa   (B)boarding pass

(C)itinerary   (D)journey   【101外語領隊】

( ) 15. I will be very busy during this weekend, so please do not call me _____ it is urgent.

(A)except (B)besides

(C)while (D)unless 【101外語領隊】

( ) 16. Prohibited items in carry-on bags will be confiscated at the checkpoints, and no _____ will be given for them.

(A)argument (B)recruitment

(C)compensation (D)decision 【101外語領隊】

解答

1.B	2.B	3.C	4.C	5.C	6.C	7.C	8.B	9.B	10.B	11.A	12.C
13.C	14.C	15.D	16.C								

總複習試題

( ) 1. It _____ raining for five days by tomorrow.

   (A) is   (B) has been   (C) will be   (D) will have been

( ) 2. Tour leader _____ twenty six years old next year.

   (A) will have been   (B) will be

   (C) shall have been   (D) had been

( ) 3. Much _____ our relief, all the passengers on the flight were saved.

   (A) on   (B) for   (C) to   (D) in

( ) 4. I _____ my breakfast when the morning call came.

   (A) had   (B) had been having

   (C) was having   (D) have been having

( ) 5. The TGV came after I _____ for about half an hour.

   (A) had been waited   (B) have waited

   (C) was waiting   (D) had been waiting

( ) 6. It _____ every day so far this month in Paris.

   (A) is raining   (B)rained   (C) rains   (D) has rained

( ) 7. There's a police car in front of our long distance coach. What do you suppose

   _____ ?

   (A) is happened   (B) has happened   (C) would happen   (D) did happen

( ) 8. Our group _____ Paris for two days.

   (A) has already been   (B) is already being

   (C) has already been being   (D) is already

( ) 9. By the time the show ends, _____ a lot about local culture.

   (A) we'll learn   (B) we are learning

(C) we have learnt   (D) we'll have learnt

( ) 10. My long distance coach driver _____.

    (A) has forever criticized me   (B) forever criticizes me

    (C) does forever criticize me   (D) is forever criticizing me

( ) 11. By this time next year he _____ from this travel agent.

    (A) will be retired   (B) should be retiring

    (C) will have retired   (D) is retiring

( ) 12. My niece has been to Sumatra and Iran as well as all of Europe. By the time she's twenty, she _____ almost everywhere.

    (A) will be   (B) would have been

    (C) will have been   (D) would be

( ) 13. She was so interested in the travel book that she _____ it for three hours before she realized it.

    (A) had read   (B) read   (C) was reading   (D) will have read

( ) 14. "I thought Spa resort hotel had already closed for the summer."

    "No, I think it _____ at the end of May."

    (A) to close   (B) closes   (C) closing   (D) to be closed

( ) 15. _____ the postcard, I ran out of the hotel to the post office.

    (A) After I had finished for

    (B) As soon as I finished writing

    (C) No sooner than I had finished up

    (D) Since I finished up to write

( ) 16. I had hoped local guide _____ me an early reply.

    (A) gave   (B) to give   (C) giving   (D) would give

( ) 17. I asked her whether the tour leader _____ a report on the coach.

    (A) is making   (B) makes   (C) is to make   (D) was making

( ) 18. Local guide told me that I _____ better take a train.

(A) would have　(B) should have　(C) had had　(D) had

( ) 19. "I have a toothache worse than ever."

"You _____ to the dentist yesterday."

(A) should go　　　　　　　(B) should have gone

(C) had to go　　　　　　　(D) must have gone

( ) 20. My coat looks rather shabby, so I ought to have it _____.

(A) clean and press　　　　(B) cleaning can pressing

(C) cleaned and pressed　　(D) cleaning and pressed

( ) 21. _____ plastics, the machine is light in weight.

(A) To make of　　　　　　(B) Having

(C) To be made of　　　　　(D) Made of

( ) 22. The Gypsy lady accused the man _____ stealing.

(A) for　(B) of　(C) with　(D) in

( ) 23. Mr. Leo _____ the travel fair in London last year.

(A) attended　(B) participated　(C) presented　(D) took part

( ) 24. When the tour member started to talk the local guide, she sounded _____.

(A) nice and easy　(B) unthinking　(C) very angry　(D) very sorry

( ) 25. Tour leader always tells very interesting _____ to make us laugh.

(A) jokes　(B) notes　(C) programs　(D) software

( ) 26. Of all the tour activities, I like _____ the best.

(A) chemistry　(B) participated　(C) piano　(D) shopping

( ) 27. His speech made a deep _____ on my mind.

(A) express　(B) impression　(C) jealous　(D) instructive

( ) 28. Leo and Janet are getting married. They are inviting many tour members to

their _____.

(A) marriage　(B) relation　(C) romance　(D) wedding

(　) 29. Mr. Leo Huang cooks delicious food that many people ＿＿＿＿ his cafeteria regularly.

　　　(A) appoint　(B) commute　(C) patronize　(D) reserve

(　) 30. Excuse me. Do you have the time?

　　　(A) Yes. It is free now.　　　　　(B) Well, maybe there is.

　　　(C) It's five thirty-five now.　　　(D) No, I am busy now.

(　) 31. When will we arrive in Tokyo?

　　　(A) It is beautiful time there.　　　(B) We will be there soon.

　　　(C) Of course, I will be back soon.　(D) Arrival time is at 9:30 p.m.

(　) 32. I reminded my tour leader ＿＿＿＿ his promise.

　　　(A) of　(B) in　(C) with　(D) on

(　) 33. Would you like a ＿＿＿＿ of tea?

　　　(A) cup　(B) dish　(C) bowl　(D) glass

(　) 34. I usually have my lunch at ＿＿＿＿.

　　　(A) lunch box　(B) lunch bulks　(C) lunch bar　(D) lunch counter

(　) 35. I mistook that stick ＿＿＿＿ a snake.

　　　(A) with　(B) for　(C) by　(D) in

(　) 36. This chocolate ice cream is ＿＿＿＿.

　　　(A) cool　(B) cold　(C) yummy　(D) hot

(　) 37. Without food, we began to ＿＿＿＿.

　　　(A) starve　(B) hurry　(C) stain　(D) soul

(　) 38. I have some crackers for night ＿＿＿＿.

　　　(A) eating　(B) cookies　(C) food　(D) snack

(　) 39. I prefer a cold ＿＿＿＿ instead of coffee.

　　　(A) soft drink　(B) tough drink　(C) hard drink　(D) shake drink

( ) 40. Waiter: _____ .

Gary: Yes, I would like have the broiled fish.

(A) Excuse me! (B) Not really.

(C) May I take your order? (D) Do you need help?

( ) 41. Would you like tea or coffee? _____

(A) Yes, please. (B) Neither, thank you.

(C) Sure, I would. (D) With sugar, please.

( ) 42. Make checks _____ to the hotel.

(A) paid (B) paying (C) payable (D) pay

( ) 43. When I moved to new apartment, my _____ changed from 07 to 04.

(A) area code (B) country code (C) ID code (D) citizen code

( ) 44. I can _____ a hotel room for you, if you would like.

(A) checked (B) argue (C) make (D) arrange

( ) 45. Do you want to _____ a message?

(A) appear (B) omit (C) leave (D) desert

( ) 46. Our room reservations are for _____ .

(A) fifteen March (B) the fifth of March

(C) five March (D) March five

( ) 47. A: I would like to book a double room for two nights from July 6.

B: _____

(A) What is your budget?

(B) Yes, here you are.

(C) I am sorry. All our rooms are taken.

(D) How much you want?

( ) 48. You might use this room _____ you keep it clean.

(A) as much as (B) as good as (C) as soon as (D) as long as

( ) 49. I have some clothes to be washed. Do you have a _____?

    (A) gymnasium   (B) safety-box   (C) room service   (D) laundry service

( ) 50. The _____ room had its windows boarded up.

    (A) free   (B) vacant   (C) triple   (D) special

( ) 51. Many people favor _____ more nuclear power plants.

    (A) to build   (B) build   (C) built   (D) building

( ) 52. A: Excuse me, Sir. Can you tell me how to get to the Twin Tower?

    B: _____. First, you have to go straight until the end of this road. Then, you

    have to turn right and you will see it on your right hand side.

    (A) Thanks a lot   (B) I will do my best

    (C) I don't know   (D) Oh, come on

( ) 53. Carol: Can I join you?

    Tony: _____

    (A) Be my guest.   (B) Forget.

    (C) What you say?   (D) You are through.

( ) 54. We could fit fifteen people in the _____.

    (A) vase   (B) van   (C) vote   (D) visa

( ) 55. This road was bumpy and _____.

    (A) unable   (B) unfair   (C) uneven   (D) unused

( ) 56. If you got caught drinking and driving, the judge has to _____ your driving

    license.

    (A) suspension   (B) suspense   (C) suspended   (D) suspend

( ) 57. If you don't' put lotion on, you will get a _____.

    (A) burn   (B) sunburn   (C) hit   (D) hurt

( ) 58. There are not many seats left for the craze horse; you had better _____ that you get one today.

(A) refer to　(B) ask for　(C) make sure　(D) set off

( ) 59. A relative of yours _____ this evening.

(A) will be coming to see you　　(B) will have been coming

(C) would come to see you　　(D) won't have seen you

( ) 60. _____ since I began to learn Italian.

(A) Six years have passed　　(B) Six years passed

(C) It had been six years　　(D) It was six years

( ) 61. He said to me, "Speak as slowly as you can."

=He told me to speak as slowly as _____ .

(A) you can　(B) I can　(C) you could　(D) I could

( ) 62. I feel exhausted, so I need to _____ .

(A) give him a break　　(B) take it easy

(C) give a chance　　(D) take a break

( ) 63. A: Do you need me to call 119?

B: _____

(A) I don't' think we'll need it.　　(B) Yes, but please don't hurry.

(C) Why don't you do that?　　(D) What does it mean?

( ) 64. Several of these earphones in the cabin are out of order and _____ .

(A) need to be repairing　　(B) repairing is required of them

(C) require that they be repaired　　(D) need to be repaired

( ) 65. One of our tour members is _____ to seafood.

(A) allergic　(B) alleviate　(C) allege　(D) hate

解答

1.D	2.B	3.C	4.C	5.D	6.D	7.B	8.A	9.D	10.D	11.A	12.C
13.A	14.B	15.B	16.D	17.D	18.D	19.B	20.C	21.D	22.B	23.A	24.C
25.A	26.D	27.B	28.D	29.C	30.C	31.D	32.A	33.A	34.D	35.B	36.C
37.A	38.D	39.A	40.C	41.B	42.A	43.A	44.D	45.C	46.B	47.C	48.D
49.D	50.B	51.D	52.B	53.A	54.B	55.C	56.D	57.B	58.C	59.A	60.A
61.D	62.D	63.A	64.D	65.A							

總綜合歷屆試題

( ) 1. In time of economic _____, many small companies will downsize their operation.

    (A)appreciation   (B)progression

    (C)recession   (D)reduction   【98外語領隊】

( ) 2. People have to learn to _____ their problems.

    (A)find fault with   (B)cope with

    (C)come up with   (D)end up with   【98外語領隊】

( ) 3. Public _____ to voting is a problem in many democratic countries with low turnouts in elections.

    (A)interpretation   (B)intervention

    (C)contribution   (D)indifference   【98外語領隊】

( ) 4. Those who _____ a quake _____ life more.

    (A)survives...cherishes   (B)have survived...will cherish

    (C)are surviving...are cherished   (D)are survivals of...had cherished

                                            【98外語領隊】

( ) 5. John's families moved to the United States. They intended to live there <u>for good</u>.

    (A)comfortably   (B)permanently

    (C)mostly   (D)temporarily   【98外語領隊】

( ) 6. I think you are paying too much for the <u>bells and whistles</u> of this new car.

    (A)important equipment   (B)basic ingredients

    (C)unnecessary features   (D)visual differences   【98外語領隊】

( ) 7. Rescuers from many countries went to the _____ of the earthquake to help the victims.

(A)capital
(B)refuge

(C)epicenter
(D)shelter
【99外語領隊】

( ) 8. There are eight _____ for the Academy Award for the best picture this year.

(A)attendants
(B)nominees

(C)conductors
(D)producers
【99外語領隊】

( ) 9. Since the economy is improving, many people are hoping for a _____ in salary in the coming year.

(A) raise
(B)rise

(C)surplus
(D)bonus
【99外語領隊】

( ) 10. The birth rate in Taiwan was at a/an _____ low last year.

(A)record
(B)recorded

(C)recording
(D)accordingly
【99外語領隊】

( ) 11. Jane completely missed the _____ of what the guest was complaining about.

(A) line
(B)goal

(C)point
(D)plan
【99外語領隊】

( ) 12. Slices of lamb are _____ or fried in butter and served with mushrooms, onions, and chips.

(A)added
(B)mixed

(C)grilled
(D)stored
【99外語領隊】

( ) 13. The caller: Can I speak to Ms. Taylor in room 612, please?

The operator: Please wait a minute. (pause) I'm sorry. There's no answer. May I _____ a message?

(A)bring
(B)take

(C)leave
(D)send
【99外語領隊】

( ) 14. She can speak English and French with _____ .

    (A)faculty   (B)future

    (C)facility   (D)frailty   【100外語領隊】

( ) 15. The <u>rustic</u> scenery appealed to him so much that he bought a house there.

    (A)rural   (B)deserted

    (C)urban   (D)beautiful   【100外語領隊】

( ) 16. His face looks like _____ .

    (A)a toad   (B)of a toad

    (C)with a toad   (D)that of a toad   【100外語領隊】

( ) 17. Gaga: Let's go Dutch.

    Melody: _____

    (A)Are you so rich as to pay for all of us?

    (B)We had better go to Germany.

    (C)Do you really want to pick it up?

    (D)Good idea!   【100外語領隊】

( ) 18. Jessica's customers complained because they had to pay twice for their _____ .

    (A)accommodation   (B)acculturation

    (C)accusation   (D)assimilation   【100外語領隊】

( ) 19. William Faulkner was a Nobel _____ .

    (A)laurel   (B)launder

    (C)laureate   (D)lavator   【100外語領隊】

( ) 20. An _____ gambler will have a hard time when deciding to stop this bad habit.

    (A)introvert   (B)invidious

    (C)inveterate   (D)innocuous   【100外語領隊】

( ) 21. The company _____ by a nationally-known research firm.

(A)the surveyed market had   (B)had the surveyed market

(C)had the market surveyed   (D)the market had surveyed

【101外語領隊】

(   ) 22. Finding an accountant _____ specialty and interests match your needs is critically important.

(A)who   (B)which

(C)whose   (D)whom   【101外語領隊】

(   ) 23. Smokers who insist on lighting up in public places are damaging not only their own health but also that of _____ .

(A)another   (B)each other

(C)one another   (D)others   【101外語領隊】

(   ) 24. Members of the design team were not surprised that Ms. Wang created the company logo _____ .

(A)itself   (B)herself

(C)themselves   (D)himself   【101外語領隊】

(   ) 25. Those wishing to be considered for paid leave should put _____ requests in as soon as possible.

(A)they   (B)them

(C)theirs   (D)their   【101外語領隊】

(   ) 26. Before you step out for a foreign trip, you should _____ about the accom-modations, climate, and culture of the country you are visiting.

(A)insure   (B)require

(C)inquire   (D)adjust   【101外語領隊】

(   ) 27. The security guards carefully patrol around the warehouse at _____ throughout the night.

(A)once   (B)odds

(C)intervals (D)least 【101外語領隊】

( ) 28. This puzzle is so _____ that no one can figure it out.

(A)furry (B)fuzzy

(C)fury (D)futile 【101外語領隊】

( ) 29. The teacher had asked several students to clean up the classroom, but _____

of them did it.

(A)all (B)both

(C)none (D)either 【101外語領隊】

( ) 30. Before the applicant left, the interviewer asked him for a current _____

number so that he could be reached if he was given the job.

(A)connection (B)concert

(C)interview (D)contact 【101外語領隊】

Now (31) as a clinical condition, the symptoms of jet lag include (32) of exhaustion,

disorientation, forgetfulness and fuzziness, not to mention headaches, bad moods, and a

reduced sex drive. Some people's circadian rhythms are so (33) disrupted that they are

on the (34) of true depression. But while it's generally accepted that there is no "cure"

for jet lag, an increasing number of treatments and products are said to be able to mini-

mize its (35) , which can last anything from a few days to several weeks.

【98外語領隊】

( ) 31. (A)organized (B)recognized (C)memorized (D)prescribed

( ) 32. (A)symbols (B)desires (C)emotions (D)feelings

( ) 33. (A)only (B)kindly (C)gently (D)severely

( ) 34. (A)blank (B)blink (C)brink (D)blanket

( ) 35. (A)effects (B)affects (C)effectiveness (D)advances

When you (36) a foreign purchase to a bank credit card, such as MasterCard or Visa,

all you lose with most cards is the 1 percent the issuer charges for the actual exchange.

Other banks, (37), add a surcharge of 2 to 3 percent on transactions in foreign currencies. Even (38) a surcharge, you generally lose less with a credit card (39) with currency or traveler's checks.

Therefore, don't use traveler's checks as your primary (40) of foreign payment. But do take along a few $20 checks or bills to exchange at retail for those last minute or unexpected needs. 【98外語領隊】

( ) 36. (A)exchange (B)charge (C)recharge (D)claim

( ) 37. (A)as a result (B)as a consequence (C)however (D)moreover

( ) 38. (A)when (B)with (C)as (D)about

( ) 39. (A)than (B)then (C)there (D)theme

( ) 40. (A)mean (B)means (C)meaning (D)material

For those who travel on a (41), flying with a low-cost airline might be an option because you pay so much less than what you would be expected to pay with a traditional airline. Companies such as Ryanair, Southwest Airlines and Easyjet are some good examples. It's so easy to fly with these low-cost (42). From booking the tickets, checking in to boarding the plane, everything has become hassle-free. You only need to book online even if there are only two hours left before departure. You can also just (43) the check-in desk and buy the tickets two hours before the plane takes off. Checking in is also easy and quick, and you're only required to arrive at the airport one hour before departure. But since traveling with these low-cost airlines has been so (44), you cannot expect to get free food, drinks or newspapers on board. There is also no classification regarding your seats and the flight attendants, who might be wearing casual clothing as their uniform, won't certainly serve you. As most of these low-cost airlines are (45), you might need to get ready for landing even after you have only gone on board for a few minutes. 【99外語領隊】

( ) 41. (A)schedule (B)budget (C)routine (D)project

( ) 42. (A)forms　(B)means　(C)cruises　(D)carriers

( ) 43. (A)pop in　(B)break in　(C)fill in　(D)come in

( ) 44. (A)inexpensive　(B)inconvenient　(C)inefficient　(D)inappropriate

( ) 45. (A)good-haul　(B)huge-haul　(C)short-haul　(D)long-haul

"That's £3.25 altogether," said a taxi driver. "Keep the change, please," replied a young lady when she handed over the money to the driver. "Thank you. Have a pleasant stay in York," said the driver after she received it with delight. This brief dialogue demonstrates __(46)__ pleasant the giving and receiving of tipping could be. Tipping has been a common way of showing appreciation to people who have served you. It is the kind of courtesy __(47)__ mostly to people who are serving in the travel and tourism industry. But sometimes things might not turn out to be so perfect. People might refuse to tip if they find the service is __(48)__ . They might have no idea about what would be the appropriate amount for tipping. In some countries, tipping is included in the service when you pay for the bill in a restaurant and that amount will be 10 or 15% of your total bill. __(49)__ they like it or not, some people might still be asked to tip or be overcharged __(50)__ tipping if there is no stipulation about how much one should tip. In cases like these, tipping might not be an enjoyable experience at all.　【99外語領隊】

( ) 46. (A)why　(B)what　(C)how　(D)which

( ) 47. (A)targeting　(B)targeted　(C)directing　(D)directed

( ) 48. (A)ungrateful　(B)unsatisfactory　(C)undeniable　(D)unexceptional

( ) 49. (A)Whether　(B)Where　(C)What　(D)While

( ) 50. (A)for　(B)from　(C)on　(D)of

In Japan, guests have to __(51)__ their shoes at the entrance of any Japanese-style accommodation. Slippers are __(52)__ inside, except on the tatami matting, so bring thick socks if the weather is cold.

Seating in the room is on cushions called zabuton arranged around the low table. In the

(53) season, there may be a blanket around the table. You slip your feet under the blanket for the (54) of a kotatsu electrical heating unit.

The futon bedding is laid out on the floor. It (55) consists of a mattress, sheets, a thick cover, and extra blankets if needed. A thin yukata robe is provided. In cold weather it is supplemented by a tanzen gown worn over it. 【100外語領隊】

( ) 51. (A)exchange (B)replace (C)remove (D)wear

( ) 52. (A)wear (B)wearing (C)wore (D)worn

( ) 53. (A)spring (B)summer (C)autumn (D)winter

( ) 54. (A)electrification (B)vitamin (C)warmth (D)wave

( ) 55. (A)extremely (B)ordinarily (C)privately (D)sensitively

Destinations can be cities, towns, natural regions, or even whole countries. The economies of all tourist destinations are (56) to a significant extent on the money produced by tourism. It is possible to (57) destinations as natural or built: *Natural destinations* (58) seas, lakes, rivers, coasts, mountain ranges, desert, and so on. Built destinations are cities, towns, and villages. A resort is a destination constructed mainly or completely to serve the needs of tourism, (59) Cancun in Mexico.

Successful destinations are seen to be unique in some way by those who visit them. Climate is one of the (60) that determines this uniqueness. Not surprisingly, temperate and tropical climates attract the greatest number of visitors. 【100外語領隊】

( ) 56. (A)dependent (B)disconnected (C)repellent (D)preferred

( ) 57. (A)amplify (B)classify (C)signify (D)verify

( ) 58. (A)concern (B)consist (C)include (D)involve

( ) 59. (A)so on (B)so so (C)such as (D)so that

( ) 60. (A)conclusions (B)specializations (C)superstitions (D)features

Many visitors to Italy avoid its famous cities, preferring instead the quiet countryside of Tuscany, located in the rural heart of the country. Like the rest of Italy, Tuscany has its share of art and architectures, (61) travelers are drawn more by its gentle hills, by its country estates, and by its hilltop villages. This is not an area to rush through but to enjoy slowly, like a glass of fine wine produced here. Many farmhouses offer simple yet comfortable (62) . From such a base, the visitors can (63) the nearby towns and countryside, (64) up the sunshine, or just (65) in the company of a good book.

【101外語領隊】

( ) 61. (A)if (B)once (C)but (D)because
( ) 62. (A)accommodations (B)replacements (C)customs (D)privileges
( ) 63. (A)explain (B)explore (C)explode (D)expose
( ) 64. (A)leap (B)mount (C)soak (D)creep
( ) 65. (A)register (B)relax (C)reduce (D)repeat

Vancouver Island is one of the most beautiful places in the world. It is situated off the west (66) of Canada, about one and a half hour by ferry from Vancouver on the mainland. Victoria, the capital city, (67) over one hundred and fifty years ago and is famous for its old colonial style buildings and beautiful harbor. It is the center of government for the province of British Columbia, so many of the people living there are (68) as public servants. The lifestyle is very relaxed, (69) to other cities in Canada, and this is (70) a lot of people to move there after they retire. The island is also popular with tourists because of the magnificent mountain scenery and the world-renowned Butchart Gardens.

【101外語領隊】

( ) 66. (A)quarter (B)position (C)coast (D)site
( ) 67. (A)was founded (B)founded (C)was founding (D)found
( ) 68. (A)regarded (B)employed (C)included (D)treated
( ) 69. (A)compared (B)to compare (C)comparing (D)compare
( ) 70. (A)hindering (B)demanding (C)attracting (D)prohibiting

解答

1.C	2.B	3.D	4.B	5.B	6.C	7.C	8.B	9.A/B	10.A
11.C	12.C	13.B	14.C	15.A	16.A/D	17.D	18.A	19.C	20.C
21.C	22.C	23.D	24.B	25.D	26.C	27.C	28.B	29.C	30.D
31.B	32.D	33.D	34.C	35.A	36.B	37.C	38.B	39.A	40.B
41.B	42.D	43.A	44.A	45.C	46.C	47.D	48.B	49.A	50.A
51.C	52.D	53.D	54.C	55.B	56.A	57.B	58.C	59.C	60.D
61.C	62.A	63.B	64.C	65.B	66.C	67.A	68.B	69.A	70.C

Note

Note

Note

國家圖書館出版品預行編目資料

領隊英文／黃榮鵬著.
--三版.--臺北市：五南, 2012.06
　面；　公分 --(觀光書系)
參考書目：面
ISBN 978-957-11-6651-3（平裝）
1.英語　2.領隊　3.讀本
805.18　　　　　　　101006744

1L32　觀光書系

領隊英文

作　　者 － 黃榮鵬(306.4)

發 行 人 － 楊榮川

總 編 輯 － 王翠華

主　　編 － 黃惠娟

責任編輯 － 蔡佳伶

封面設計 － 陳翰陞

出 版 者 － 五南圖書出版股份有限公司

地　　址：106台北市大安區和平東路二段339號4樓

電　　話：(02)2705-5066　傳　　真：(02)2706-6100

網　　址：http://www.wunan.com.tw

電子郵件：wunan@wunan.com.tw

劃撥帳號：01068953

戶　　名：五南圖書出版股份有限公司

法律顧問　林勝安律師事務所　林勝安律師

出版日期　2007年 5 月初版一刷
　　　　　2010年 6 月二版一刷
　　　　　2012年 6 月三版一刷
　　　　　2016年10月三版二刷

定　　價　新臺幣350元